the

Colonel

MAHMOUD

DOWLATABADI

DAWLAT'ABADI

Translated by Tom Patterdale

MELVILLE HOUSE
BROOKLYN, NEW YORK

The Colonel

Translated from the Persian, *Kolonel*, and first published
in German by Unionsverlag, Zürich, 2009

This edition is published in agreement with Haus Publishing, London

© 2009 Mahmoud Dowlatabadi
Translation © 2011 Tom Patterdale
First Melville House printing: April 2012

Melville House Publishing
145 Plymouth Street
Brooklyn, NY 11201

www.mhpbooks.com

ISBN: 978-1-61219-132-4

Printed in the United States of America

1 2 3 4 5 6 7 8 9 10

Library of Congress Control Number: 2012934610

PRAISE FOR MAHMOUD DOWLATABADI
AND *THE COLONEL*

"A demanding and richly composed book by a novelist who stands apart." —*Kirkus Reviews*

"Dowlatabadi combines the poetic tradition of his culture with the direct and unembellished everyday speech of the villages. With this highly topical new novel Mahmoud Dowlatabadi, Iran's most important novelist, sheds light on the upheavals, which haunt his country until today." —Man Asian Literary Prize nomination citation

"We are ... fortunate to have this passionate and informative fable of the Islamic revolution in our hands.... [translator Tom] Patterdale is to be commended for his immaculate [notes], which do not omit a single reference in the text to Persian mythology, place-names or historical and political figures. His equally precious afterword informs us that *The Colonel* has 'never appeared in its original language' in Iran.... It's about time everyone even remotely interested in Iran read this novel." —*The Independent* (London)

"*The Colonel* is a page-turning panorama of Iranian mental anguish, producing visions and nightmares like dark exotic blossoms." —Angela Schader, *Neue Zürcher Zeitung*

"This novel has what it takes to become a strong and irresistible window into Iran." —*Die Zeit*

"... a very powerful work." —Michael Orthofer, *The Complete Review*

"... because of its honesty and indeed brutal clarity of language the novel has so far not been published in its original language, Persian ... [an] honest and truly literary account." —English PEN

PRAISE FOR *MISSING SOLUCH*

"Whether that is a question of dialect or tone, it's clear that Mr. Dowlatabadi approaches the world of his own childhood—he grew up in the village of Dowlatabad in northeastern Iran—with unsentimental respect. *Missing Soluch*, in the violence and the unceasing vicissitudes of its agrarian plot, brings *East of Eden* to mind, but has none of Steinbeck's teacherly symbolism.... Dowlatabadi knows a world that has seldom overlapped with the modern novel.... What makes this book stirring is the way Mr. Dowlatabadi has limited his palette, self-consciously but realistically, as only a modern would."   —Benjamin Lytal, *The New York Sun*

"An outstanding master achievement."   —*Der Spiegel*

"... beautifully and incisively rendered, and imbued throughout with hope."   —*Publishers Weekly*

Translator's Note

In the original Persian, the title of the book is *Kolonel*, a word derived from the French "*Colonel.*" There are two colonels confronting the reader in this book: the nameless colonel of the title and his *alter ego* in the photograph. Both are referred to as *Kolonel*. The Persian for 'colonel' is *sarhang*, but there was one colonel who was always known as *Kolonel*. This was Mohammad-Taqi Khan Pesyan* who, in recognition of his training in Europe, was given the nickname *Kolonel*. Any educated Iranian would know who this was. His story can be found in the Notes, which begin on p.233 (Notes are indicated throughout the text by the symbols * and †). To help the reader distinguish between the two colonels, I have referred to Pesyan as 'The Colonel', while the protagonist remains in lower case.

Dowlatabadi's language shatters the Persian literary conventions. It is rough and ready, the language of the street and the barrack room. Like the great 11th century Persian epic *Shah-nameh*,† it avoids the use of Arabic words imported into Persian. In an effort to reproduce this in English I have tried to use Anglo-Saxon words in preference to Latin.

Tom Patterdale

I'd better put my cigarette out first...

This was perhaps the twentieth butt that he had stubbed out since nightfall. He was feeling suffocated and he had smoked so much that he had lost all sense of taste. The cracked pane in front of him had steamed up. It was unusually quiet.

Every knock at the door broke the caressing silence of the rain. There was nothing but the sound of unremitting rain drumming on the rusty tin roof, so unceasing that it amounted to silence.

Only once in my lifetime do I remember seeing these roofs in the sunset. I remember it well...

In the evening after the rain, just after sunset, the ochre of the rooftops glowed with melancholy beauty, in those days when the first grey hairs had started to appear on his temples. In those days he still walked upright, with his head held high, and he could feel the earth under his feet. He had not been old and worn out then, his cheeks had not yet sunk in and the worry lines had yet to furrow their way across his brow.

Now that these gentlemen have come... I had better put out my cigarette first, then get up and throw my raincoat over my head. Then I can go to the door. Knock away, knock, keep on knocking, whoever you are! It's been years since I've heard any good news and I'm certainly not expecting any now, at this ungodly hour of the night. Let's see now, if this old clock is right, it must be about half past three in the morning, and just look at all the fog on that cracked old window... Knock, knock, my friends. Knock hard enough to wake the dead in their graves. But I am not going to take a single step out into the yard before I've put my raincoat over my head and my galoshes on my feet. You can see for yourselves that the rain is coming down in buckets. Besides, I need to switch on the outside light before I come downstairs. Do you want me to slip in the dark and put my shoulder out...? I'm coming. I just hope that Amir's basement light isn't on... I must not get muddled. I must stay calm and try not to appear upset or frightened when I open the door. I absolutely must not bat an eyelid or let my mouth shake. But I can't stop my left eyelid twitching. As soon as I concentrate on anything, it starts fluttering. It's just this weary old left eye...

"Yes, yes, I'm coming... Just a minute..."

Why should he need to ask who it was, banging on his door at this ungodly hour? It's not that he didn't dare ask the question. No. It wasn't like that at all. It was just that he knew that, in the end, it made no difference. He knew full well that nobody knocked on a locked door in the middle of the night without a reason.

There's no escape... Take a deep breath... And try not to think about the number of cigarettes I have smoked all day. Stay calm; don't do any of those stupid things I do when I'm wrong-footed. I must be in full control of myself when I open the door. My puffing and wheezing might be seen as panic, so I just have to take a deep breath. Then, I shall open the door quite calmly.

"Colonel?"

"Yes, yes..."

"Is that you, Colonel?"

"Who else did you think it would be?"

"Well, why don't you open the door?"

"All right, all right, I'll open it. I'm trying to find the key.

Ah, I've got it. Oh, no, that's the key to the safe. I'll have to go and look for the right one. Sorry, just give me a minute…"

Where could I have put it? On the ledge or on the table? I always keep the key in my pocket, because… well, just in case. But I haven't left the house since I got back this afternoon, so I didn't have to change out of any wet clothes. Unless I put the key with my prayer beads and lighter – that German petrol lighter that doesn't work any more – on the mantelpiece, next to the photo of The Colonel. Yes, that's it.

There it was, right beneath The Colonel's shiny black field boots, next to the passport photo of Mohammad-Taqi, which he had had taken for his driving licence. He had placed the photo there two, maybe three, years ago, next to The Colonel's shiny black boots so that he could get used to looking at his son.

Yes, I want to get used to seeing my sons' pictures…

In truth the colonel had made this decision for his own self-preservation. By positioning his son's photograph at eye level he would force himself to ride out the great wave of emotion that welled up from the depths of his heart to invade his mind. He believed that as long as Mohammad-Taqi's photo was where he could see it, he wouldn't run the risk of forgetting the boy. He tried to persuade himself that by always facing his son, he was facing the barrage of emotion that wanted to destroy him. It was just like "engage and confront" in army exercises. *Or like war. A decisive blow has to be delivered where the enemy least expects it. You can only parry an attack if you are prepared.*

He had kept the full-length portrait of The Colonel before his eyes for half a century. He had also felt an urge – yes, even a longing – to push his wife's photograph into the left-hand corner of the frame, right beneath the point of The Colonel's sabre, so that he could look at her as well. *But I couldn't… I still can't.* But he had managed to position Parvaneh's photo right beneath The Colonel's boot. That was different. Three days and three nights after she had left the house and never returned, he had placed Parvaneh's photo next to Mohammad-Taqi in the right-hand corner of the frame. For almost two months now, he had been trying to get used to seeing the little photo of his daughter – and the one of Masoud, whom they called Little Kuchik at home: *Ah yes, Kuchik. Maybe it was because of his bushy black eyebrows and low forehead that the children had nicknamed him Kuchik Jangali…*'*

"I've got the key, I've just found it. I'll open the door now. I'll be with you in a second. Come in. Good evening!"

The pale reflection from the neon light in the shrine to the young martyr[†] on the street corner opposite lit up the colonel's face like a moonbeam and fell on the olive green parkas of his visitors. Merging with the drizzle, it formed a white mist, which glinted off the men's epaulettes and the peaks of their caps. From their silhouettes, the colonel could see that both men were young and carried rifles slung over their shoulders, which was probably why the colonel did not even hear himself wish them a good evening. He found himself doing it again. He gave himself up and waited for these two youths to say something, anything, and to do with him whatever they pleased.

They did not take long. One of them took a torch from a deep pocket in his parka and, even though he could see the colonel's face perfectly well by the cold light from the shrine, he pointed the sharp beam at him, flashed it round the rain-soaked yard and, before it could reflect off the water in the pond, shone it down on the colonel's wet galoshes and then switched it off, as if waiting for his companion to make a move.

The colonel was full of questions. As he stood there in the rain, hunched and stooping, with his rigid, frightened gaze, he looked just like a question mark written by a child with bad handwriting. But no question came to his lips: not a single word could he utter. He could not even remember the simplest of greetings. He just stared at the two young men, still standing outside, who seemed to be inspecting something somewhere in the rainy reflections from the shrine.

They could think whatever they wanted, but what was preoccupying the colonel, quite apart from the fear flowing through him like a river, was that these two were the same age as Mohammad-Taqi and Kuchik. All he could think was that if Mohammad-Taqi had lived, he would have been twenty-one in March, on 3rd March 1983 to be exact, and that Kuchik Masoud, if he were still alive, would now be about twenty-six.

What could I have done? What should I have done? There was nothing, nothing that I could have done. Things were out of my control by then. The children had grown up. They knew their own minds and felt no need to listen to anything I had to say to them. Come on, could I have ordered them not to be so hot-headed? There was a revolution on then, a revolution, you know, and it was every man for himself. Except the young, you can't say the young were driven entirely by self-interest. The young were all trying to find themselves in the revolution, trying to give some meaning to their lives. Revolution gave them a thrill and kept their adrenaline going. They were riding a wave of excitement, like a dove that flies higher and higher to reach the sun, until it burns up – that's the acme of truth for youth! The revolution carried my children off and I have no idea at what point any of them got burned, or may still be burning, for that matter. We should feel sorry for our immediate neighbours, our fellow townsmen and fellow countrymen, if any of their young men should come back from the edge of immolation only half-burned, if they descend from that height only to discover that the truth they have found is nothing but specious doctrine and bogus ideology... Then this glowing, molten wreck turns into a stream of raging fire...

"Now then, lads, don't stand outside in the rain, come inside."

What else could he have said? Even though they had not shown the colonel their identity cards, he could hardly object to their coming in.

The fact is, I'm frightened, I've been very frightened for a long time now...

Perhaps he should have left the yard gate unlocked. The very thing that could happen if he left it unlocked had just happened. Locking the gate had become second nature to the colonel. It was not so much a conscious act of securing his property now, but just a habit born of fear.

I am afraid, my friend, I am afraid. I don't know of what or of whom, but I feel that people are something more than just the clothes they wear. I feel that man comes naked into the world, and most of the time I can't help seeing myself as naked, too. All the good manners and politeness in the world actually tell you nothing about people. When I see through people, I'm shocked at what confronts me, because they remind me of herds of wild, stampeding buffalo – I probably saw them in a film. I screw my eyes tight shut to keep the image out, or rather they shut by themselves, out of sheer fright, as I see herds of men with strange horns growing out of their heads coming to destroy everything, including me, this little heap of bones. A nightmare, my friend.

"My good fellow, why don't you come in and sit down? Oh, yes, I should warn you, those bentwood chairs are clapped out and they crack like a dry poppadom when you sit on them, but as they used to say: what we have is what we have, and a guest is a guest. Anyway, please have a seat!"

They will sit down, won't they…? Yes, a seat for the gentlemen… A towel, maybe…

He could have fetched a towel to dry his rain-soaked white hair and wipe his face and neck, but it was too late. He had thought of it too late. It was all he could do to light a cigarette and sit down on one of the opium-coloured chairs, with his back to the stove. A kind of calm was creeping over him, even though he was having to hold his left hand to stop it shaking. Even worse was the way his cigarette would not stop twitching; there it was in his hand, it seemed to have acquired a life of its own… *This is a small town. It hasn't grown like all the others; everyone knows everyone else here. If I could just control my nerves and gather my wits for a minute, I am sure I'll know who my visitors are, or at least know their parents. Although I wasn't born here, I have lived here so long that my Parvaneh was born in this town. Amir, the eldest, was no more than fifteen when we moved here, and the middle boys were so small that in no time they spoke like the locals. If my mind doesn't fail me, I'm sure I'll be able to get my visitors to admit they know Mohammad-Taqi and Masoud. Maybe they were friends, even. I bet they were at school together, sharing a desk. Or if not, they must at least have run across one another during all the ballyhoo in the revolution...*

His guests were silent and kept their faces averted, as if they were embarrassed to be there. Finally, the one who reminded the colonel of Mohammad-Taqi – or did the colonel only wish he did? – could stand it no longer. He got up and went over to the big portrait of The Colonel and stood staring at Mohammad-Taqi's photo for a long while, with the hood of his parka hanging down over his back. Meanwhile the other lad, whom the colonel thought was the very spit of Masoud, just sat opposite him, with his arms crossed and his elbows on the table, gazing in silence at a threadbare corner of the old red table cloth.

One would think that boys were born coy, but there lurks within them a dreadful, perverse force that can, in the blink of an eye, turn them into savage beasts, beasts that since the beginning of history have been easily drawn into committing the most appalling of crimes, just to prove themselves. They follow their orders to the letter and call what they do acts of heroism. Can we blame them? What about us, the people who send these unformed lumps of soft putty out onto the street, where they fall into the arms of the first merchants of villainy they come across? And we just sit back and wait for them to be turned into rods to beat our own backs...

"My Mohammad-Taqi was in his first year of medicine..."

"I knew him, yes, I knew him..."

Maybe the conversation had gone like that, or maybe it hadn't but, from the way the young man was standing, the colonel assumed that he had known his son. He wanted to believe that he had met Mohammad-Taqi, even though he doubted that knowing or not knowing someone like him

| 8 |

would make any difference to his situation, whatever it was. But, just for a moment, the thought took the colonel's mind off the maelstrom of his thoughts.

He's just as impatient as Mohammad-Taqi was.

Which was probably why he did not linger in front of the photograph, and the colonel did not think he would spend much time looking at Parvaneh's photo either. Instead, the youth sat down, checked his watch and glanced at his colleague. It seemed to the colonel that the young man must be worried about the time, for time had passed and nothing had been explained. As for the colonel himself, he was unnerved by their uncertainty and gaucheness. He still did not know where the blow was going to fall. He just had to wait for it. The only thing he was sure of was that these young men – *they looked wrecked and melted by their return to earth from the sun* – had not come knocking at his door to pour balm on his wounds. All he could do was wait. And so he waited, until one of them spoke:

"Right, we're taking you to the prosecutor's office."

"The prosecutor's office?"

"It'll all become clear when you get there, colonel."

Now, whatever I do I mustn't look surprised or appear indignant. I need to behave myself. I've been telling myself for ages that I mustn't boil over and lose my temper. I mustn't let anything faze me ever again. No, whatever happens, I mustn't be surprised. It's the only way of steeling yourself against nasty bombshells. I live in the past anyway. Maybe it's to do with my army service under the Shah, or Kuchik going to the Iraqi front, or what happened to my wife… or Parvaneh… I don't know. It could be one of a thousand things. But the butterflies in my stomach I can't do anything about. Not a thing! Look at me, I can't even go downstairs without locking the door behind me.

It's lucky I didn't leave my hat behind. It's on my head. Just to be sure, I'm putting my hand up to my head to touch it once more. I've got enough of my wits about me to realise that I need to turn up my coat collar to stop the rain wrapping itself round my neck like a chain. And of course I mustn't let these young men find out that Amir's in the basement. It probably doesn't matter, but I have a feeling that my Amir's hiding himself away there for over a year might raise the odd doubt or two and give rise to some curiosity, or even suspicion. There is just no logical reason for an ex-political prisoner, particularly one under forty, to hide himself in the basement of his parents' house, turning himself back into a prisoner, as it were, and cutting himself off as much as he can from his own family. Such behaviour is bound to make the authorities suspicious, especially with a chap like Amir. Amir isn't really crazy. I mustn't even think about him. Many times I've heard him talking to his sister Farzaneh. She does bang on a bit, and she gets carried away with sisterly concern. She's the same sort of age as Amir, so when she gets the chance, she comes and sits at the top of the basement stairs and starts pouring out her heart to him.

"Why are you sitting all hunched up, brother? What is it? Has the world come to an end? First of all, it hasn't, and secondly, plenty of other people like you are out of work. That's no reason to creep into a corner and shut yourself away like a leper. What's up, Amir, my darling brother? At least think of Papa. He's really aged since we heard about Mohammad-Taqi. You mustn't be the end of him. Papa has had a really hard time, as you know better than any of us. You are the eldest son, after all, so you've got to start thinking about the family a bit more, about us. I'm just a married woman, I don't have a choice. You know very well that my husband, Mr Qorbani, has banned me from coming here. My son is getting wind of things and his father's started quizzing him. The boy can't hold his tongue and he says things. He's only a child, after all. He doesn't understand. And my daughter. And the baby is always in the way. And Qorbani Hajjaj* is a worried man, he suspects everyone and everything. But I can't help myself. If I don't come and see you, I'm so jumpy and ill at ease that I feel as if my clothes were on fire.† Look, brother, I have to put up with my husband and obey him. I may just have to stop coming here to see you. Because Qorbani says that if I come here it will go on his file and he'll have problems. Hajjaj is worried about his position, because they're taking an unpleasant interest in him. It could cost him his job, he says. Tongues are wagging and they have given you and our whole family a bad name, brother. You know only too well, brother, that having a bad reputation you can't get rid of is a worse fate than having a roof fall on your head. Every memorial service for these young men I go to, the women are talking about you. Some of them have sharp tongues, bro. But I can't not go. When you get a bad name like that, you want to run away from yourself. I want to tell everybody a hundred times that I am someone else, not the person they think I am, but in my thoughts I am always with you!

So, my dear brother, I have to keep away from you, or rather… from myself. But every time I see you or think of you, every time I think of the state Papa is in, shrunk to the size of a pullet as he is, I get a lump in my throat, my heart wants to burst and I want to melt away, I want the earth to swallow me up. Amir, Amir… my darling brother, just say something, just answer me, for heaven's sake. You're going to be the death of our father if you carry on like this. Look, you were such a good boy, why did you suddenly go this way? You always used to give good advice to people and taught them things. Your pupils gathered round you like moths to a flame, they loved you like an elder brother. You're already getting grey hairs, dear brother!"

I could hear her going on like this while I was rereading, for the hundredth time, the story of Manuchehr and Salm, Tur and Iradj, who had become so familiar to me that I could imagine myself caught up in the tangled mess of their lives.* Recently I'd noticed how Amir had become even more cross-eyed: his expression was more vacant than ever, and an air of something between shame, panic and doubt – in any event an emotion that went beyond despair – had taken up residence behind his eyes. His long greasy hair fell over his shoulders and streaks of grey had appeared, not just on his temples, but in the middle of his head as well. I saw my son through the frosted glass of the basement door, and he was shrivelling up and growing old in front of my very eyes and I could do nothing for him. For some nights I had been hearing him scream and I felt for him in his frightening nightmares. Visions of catastrophe, of people falling off a high roof, or off towering rocks down into a hole, into nothingness, of young men plummeting into the black abyss of despair, dreams of distorted faces that had seen pain, only pain. Dreams of wild cries of despair, dreams of fathers taking their sons to the slaughterhouse to end it all, and of women ripping open their wombs so that no seed should take – and this was all that they could do, nothing else… And screams, silent screams of despair, muffled as if through cotton wool.

Horrible chimeras plagued him. It took a lifetime for me to get used to witnessing all this without going crazy myself. But Amir still hasn't managed to treat these horrors as normal. It seems to me that he's tormented by a sense of guilt, like a broken bone sticking through a wound. Amir is still a boy to me, but not so young that he will take my advice any more. As time passes, we seem to be gradually losing our common language. He isn't interested in a heart-to-heart and I'm too ashamed to talk. What could I say to him that wouldn't seem forced or contrived? How can an entire nation endure so many long silences and so many unspoken words?

That leaves only Farzaneh, who comes over whenever she can get away from her husband, and tries to draw Amir out in her artless way, because she can reduce big worries into little words and is less anxious about exactly how she should put things. Farzaneh just sits down on the top step of the basement stairs, holding her baby on her knee like a good woman, and weeps quietly as she speaks to Amir and, if I pay attention, I can just make out what she is saying:

"I'm dying of grief, Amir, at least have pity on me. I can't bear just watching you waste away in front of my eyes... I've now lost all of you, one way or another. First Mohammad-Taqi, then Masoud, well... we have no idea what happened to him and I'm beginning to lose hope. And our Parvaneh... Parvaneh... my little sister, Amir! Nothing is clear, nothing is certain on this earth except death: death, which has now lost face, lost its dignity. Whenever I imagine the day when they'll bring in Masoud's corpse, or at least his dog tag, I just laugh, because I won't know what to do about it. And whenever I think of the day when they brought in Mohammad-Taqi's body, and I didn't know what to do, I just cry. Death and dying, there's so much death… All my brothers… Just look what's happened to us all, that I can talk about death so openly and shamelessly. What will happen to our sister, Amir, our little sister? The town is full of shrines to young men and coffins are being carried through the streets and the roads are wet with blood and my husband has become an agent of death, now that he's decided to do… God knows what! There is such a lump in my throat, little brother, that I can hardly breathe and you… so silent, so silent… rescue me from this despair, little brother, Amir, Amir! I can see you withering away and it's just killing me. At least say one word to me, please Amir, just one word!"

No! I cannot believe that my Amir has lost his mind. No, it cannot be! But those crazy dreams, those terrifying nightmares of his…

The colonel was not altogether wrong since, even after Amir had had these horrible dreams and nightmares, he did not behave oddly but just sat on the edge of his bed smoking, wiping the sweat from his brow with an old hand-kerchief. He had even heard Amir saying to himself, "I can cope and I will try to cope, if these nightmares will just let me." And, even more unequivocally: "I haven't lost my wits, I swear I haven't." The colonel believed that his son could still think straight and that he was trying to be strong. All the while, Amir had kept working on a bust of Amir Kabir* – the colonel had seen its outline through the dusty basement window. So how could he despair of his son?

It was I who introduced him to Amir Kabir and told him that he was a shining example to our nation. Wasn't I right to do that? And why not? But… there are moments when I feel ashamed, even brow-beaten, for having introduced my sons to these free-spirited and patriotic figures, and I feel that I have in some way betrayed them. It's just as well that those moments soon pass and don't take root in my head, because I tell myself over and over again that I have done my duty to my sons. Sometimes I go further and pride myself that I have imbued them with all the progressive ideas of the last century. A young mind hungers for new ideas and, as a father, I had no right not to respond to that perfectly reasonable need. What else keeps a nation alive? So why should I blame myself? What else could I have done? Should I have lied to them? I admit, yes, that sometimes I held the truth back from them and that sometimes I inculcated things into them… But who can tell what they would have found out on their own? After all, nobody can pull the wool over the eyes of the young. No, I've got nothing to be ashamed of, and I shouldn't allow myself to think that I've let my sons down in any way. Why should such an idea have ever entered my head? My sons, my sons, what have we come to that we have to regret having done the most reasonable thing one could have done?

"Papa, papa, my head is bursting!" How many times had the colonel heard this plaintive cry coming through the walls and windows of the basement, over and over again, as his son wept bitterly and held his head in his hands. Amir seemed drained after each nightmare, exhausted as if running a fever, and could not make sense of anything. He guessed that his son had got himself into such a state that he did not even want to think any more. Not that he could stop himself, the colonel suspected. Amir had not lost his mind and Farzaneh was wrong if she thought that he had. The colonel reckoned that she should not muck him about the way she did and that she certainly should not drag up what his brothers and sister said about him, which only set him off again. He was certain, or at least he thought he was certain that, apart from those brief moments of desperation, Amir had dispelled all thoughts of his brothers and of his sister Parvaneh, perhaps because he had lost the courage to think about the tragedy or, worse, that he had been infected by doubt, by the leprosy of doubt and resignation. The colonel was aware that once someone has fallen into a deep slough of despond, it is virtually impossible to get out of it. You can twist and turn all you want, but in the end, you succumb to the giddying confusion of it all and throw in the towel.

"I am the answer to a riddle that I have set myself, to which the only answer would seem to be death. I am having doubts not only about where I belong in my own country, but even about my own humanity. Who am I, what am I, where do I belong?"

The colonel must have heard Amir say all this. How often had he felt the same thing himself, just what one should never allow oneself to say? He could read his son's words on Farzaneh's face, after all. Farzaneh bit her lip and wept in silence. She had lost weight, but she still reminded the colonel of her mother, with her light auburn hair, her greenish eyes, her smooth forehead, her elegant lips and her delicate little chin. But now her face bore the marks of confusion and failure. Reflected in it, the colonel could see the state that Amir was in; the state that they were all in.

"You're lost to us all, my sister, and I, Amir, have lost my faith."

He knew, he knew perfectly well, that his son was changing, but he absolutely refused to see this as him losing his mind. He could read Amir's metamorphosis from his squinting eyes, which mirrored his descent into paralysis and lifelessness. The only signs of life left in him were of fear, shame, despair and failure. Now and then, his hopes were raised by seeing the outline of his son through the frosted glass of the little door, as he worked on the bust of Amir Kabir. That must do him some good. But he regretted that he had not said anything to Amir about all the comings and goings in the house of Khezr Javid, the Immortal Khezr.* He worried that Amir appeared to be having nightmares more and more frequently. Should he have warned Amir not to let Khezr Javid come and visit him at the house? The colonel mulled over this question, rebuking himself for his passivity.

For a long time now I have been trying hard to keep calm and not get upset, to take everything in my stride and not be surprised by anything. If I'd said something to Amir about Khezr, could I have prevented what happened, or at least delayed it? No, gentlemen, my son wasn't a child anymore!

Now, am I sure I locked the door behind me? Yes, I can feel the key in my coat pocket. But did I lock it properly? Maybe, maybe not. I can't honestly remember. How can I be sure? Not being sure is what starts me worrying so…

It was clear to the colonel that he would have to walk in front of the two policemen. He knew the form as well as they did: anyone arrested for a crime, whatever it may be, was required to walk between and slightly in front of the arresting officers. It had been like that since the beginning of time, and it would go on being like that.

That's as may be, but I must make sure I've locked the door behind me…

The colonel was too old to want to go against these unwritten rules. His back was bent in a stoop, his head hung low and he was staring in front of his feet. He could feel his grey hat pressing down on the tip of his nose, while his coat tails seemed to grow longer, dragging in the mud of the alleyway and wrapping themselves round his shins.

"This way, Colonel."

Yes, that's just it. I just have to go along with them.

They had reached the end of the alley, and were turning into the main road. On each corner stood another brightly lit shrine to a young martyr, casting its glow out into the main road. They were getting to the town square, with the prosecutor's office on its western side. Passing between two more shrines on either side of the entrance, they climbed the steps. The stairway was dark and silent, lit only by a naked, lifeless bulb hanging from the ceiling. 'So much for their economy measures', the colonel thought, treading carefully, as befitted his age, on the staircase, which was wet and muddy from all the comings and goings.

Even before his dishonourable discharge, the colonel had not been one for gambling or such things as bridge or snooker. He had never even held a cue in his hand. Yet he knew that the upper floor of this building had once been a snooker hall. In his youth he had played the *setar*,* and he still wanted to play; he had recently got a pair of doves and he was not unfond of his daughter Parvaneh's pet canary. In vain, he now tried to remember how to play snooker, even though he had not seen it played more than once in his life. And indeed, now that he saw a man sitting behind a table covered with a green baize cloth – *he's the spitting image of my son-in-law Qorbani!* – with another two lads on the other side of the table, he was certain that this must have been one of the old snooker tables, with the cushions sawn off, that the prosecutor's office was now using as a temporary desk. The two policemen who had brought him in sat down on either side of the table.

"Were you an officer, Colonel?"

"Yes… I was."

"If you want to take the body and bury it yourself, you have to make a contribution to our funds."

"I see… of course."

"Everything is ready. Two men will accompany you and stay with you until the end of the funeral. Kindly sign here, and here…

"Yes… kindly… certainly… yes sir!"

I think I was saying earlier that for a long time now I've given up expecting any good news. But is it too much to ask that they don't give people bad news at such an awful time and in such a dreadful place? Well now, at this time of night, how can I bring more disgrace on myself? Of course…

Of course, the colonel knew full well that the point of dragging him there at that ungodly hour was to ensure that the whole matter was over and done with by dawn. Anyone with half a brain understands certain things without needing to have them spelt out. It made sense to cooperate with the court officials and not ask awkward questions. The colonel had learned and inwardly digested that Parvaneh's funeral had to take place without any fuss and in secret and that the first step in this direction would be to stop up his own sobbing and try instead to conduct himself in a calm, dignified and becoming manner with a certain degree of meekness and submission, while somehow standing firm. In sum, he did what was required of him. In any case, their clipped tones and matter-of-fact attitude scotched any thoughts of extravagant mourning. So, instead of getting worked up, the colonel just stood there for a while, stunned.

Unable to find a pay desk, he came back to the snooker table and fished out all the notes he had in his wallet, of small and large denominations and, not knowing exactly how much he owed, slapped the whole bundle down on the green baize. With any luck, that would settle the matter. But what still niggled the colonel was that he had made a mistake about the snooker business. About thirty years ago – or was it even longer? – around the time of the Mossadeq affair, one autumn afternoon he had gone to a snooker hall with one of his fellow officers, who not long after had been shot. They were both lieutenants and were strolling along Lalezar Avenue* when his friend suggested they go in and play a couple of frames. The colonel knew nothing about snooker and, not surprisingly, lost. But he could vividly recall every detail of the hall, with its green baize tables, the brightly coloured balls, the perfectly formed wooden triangles, the finely turned cues, the little pieces of chalk and the empty lemonade bottles, and his friend telling him that the game had originally come from Russia. And so he approached the man sitting behind the table and said, as if he were making a confession:

"I made a mistake… a mistake… forgive me; I forgot that I did actually play snooker once."

"I beg your pardon?"

"Nothing, sir… nothing… it just came out. You see, I just can't help saying things sometimes. Something in me makes me want to rake over all my past sins and tell someone about them."

Somewhat taken aback, the man behind the table stared

blankly at the colonel, looking long and hard at his face as if there was something odd about it. Realising that the man hadn't the faintest idea what he had been talking about, the colonel turned away. He could not possibly understand what was going through the colonel's mind and why he was talking in such a random fashion. He was sure that if the fellow had been in his shoes, he would have started thinking about things, too, and would have reflected on his past and would have tried to find the reasons for his sins and, at least, would have undergone some sort of self-examination.

What possible reason can there be for thinking that I have sinned in the past and that I am now being punished for it? How can anyone else possibly understand how, with every breath and with every step, I am drowned and suffocated by a feeling of guilt? It has got such a grip on me that I feel that my entire existence is under question. It's so powerful that I don't know what to do with myself. It's got to the point where I imagine I am being followed around by a pair of invisible policemen who watch everything I do. I suppose I can be thankful that, since my stomach ulcers, I've given up drinking. And after killing my wife, I've lost all interest in women. So there's no danger of me even looking at one or, God forbid, disgracing myself by falling for her charms. I'm not involved in any business or wheeler dealing, so I'm not mixed up in any thieving or swindling. As to what I live on, I'm drawing on a little nest-egg that my sons and I put aside. If anyone wants to investigate me, they'll find that I've not taken even so much as a packet of cigarettes off my daughter, now the wife of Qorbani Hajjaj. Nor have I ever left Yousef Noqli's teahouse without paying for my glass of tea. I don't believe in living on tick. And don't even get me started on my setar-playing. I used to play all the time and I still want to play, *but my hands are now so unsteady that I can't control the thing. I haven't touched it for years now, and it just sits there in its old case on the wall, with dust as thick as your finger on it. Even the policemen didn't react when they saw it. What else? Two important things: I have committed two mortal sins in my life. One was killing my wife and the other was disobeying the order to join the Dhofar campaign.* I killed my wife, that's true, and I didn't go to Dhofar, that's also true.*

Why should I have cared that the British didn't want to leave the Sultan at the mercy of some rabble of barefooted peasants? Why should I care that they wanted to give us the honour of being their comrades-in-arms and saddle the Shah with the costs of the campaign? I just knew that I had to say no, and I did exactly that.

The man behind the green baize table suddenly got up. Holding his stomach in, he stood bolt upright. His new tone showed that he was beginning to get irritated: "Well, what are you waiting for, it's nearly morning?"

The young men sprang into action. One of them took the colonel by a scrawny elbow and spun him round, while another shoved the receipt for the money into the colonel's coat pocket:

"All ready, Colonel."

"I know, Sir. I know."

* * *

"Dhofar is an important and prestigious posting, Colonel! It is a mark of the esteem in which His Imperial Majesty holds patriotic officers like you. I congratulate you."

"Sir, I…"

"Good luck, Colonel!"

"It's just that I still have to sort out a family problem, sir, as you are aware."

"Put it from your mind, Colonel. There is no getting out of it. That's that."

"But, General, it's my wife…"

"You must consider the consequences, Colonel, since she shares your name. Don't forget that your wife comes from a very prominent family…"

"But, Sir, I am just a simple soldier…"

"We are all soldiers, Colonel. Haven't I made myself clear?"

It was night when they summoned the colonel to headquarters. Night is when crimes are committed, he thought, and night is also when they are planned and the evidence is buried. Criminals fear the light of day and try to wash the evidence off their hands before dawn and hide their guilty consciences from their fellow men. And so it was, that night, that the Colonel decided on crime. He would absolutely not obey the order of posting. As he took the written order from the general's puffy white fingers, he decided to kill his wife. He could not bring himself to fly to Dhofar to slaughter a bunch of hungry rebels on the grounds that they were "a Soviet threat." He could no longer go on living the lie that he had been forced to live.

It was a pimp of a lie! I tucked the folder with the order in it under my arm, about-turned, marched out of headquarters and told my driver to get out of town and take me straight home. Maybe I'd lost my senses, or was it that I'd finally come to them at last? What are one's senses, anyway?"

"This way, Colonel."

"Yes, yes, of course…"

He knew everything was ready. He had hung about too long and it was time to go. He had to go the length of the snooker hall to the door, through the door and down the steps that he had come in by. Outside, waiting in the rain beside the ambulance, he could just make out the two young men who had come to his house. The barrels of their machine guns were shining in the light from the martyrs' shrines as they pulled the hoods of their parkas over their heads. Their trouser bottoms and boots were soaked and spattered with mud. He remembered that the younger one had rubbed at the sparse hair on his face, while the cheeks of the more grown-up one were already endowed with a decent black beard. And now the colonel was watching the ambulance, as it was being washed by the rain, to see how the next stage of the proceedings would begin.

"You sit in the back, Colonel."

The driver, whom the colonel had not noticed – though this was nothing to do with his short-sightedness – was raring to go. Young drivers these days generally drove fast and nipped through the traffic, not at all like the old lorry drivers after the war, who made a point of driving in a very dignified and ostentatiously sedate manner. For instance, whenever they stopped off at a roadside teahouse, they seemed to shed a huge load of responsibility from their shoulders as they got down from their cabs. They always wore a silk neckerchief and, as they got down, they always had one hand hooked onto it as, with great dignity, they took a leisurely turn round the lorry and, after giving orders to their driver's mate, lumbered off to the little stream beside the teahouse, where they squatted down to wash their oily hands and faces, never taking their eyes off the lad who was seeing to the lorry.

But today's young drivers had different ideas about life. Most of them seemed to be rude and flippant, even those who drove ambulances. They were as arrogant as cats that had been told their shit had some use. They didn't give a damn about their passengers and just kept their foot on the floor. It didn't matter if it had been raining and the potholes were full of water; they couldn't be bothered to avoid the bumps or think about an old man perched on the narrow bench in the back, clinging on to his daughter's coffin. The colonel was aware that, by giving his daughter a coffin and an ambulance, they had shown him some respect, but he also noticed that the driver could not care less, and was driving as if he was delivering meat to the butcher's. No question about it – quite unwittingly on his part, he had got this chap out of bed, even though he was supposed to be on nightshift, and now he would be cursing the colonel under his breath all the way to the cemetery.

And again he fell to thinking that, if he had not killed his wife, his daughter would not be lying there in her coffin now. But he knew perfectly well that persisting in this line would get him nowhere and that nothing was going to change. The truth that was now staring him in the face was that Parvaneh was lying in a coffin that smelt of blood and guts and, with every bump in the road, her skinny little body was flapping around in it like a half-dead fish. Parvaneh had been young and the colonel could not imagine her without her grey school smock. He could even picture the outline of her bony shoulders through it. So much about Parvaneh reminded the colonel of the little canary which, from the first day, he had named after her. Perhaps he had become so attached to his motherless daughter through having had to bring her up on his own, loving her both as a father and as a mother. He saw her as a fledgling that he was teaching how to fly. He had once heard that young birds lose their way in storms, especially at dusk, and get blown off course into unfamiliar country. He saw all her comings and goings in this light and, when she disappeared, he imagined that the wind had carried her off and lost her.

The wind confuses them, makes them giddy. I am no professional pigeon fancier, but I know this much, that young birds get lost in the wind, particularly in a west wind. It confuses them and makes them giddy, it ties them up in knots and they lose their sense of direction and, in their struggle to find their way, they break their wings. And in a storm there is no shortage of hawks and vultures looking for prey.*

The night that Parvaneh failed to come home, the colonel had a premonition that the wind had taken her, and he could not help thinking how many pigeons with bloodied wings he had seen over the years. So he waited, which was all he could do. Which in fact was not doing anything, but just a state of mind. A state of mind that our fathers and forefathers have passed down to us like some painful legacy. Waiting, endlessly waiting… And now he was waiting to get to the graveyard, in the hope that, as she was being consigned to the earth, he could pull aside Parvaneh's blood-stained shroud and see her face one last time.† Of course, he could uncover her right here in the ambulance, but he was worried that this breach of the rules might have unpleasant consequences, both for him and for the others. He could imagine her face and he could even feel how she had become almost weightless in her innocence, more so than she had ever been in her life. This feeling only served to heighten the pain, making it so acute

as to almost tip the old man over into madness. But because
he knew he had to remain calm and composed, he forced
himself to suppress all thoughts – impossible thoughts – that
his daughter was alive, as it was obviously out of the question. Experience had taught him that outpourings of grief at
the death of a loved one come from remembering moments
in their life. So, the only way for him to hold back his grief
would be to resist thinking of her as alive. This was anything
but easy, and required complete control over his nerves and
over his mind. He was determined to shut out any thoughts
of his daughter when she was alive until after the funeral,
when everyone had gone away. And so he tried to imagine
Parvaneh as a dead fish on a river bank, wrapped in a dirty
cloth, which flapped this way and that every time the ambulance hit a bump in the road.

*But… was it really because I disobeyed orders, was arrested
and went to prison, that I could not do my duty by Parvaneh,
my youngest child? After all, Farzaneh, her elder sister, was busy
looking after her husband, and my boys had all gone their own
ways. Amir was in prison, Mohammad-Taqi was trying to get
into university and Masoud was a complete loner. Oh my poor
children… at least one of you might have taken better care of
yourselves. It's not as if you had to bear the whole weight of the
world on your shoulders! I am not as strong as you may think I
am. Do you want to take on the whole world? Life is not about
winning, you know… But whenever I tackled them about this,
they always had an answer up their sleeves.*

"But we get it all from you, papa, you are one of the few
officers of the Shah who refused to go to Dhofar. You were
the only person who told us all about Mossadeq and how he
nationalised the oil industry."*

I walked a very straight line, my dear children. But none of you cared about the others and you all went charging off in different directions. What's the matter with you all? You're all one family, but you bark up different trees! What is it that you are all after, that keeps you so much at each other's throats? Are you all living on different planets?

No, in fact they were living on the same planet. But each of them reckoned to have found their own answers to life. They showed me respect but, at bottom, they did not believe in me. When it came down to it, they saw me as an officer of the Shah, although they granted that I'd had no part in the crime that was Dhofar. But even that couldn't prevent them from regarding me as a creature of the old regime.

They knew all about the pyramid structure of the Shah's army, but I could never get them to accept the truth. My children did not despise me, but I felt their contempt deep within me. Maybe they were brighter than me and were simply foreseeing the day when their father, the great patriotic military man, would end up as an old pigeon fancier and a *setar* player who couldn't even play any more. And if I hadn't killed their mother, would they even pay me the slightest attention nowadays? Who knows? But I did kill my wife, and it wasn't difficult. Which was how I ended up going to the detention barracks without a care in the world.

"Did you really kill your wife, colonel?"

"Yes, I did. Does that surprise you?"

"And you didn't go to Dhofar?"

"As you can see, no."

* * *

"We're here, colonel. Please step down."

"Yes, all right, just a minute."

The back doors of the ambulance opened and practised hands pulled the coffin out. The coffin was light, very light, feather-light. They put it down in the mud next to one of the graves and stood aimlessly around it. In the darkness, one could not make out which prominent family the grave belonged to. It was still raining, which was probably why the driver hauled himself over to the passenger side, stuck his head out of the window and told one of the policemen, whom he addressed as Ali Seif, that it was time to get back. This was when the colonel learned the policeman's name, and he made an effort to keep it in his head. He thought that it was perfectly natural for the driver to want to get back, as he had done his job. He had taken a lot of trouble, coming out of his way over the muddy, bumpy track up the hill to the graveyard. Ali Seif said nothing to the driver, or perhaps he did and the colonel did not hear him above the hissing of the rain. The driver started to move off and they all knew that he would have to reverse first to find a wider space to turn round in. They kept staring at the ambulance as it went off, clearly worried that one of its back wheels would slide off the track and get stuck in the mud. Only when it had got to a clear space, turned round, accelerated down the hill and disappeared did they breathe a sigh of relief. They looked at each other and then realised that they were still some way from the mortuary, where they needed to wash the body before burying it. The colonel, in some puzzlement, supposed that the driver had made a mistake and taken them to the graveyard first, instead of to the mortuary.

Of course, it was nothing to do with me. I had never felt the need to commit to memory the geometrical position of the cemetery. I was under arrest when my wife was buried, and at Mohammad-Taqi's funeral I had my head buried in my shoulders and, apart from sun and dust, I couldn't see anyone or anything in front of me. I had lost all sense of direction. That day was the first time that I felt no wish to look the world in the face.

* * *

They had brought Mohammad-Taqi back from Tehran – it was late January or early February 1979, in the throes of the revolution. At that stage, Amir was still a strong and upstanding young man, not the resigned, one might almost say the confused old man that he later turned into. Without breaking down or letting his grief get the better of him, he knelt down beside his brother, bending right down as if to sniff his brother's bloodied shirt. Then he stood up again in manly fashion, straight and proud, turned away and took his place alongside the others. The colonel would have expected no less of him. Farzaneh looked as if she were walking on coals and Parvaneh circled round her brother, like a moth flying into a guttering candle flame.* It was there that the colonel felt that his little daughter's heart was broken. He asked himself why it is that love and affection are like an abscess that is only lanced by the death of one's nearest and dearest, then wondered what on earth had made him come up with such a horrible analogy of love. He had had no time to dwell on this, though, as little Masoud had gone mad at his brother's martyrdom. He had thrown himself on the bier, weeping and wailing, and had then stood up, held up his clenched fists in the air and, with the veins in his neck bulging, bellowed out, "Oh my God!" The colonel heard Masoud's screams but, over the angry shouts of the crowd, he could not make out what he was yelling. At that moment, it dawned on the colonel how many people had prior claims on the blood of his children. Something within him snapped and he was overcome by a feeling of bitterness and alienation from the proper emotions of a father whose son has just been killed. He cracked up, turned away from the world and became a hermit in a corner, far from the madding crowd, there to end his days. He felt as if his spine had broken and he could not walk upright; then all of a sudden, he felt Parvaneh throwing herself into her father's arms. For a moment, the colonel had to forget his own misery and he took hold of his daughter's little shoulders to try and still the alarming, sobbing convulsions that shook her whole body from head to foot.

* * *

"We should have taken her to the mortuary first, Colonel."

"Yes, I thought so too. We should have. Let's take her there now… You lead the way."

The bier weighed no more than a pigeon's wing. Even so, the colonel wished that he had brought Amir to hold one of its feet. It might not weigh much, but the done thing was for four people to carry it on their shoulders. Ali Seif solved the problem. He got the colonel and the other fellow to carry one end on their shoulders, while he supported the other end on his fists, balanced on his barrel chest. And so they trudged off through the graves in the mud and slush. When they found the mortuary and had set the coffin down, the colonel felt his sweat pouring out of his ears. He was soaked through, as much by sweat on the inside as by rain on the outside. He looked as though he had just been fished out of a river.

Once more, the three of them found themselves standing aimlessly beside the coffin. It was dark as a tomb inside the mortuary and they could scarcely make one another out. As they hung about, uncertain what to do, it struck the colonel that the policemen must be exhausted, and possibly even a little spooked, by all this miserable portering, even though they probably would not admit it. They were all tired, each in their own way. They were all waiting for someone to break the silence of this deathly blackness. The only sign of life was the sound of their heavy breathing, like criminals about to embark on a job. The chilly, airless atmosphere in the ante-room, with the rain battering down on the mortuary's rusty tin roof, made his skin creep. The bulging walls were wet and clammy. Reeking of a mixture of damp, decay, camphor and cedar-leaf oil, they felt swollen by the remembrance of endless hideous deaths. This was not like the rain and mud outside. The dampness on the floor here seeped through the soles of their shoes into their feet, worked its way into the flesh and up into the guts and sent a shiver of nausea right to the marrow of their bones. And the silence, the silence of the ghosts… The colonel imagined himself and the two police-men as coagulated and frozen solid, like exclamation marks, beside the coffin. His sight seemed to have mildewed over, his breath stank of decay and his body felt as if it was decom-posing into cold slippery sweat and was about to freeze solid.

"You need someone who's next of kin, Colonel; the body has to be washed by someone next of kin, like a mother or a sister."

Ali Seif's voice hit the colonel like a slap in the face and hung there for a moment until the echo died away. Of course, he knew perfectly well that the laying out had to be done by a close relative, but it vexed him that nobody had thought about it earlier. What could be done about it now that the ambulance had gone back? Why had they not told him before? How could nobody have thought about a body washer when they had sat him down in the ambulance, with no idea where he was going, next to his dead daughter? *Isn't body washing the most basic part of their job? What are they bloody paid for? They shouldn't break things to people so suddenly and with such bad timing, when they should have thought about it beforehand. But it's no good worrying about that now; I need to get on with it.*

"Yes, colonel, you need to sort this out. We'll stay here until you get back. Go and fetch her sister. Have a think, and bring whatever else you need. But we haven't got all night, you know."

"Yes, I know." *I know that we have to get this thing over with by daylight.* "But where can I get a gravedigger from? Some out-of-work fellow off the street, maybe?"

"No."

"Oh, are there graves already dug, then?"

"That's a thought, but no. We'll help you dig. But we need a pick and shovel. Where are we going to get them from?"

"I wish you'd thought about that before the ambulance went off. I wish I had had my wits about me at the time, but then my wits aren't what they used to be…"

The colonel's problem with his wits was that he had got used to living in the past and thinking about nothing else. The past had such a hold on him that he had grown afraid of dealing with what was happening under his nose. This fear of the present and living in the past had become a habit. Perhaps it was just an instinctive retreat, a defence against events.

In occasional idle moments, his thoughts wandered back to the story of Rostam and Ashkabus, those ancient enemies of the Shahnameh, and he would lose himself in the story of their battle, which he never tired of… Really, he ought to have given his children names like Paridokht and Ashkabus.* He was fully aware of this involuntary tendency of his to dwell on the past, and it bothered him that even now it might make him forget what it was that he had to fetch. And so, as he walked back home, he kept repeating aloud to himself, "pick and shovel; Farzaneh, shroud, pick and shovel; Farzaneh, shroud…"

"Right, gentlemen… I'll leave you in charge of my daughter until I get back."

The colonel left the mortuary without bothering to wait for an answer. He knew perfectly well that there could be no answer to what he had just said and, when he thought about it, he realised that there was no need to have said it. But then, is anything we say ever really necessary, and are all words to be weighed in the balance of reason? No, most things we say are to stop ourselves worrying and to keep a lid on our own fears, so that, in time, they become just a habit. *It's like when, without thinking, we tell one of our boys — let's say my Kuchik — who is heading off to war, to take care. Well, really, as if he wouldn't take care if we didn't say it!* In effect, aren't we just trying to say that the war should look after him? No, since the war has not undertaken to take care of anyone. So, even though we know that what we say means nothing, we still say it, just out of a wish to stop our loved ones from worrying. Otherwise, could there be anything more moronic than a man of the colonel's age asking two young warriors to look after his daughter, a girl who was asleep for all eternity in her coffin? After all, they had not looked after her very well when she'd been alive, had they?

It's stupid, just stupid; either everything is stupid, or I am an idiot!

When young Masoud had been about to set off for the front, the colonel, without thinking, had said to him, "Take care of yourself, my boy." The instant he said it, he was all too conscious of the fact that war was some kind of poisonous, carnivorous plant. You could make it responsible for anything, except for the lives of the people caught up in it. Apart from anything else, anyone could tell that, if war was going to be answerable for people's welfare, then war would not be war. It would be something else. *What else could I have said? Any fool can see that if someone's worried about his own welfare, he is hardly going to go to war!* So, if he had really wanted to dissuade little Masoud, he should have said something quite different to him before he had set off, and come up with some far more persuasive arguments.

But I was firmly of the view that my children, each in their own way and independently of me, had the right to form their own set of values and standards, even though Masoud had persuaded himself that his entire family was beyond the pale, including me, his own father. Sure, I believed in independence for my children, but it's a bit late to do anything about it now, even if I wanted to, isn't it?

Am I going the right way? It looks right.

Yes, he could see the city lights in front of him. It was

lucky that the city was out of range of Iraqi missiles, other-wise there would have been blackouts and the colonel would not have been able to find his way. By now, though, he was sure he was on the right track, heading towards the entrance to the narrow street which, after several twists and turns past a number of cul-de-sacs, eventually emerged into the square in front of the town hall and carried on to the little alley where his house was. He did not have to go through the square, though. Another way was to climb a grassy slope, taking care not to slip on the wet, rotting grass and then go down to a big hollow, which was not very deep but was always full of mud and rainwater, where he had to watch his step. After going round the hollow, he reached his alleyway, a little alleyway that was just made for a fine spring day when a man could take his stick and go out for a walk. For no sooner had you emerged from it than you could see in front of you the meadows on the foothills ablaze with flowers, and inhale the breeze that came down the mountains to fill the lungs, blowing away the accumulation of cheap cigarette smoke, and sucking in the delight of being alive. These were moments to be savoured, when no black clouds hung over the sky, and the sun did not seem to have swallowed itself in grief. Not like these days, when the sun seemed to have been buried for ever and there was nothing but the irritating drip of incessant, soul-destroying rain.

As the colonel turned into his street he knew that he had to be careful how he went at this late hour, and have some answers ready for the young men who hung around on every street corner like goats, seeing conspiracies and plots in the most everyday comings and goings. It was as if they were training to be detectives, practising on the passers-by. To lend weight to their dangerous game, they had to imagine that each of the passers-by had committed some criminal act. At the very least, they were involved in adultery or drug smuggling, or visiting a cache of weapons, or were linked to people who were plotting to overthrow the regime. Perhaps the colonel was getting carried away, but the fact was that he had no wish to make his problems any worse and, if he was letting his imagination get the better of him, he chose to see it as some passing compulsion that was not natural to him. It grew out of the atmosphere that pervaded the streets and alleyways where he lived. He regarded the fear and insecurity that this atmosphere provoked in him as a kind of necessary training for life which, like it or not, everyone was forced to be inoculated with. Take the sensation of fear, for instance. You can be frightened of something without knowing what it is. Looming over your head, you fancy you see a sword held in an invisible hand, and you have long felt its steel in your bowels. This feeling is irrational, and you cannot shake it off. *Because you fear being spied upon, you end up believing that you really are being spied upon. But if this turns out not to be so, you still have to ask yourself why you can't stop imagining that it's happening. Where does this corrosive and exhausting feeling that constantly tells you that every eye is watching you come from?*

* * *

"Yes, sir, yes, it's me. I'm going home to get a pick and shovel. No, my mistake. I'm actually on my way to my daughter's house first… no, sorry, that's wrong, I mean I'm going to my son-in-law's house to borrow his pick and shovel. I'm sure you know him, Mr Allah-Qoli Qorbani Hajjaj."

Another voice came from a dark corner: "Let him go, it's only *the colonel*." The mocking, sarcastic stress on the word "colonel" seeped like poison into the colonel's bone marrow.

Yes, my friend… you must be right. I know that in this country the person who's invariably right is the one who can fix his bayonet fastest and hardest. Right? Did I say "right"?

In any small town you can always find someone who is different from the others and who, as chance would have it, also has an unusual name or a nickname. Such a creature becomes the butt of jokes and is mercilessly baited because, for whatever reason, he is on a different wavelength to everybody else. They treat him as a half-wit and a nutter. The young man who had recognised the colonel clearly saw him as just such a person. The colonel did not see himself as a nutter at all, but he was in no mood to bother about what other people thought about him. Without glancing round he carried on, trying not to be sidetracked by stray thoughts. Any moment, if he wasn't careful, he would trip over and sink up to his knees in a muddy pothole. So, instead of worrying about the jokes and sneers, he concentrated on every step of the way to the house of his son-in-law, Allah-Qoli Qorbani.

Of course, he knew it was far too late to be calling but there was no other way, so he rang the bell. Ah, yes, the bell – the house had only just been built and, as far as the colonel could remember, the bell had not been connected yet. He would have to bang on the new ochre-painted steel gate with a stone, a shoe horn or a penknife. It was obvious that to do such a thing at that late hour, just before the dawn call to prayer, would give those inside a fright. Then again, he thought, anyone sleeping safe and sound in their own home should expect alarms and frights as a matter of course. Because we all, rightly or wrongly, learn to live with such frights; we are subconsciously primed to expect the next alarming event, as a kind of defence mechanism against living in a constant state of insecurity and blind terror. And isn't this anxiety bound up with our abiding fear of death? Of course, it seemed natural to the colonel that nobody expected to die. By forgetting that death is decreed, one can bear the weight of the world on one's shoulders and live a little. At the same time, he thought, everyone, in his own mind, without actually facing up to it, must be waiting for death. Of course, mused the colonel, everyone expects to die, even if they won't admit it. It can happen to anyone that the grim reaper comes banging on the door just before the dawn call to prayer. Even Allah-Qoli Qorbani Hajjaj must believe that.

"Who is it? Who's there?"

It was the shaking voice of his daughter Farzaneh. There could be nothing ordinary about all this commotion at the door. The colonel's family had experienced more than their fair share of fear and alarm, and anxiety was a constant part of their daily lives, yet none of them had ever got used to it. As she spoke, Farzaneh's voice betrayed her growing sense of unease. It was as though, even before she had been woken by his knocking, she had been with the colonel in his nightmares and had seen all that he had seen. The old man felt sorry for his daughter and felt that he ought not to keep her in suspense any longer. He needed to steel himself for a talk, however brief, with her. He wanted to put her mind at rest, but what should he tell her? Would the news that he had to break to her do anything to calm his Farzaneh down? Not likely. When he thought about it, he felt empty inside and wished that he hadn't knocked on the door. But who else could he turn to? Who else was as close to him as Farzaneh? It was too late now, so he had better stop agonising over it. There was nothing else for it.

"Papa, papa... Is that you?"

"Yes, it's me, my dear."

"What are you doing there, why don't you come in? And why are you standing there looking so worried?"

The first "why" was clearly a reproach to the colonel for knocking the house up so late, but Farzaneh had quickly picked up the undue harshness of her tone and softened it by asking how he was. He was not offended by her tone, though. However old and grumpy fathers can be, they never let go of the capacity to forgive and indulge their children, and he did not have it in him to get angry with her. It was not his children that the colonel was angry with, but with their lives in general. *Oh, Lord... we seem to spend our entire lives in not knowing what to do, and putting off to tomorrow what we need to do today...*

The colonel could not think how to break the news of Parvaneh's death to his surviving children. What made it all the more difficult was that here he was, at this hour, having to tell his daughter that her younger sister had been killed and then having to ask her to come with him to the cemetery to lay out her body. He lost his nerve; he couldn't possibly tell her, not now. He would just have to get a grip on himself and tell her something else. But what?

"Er, Farzaneh, my dear, you had a pick and shovel here once, didn't you? You must have a pick and shovel here somewhere, mustn't you?"

The colonel's daughter stared at her father in astonishment.

She was quick-witted enough to smell that something dreadful had happened. The colonel had not been far out in thinking that everyone expects dreadful news sooner or later. And Farzaneh had been at the eye of a storm of tragedies of late. If she could only get over her amazement and open her mouth, she could force him to be frank with her and satisfy her quite justifiable curiosity. But the fact that Qorbani chose that moment to wake from his usual deep sleep left him still in the tangle. Qorbani harrumphed and called to his wife – calling her "Kuchik," the family name for Masoud – and his tone made it clear that he wanted to know where she was and who was at the door and what she was doing. Before Qorbani had time to sling a coat over his shoulders and come out onto the verandah of his new house, the colonel asked her again for the pick and shovel. Fearful that her husband would say something rude to the colonel, Farzaneh quickly forestalled him by turning her back on her father and running down to the basement, explaining to her husband on the way that the colonel just wanted to borrow a pick and shovel.

When he comes home at night, or early in the morning, his sweat smells of blood, Papa. His shirt, his vest, even the hair on the back of his hands smells of blood. I have seen bloodstains on his overshoes, and I've cleaned them off myself. Sometimes I've even seen blood on his trouser bottoms. I've seen all this with my own eyes and I'm sure… absolutely sure that…"

Farzaneh had said this to her father more than once. When the colonel saw that Qorbani had not been surprised by his banging at the door, or by his need for a shovel, he began to think that Qorbani might know what was up… And his suspicions became stronger when Qorbani simply ignored him, his own father-in-law, turning up in the middle of the night, and went back inside, muttering something sarcastic about the baby crying. He called his wife inside and, leaving the door half open as he went into the hall, gathering his coat tails, he paused:

"It looks as though nothing will ever make this rain stop."

* * *

What was it that Amir had said on that rainy day when he had been sitting on the old velvet sofa next to the stove with his legs casually crossed, smoking his pipe and with that Bolshevik cap on his head that he refused to take off, even indoors? How he had banged on, so pretentiously, so much so that Qorbani had believed that his brother-in-law fancied himself as some sort of leader. What had happened in that room? The colonel had seen how Qorbani had slipped out and, without telling the family what he was up to, rustled up a crowd and brought them back to the colonel's house to do honour to his son, the returning hero who, "After enduring years of imprisonment and torture, here he is once more, with his head held high. Having depended on the unstoppable momentum of the people to secure his release from gaol, he is now going to mobilise that same force to overthrow this government of tyrants and oppressors and make this part of the country tremble with fear!"

What a speech! No doubt Qorbani had learned this humbug and windbaggery from newspapers, which at that time had made a sudden U-turn from their former line. I hope I never read words like that in a newspaper again, let alone in a novel, for those kind of hollow, weasel words aren't even worthy of a piece of fiction!

And in no time a crowd of people, "simple gullible people," as if they had suddenly been woken from a deep sleep, some with umbrellas and some without, began to beat a path to the colonel's house in the pouring rain. The colonel, stunned and silent, looked on as tray after tray of fruit and pastries were delivered, ordered by Qorbani and his cronies. After a while, so many people had piled in on top of each other in the courtyard, and even in the alley outside, that there was no more room for them. He noticed that Amir had been dragged out of the living room onto the verandah to give a speech of thanks. But the crowd wanted more. The place was not large enough for such a huge gathering, nor was there a loudspeaker, but it did not matter. That was the sort of thing that Qorbani was used to dealing with, and before Amir had had time to think, he was being swept along by the crowd to the town square. Amir, whom Qorbani claimed had "risked his life, all his worldly goods and his reputation to further the cause of the revolution" – more weasel words – was hoisted up onto a dais, fully equipped with a lectern and microphone. Helpers were even hauled in to hold umbrellas over his son in the rain, which was still drumming down mercilessly through the barrage of slogans and clichés that bellowed out in broken fragments from the loudspeakers: "Oppression… inflation… oil… fatherland… workers… proletariat… dictatorship… ism… more isms… and freedom, oh yes, we mustn't forget freedom." And the people suddenly found they had a talent for listening, for harmony and conformity. Raised fists and slogans, a scuffle or two at the edge of the square, a couple of random shots, shouts of "make way," and then Qorbani and his boys forced a passage through the crowd for Amir to a big car that was waiting there with its doors open. It had been borrowed from a showroom belonging to one of Qorbani's new best friends.

Back in the house, the colonel opened his cigarette case, lit one and stared silently at his son… Amir hoped for at least a brief look of approval from his father, albeit mixed with the customary measure of mistrust. He wanted to know that he had impressed the colonel and had finally persuaded him to believe in his son. Perhaps it was this burning, yet unspoken, urge that prompted him to ask: "What did you think, Colonel?" But the colonel did not give him the answer he wanted. He just closed his cigarette case and tried to suppress the faint smile that played across his lips, a smile that made Amir blurt out, "It's the revolution – we've got a revolution!"

It was the revolution, yes it was. And now I'm not sorry that I didn't say anything about Parvaneh's execution to her sister. If I'd told her, I'd then have had to ask her to come and wash the body and lay her out. It was just as well I didn't have to tell her and ask her to do such a thing. I'm not just not sorry, I'm quite glad about it now. I'm bloody sure that if I'd said anything, Qorbani would not have let her go. It would have been a bloody disaster… So now…

So now he had to find a quick way of putting Farzaneh's mind at rest.

"With all this rain coming down, you could get flooded out if you didn't have a pick and shovel to hand," he said to her, as casually as he could, while laying the pick and shovel together to hoist them over his shoulder. Without waiting for an answer he turned round and set off.

But he had only gone a few steps when a terrible, keening wail of sorrow and grief broke from his daughter and made him shake at the knees. He knew that, if he did not keep a tight grip on it, the cat would be out of the bag. He stopped and waited in the rain. Farzaneh did not say anything in particular, didn't ask any questions. She did not even beg him to stay. In a voice that shook from the searing dryness of her throat she uttered just one word: "Papa!" Her voice froze his whole body and, for a moment, he stood nailed to the spot. But then, like someone fighting desperately for his life, he tried to pull himself together. Knowing he was invisible in the darkness of the false dawn, and relying on his old age and deafness as an excuse, he pretended not to hear her. The incessant hiss of the falling rain helped him in his ruse. He turned into a dark alley and disappeared out of his daughter's sight, back into the darkness and the rain.

On the way back to his house, so as not to forget, he kept repeating one word over and over again: "shroud." He hummed it out loud all the way: "shroud, shroud, shroud, shroud." As he turned the key in the lock he had to break the rhythm, but after opening the door and stepping into the courtyard, he picked it up again, but this time whimpering the word, like a dog shivering in the cold, wailing the word out, with long pathetic pauses: shroud… shrou…oud… shrou…oud. He carried on whining softly as he switched on the light and opened the chest and rummaged through blankets and his old abandoned uniforms until he found a length of canvas at the bottom. His soft whimpering was like a camel pack, on which he was loading all the burdens of his misery, sending them off to their fate. His only worry was that he might get so carried away that he would forget to collect the pick and shovel, which he had left propped up by the gate. He told himself never to let himself become so absent-minded in such a situation.

I'll never allow myself to get absent-minded! I have made up my mind to keep a cool head through this awful business. I'll wrap up the shroud, just like the country people wrap their lunch in a cloth, and sling it over my shoulders, with two corners tied round my chest. I'll stick my hat on my head and I'll put the pick and shovel on my shoulder, just like the Khorasani peasants I've seen in Birjand* and I'll roll up my trouser bottoms, just in case I trip over them. My overcoat, I'll have to do something about that... but before all that I've got to switch off the lights and lock the door. I can't help it, this door locking has become an old habit and I can't do anything about it, but... oh, nothing...

It was not clear why he could not bring himself to look the photograph of The Colonel in the eye, or even in the boots. He just felt a sense of shame, which prevented him from raising his head to look at him. He thought that the smaller and more abject he became, the greater became the distance between himself and The Colonel. He felt he had lost the capacity for friendship with him, that they no longer had anything in common. If the day ever came when he could no longer look The Colonel straight in his bright black eyes when he spoke to him, he would die. He knew that with every step that he took away from The Colonel, a man who throughout his life had embodied all his ideals, he was moving one step closer to his own death.

Yet he must be able to see the bind I'm in. If the person closest to you can't see the problems you're having, what can you expect from anyone else?

He thought that it was nearly time for the dawn call to prayer, but the false dawn had fooled him. The blackness of the night was made even darker by the heavy clouds. The rain beating down on the tin roof rasped his nerves.

Is that Amir? Is that his voice I can hear? "Amir... Amir?"

He would have to turn back and go down to the basement. There was nothing else for it. Hearing Amir speak was becoming quite a rare event. This was only the second or third time since Amir had retreated to the basement that the colonel had heard him clearly. Going down the steps to the cellar now, he called Amir's name once more, this time loud and clear. But he got no answer, no proper answer, just a string of broken syllables, like the noise someone might make who had just been struck dumb. Odd, frightening gargles. The colonel was so distracted that he realised he had forgotten to turn on the light. He reached out for the switch. The basement lit up and he saw his son huddled on the wooden bed with its rumpled sheets, an old army blanket over his head. He was shaking all over and staring blankly into space – his squint even more noticeable now – as if dazed. He was so wrapped up in his own misery that he had not even noticed his father coming in. The colonel stood and looked at him. Sweat was running down his forehead and his long unkempt hair was matted together. He seemed to have been fighting with his demons in a nightmare. His body twitched convulsively as if struggling against terrible forces from another world, against things that were so unspeakable that he could not bring himself to say what they were.

The colonel had to sit down for a minute to rest. He lit a cigarette, pulled up his stool and, sitting with his back to the half-finished bust that Amir was working on, he could see half of Amir's face. He proffered him the cigarette. He knew that it would be better to get him a glass of water first, but it was too late and Amir snatched the cigarette from the colonel's hand. As he dragged deeply on it, the colonel noticed that Amir's lips were as dry and cracked as a flake of bark. Amir held the smoke in his lungs for as long as he could and, when he finally exhaled, it had mingled with his own damp breath and came out like a jet of steam. Neither of them could think of anything to say. So this, then, was his son – a broken man with grey hair sprouting on his forehead, shattered, desperate and ill.

Amir suddenly seemed to come to, but even when awake he could not seem to escape his nightmares. His lips did not move, and neither did his face, but the colonel could hear his voice, a voice that was broken and changed, as if he were conversing with his bones:

"...the madman, that same madman that I once saw in Birjand, the one they called the Caliph.* No-one knew where he had come from. His face, his eyes, his beard and even the hairs on his temples were dark blue and they said that he would never age and that he had never been any younger than he was now. They said that, to avoid his evil eye, you had to give him alms every time you passed him. They said that a look from him brought a curse and that his breath was poisonous. Yes, that's right, it was him. He was sitting in a porchway and pissing blood. He was pissing blood into my eyes and I couldn't shut them. It had run down to the corner of my mouth and in through my clenched teeth. Clotted now, it was blocking my throat and I was choking while I was forced to look at his cock, which he had sliced up with a barber's razor. I had seen this all with my own eyes when I was a boy. He had painted a face on the tip of his dick and now he was ripping it up with a razor. Then the police came running up. They bundled him into a droshky and carted him off to hospital and we all thought he'd bleed to death. But a week later he was back under the same porchway, sitting on the same charpoy. He'd got himself another razor and was weeping and preparing to mutilate his cock again. He was acting like a man possessed. Now and then, he wiped the snot off his nose with a handkerchief and kept maundering on in a whiny voice. I saw it all myself in my childhood, or maybe in some other childhood, perhaps in a previous incarnation several generations back. But I was seeing it now, and I couldn't do anything about it and I couldn't stand it. I was in agony from pain and pus and suffocation and just wanted to die, but... there was worse to come. The Caliph laid his dick on a piece of black stone from an old tomb, got another sharp stone and... ugh! My skull was bursting and I was yelling, but the Caliph kept beating me about the head with his sharp stone until it was all mashed up and I was still screaming and screaming and I pulled at a cord that was round my neck until it was tight round my throat and I couldn't move, because I was squashed. But I could still feel the Caliph beating and bashing me all over with that piece of stone, which had probably come from a tomb in a cave, trying to break every bone in my body, and my mouth was full of blood and shit and I couldn't shout, but I could hear the cries coming from the throats of the people in their streets, in their alleyways and in their homes, as they were crushed between those two little pieces of black gravestone. Voices... screams. I had lost so much blood and I had vomited up so much blood that I was fainting. I'm amazed I didn't die."

"Ah, colonel, it's you. I'm not dead, am I?"

"No, not yet, my son."

The colonel's reply to his suddenly aged son came from

the creaking of his own bones. Sitting there dazed, with his teeth clenched, he seemed incapable of further speech. He was struggling to keep his composure, telling himself that he must not be shocked or surprised by anything, whether it was by Amir not calling him his father or by his disinhibited obscenities. The colonel had begun to think that the strangest things could happen in life, and that mankind had been created to go through life in a string of bizarre experiences, then to die with its eyes wide open in amazement, proud of never having been shocked by anything.

So why should he now be shocked to see his son reduced to this state – his eldest son, who had witnessed his mother's murder so manfully that he had become almost an accomplice in the deed? Just for a moment it crossed his mind that he should take Amir to hospital, but he dismissed it immediately as pointless. He remembered that the city hospital was overflowing and that the only psychiatrist had gone mad and had been locked up in one of the cells of the Tehran mental asylum, accused of being a spy, and was undergoing 're-education.'

He decided to tell Amir the news that his sister had been hanged, thinking that the shock might shake him free him his nightmares. After all, you were supposed to be able to snap people out of shock by giving them another one. It was no fault of the colonel's that he had never been a psychologist. There were other reasons that prompted the colonel's decision. It would soon be morning and he had to get on with burying his daughter because, if he hung about any more and did not get back in time, it would be too late and he might lose her. He also thought of taking Amir with him: for one thing, he could do with a hand burying her, plus it would be a good way to get Amir out of the house for some fresh air. More than ever, he was deeply anxious about leaving Amir alone. If he didn't take Amir along with him, he would not be able to concentrate on the job in hand. He took the plunge:

"Parvaneh has been hanged."

"Really?"

That was all he said. He just looked at his father, as if frozen. The colonel saw a frightening change come over him, as his whole face took on the expression of an old man now at peace. There was a long silence while the colonel sat quietly, waiting for Amir to react. Amir finally took his eyes off his father's face and hung his head. Then, as if totally unaffected by the news, as if struggling with a geometry problem:

"Wasn't she too young to be hanged?"

The colonel had no reply to that. He took his watch out of his waistcoat pocket and studied it to work out how long it was left before the dawn call to prayer. Putting it back in his pocket, he felt for the knot holding the shroud together. As if giving his son an ultimatum, he pronounced his last word on the subject:

"I'm going to the cemetery. I'm going there to bury Parvaneh. Are you coming with me?"

Amir, still staring blankly in front of him, drained of colour and petrified, suddenly began to shake. His whole body shook stiffly, as if he was having a bout of malaria. His teeth started to chatter and his hands began to punch one against the other, as if some outside force had hold over them, as he tried to grasp the blanket and wrap it round his scrawny body and lose himself in its folds. To the colonel, this was not a cold fever, but fear – dread and horror – that sought refuge in the old blanket that protected him from his nightmares. Amir's whole face was now hidden and panic had turned him into a shaking wreck. The colonel could just hear his voice, muffled by the damp warp and weft of the old blanket:

"No, I'm not coming. I'm nobody's brother. I'm not anybody. I'm nobody. I don't even exist…"

The colonel was already on his way down the stairs when he wondered why he hadn't warned Amir about the "Immortal Prophet Khezr Javid." He should have put his foot down. He would have been perfectly within his rights; it was still his home, after all, and he had a duty to act against suspicious types who drifted in and out of his house. But what Amir had said was ambiguous. What did he mean by saying that he hadn't got a brother? Was it just him being mad, or did he mean something else? *Was he trying to get at me? Was he trying to make me feel even more wretched than I am? What was he driving at? What did he really mean? Was he aware of the venom behind his words? Was he saying that I'm not… not the father of all my children? Has my son become so heartless and cruel as to bring up my wife's whoring – his own mother's whoring? All right, so I killed her, I killed Forouz; right in front of him, I killed my wife. So everything needs to be scrubbed and purified now, does it? Why, why? I've absolutely no doubt in my own mind that none of my children are bastards, no doubt at all. If Forouz had wanted to break the rules, she'd never have agreed to those two operations. And in any event, I'd have noticed. Gut feeling and animal instinct don't lie. No, I loved you all and I love you still. Why else do you think I regret not warning you about Khezr Javid, or why would I be feeling so much love for my little daughter Parvaneh? So much love that I feel I shall die if I return to the cemetery and find that they have already buried her without my seeing her for one last time? Come on now, don't be so foul to me!*

* * *

As the colonel made his way along the muddy streets in the rain, holding the pick and shovel firmly on his scrawny shoulder, his thoughts were never far from Khezr Javid. At times he even felt that "the immortal one" was following him in the darkness and mocking him.* He could picture him standing before him right now: with the collar of his raincoat turned up and the brim of his hat pulled down over his forehead, his coat belt tied at the waist and his shoes shining, as always, in spite of the rain and mud. For Khezr Javid moved in mysterious ways and appeared to walk on air without his devilish shoes ever getting wet, no matter how hard it rained. On the many occasions that the colonel had seen him come to the house he never seemed to be the least bit wet. Incredible! Even on that fateful evening – was that the last time he had seen him? – it had been raining.

The colonel had been sitting on his bentwood chair by the window, looking out and listening to the rain falling into the pool in the courtyard. He noticed that the black cat that usually sat on the edge of the pond was not there. It must have hidden itself away in a corner, out of the wet. This time, Parvaneh opened the door to Khezr Javid. She had rushed out into the courtyard and lifted her face to the rain as it ran down in heavy drops over her cheeks and forehead, enjoying the game as if she were a small girl. As he looked on, the colonel felt embraced by the warm feeling of sharing in her simple pleasure.

Khezr Javid knocked on the gate. Parvaneh opened it and, without looking at him, hid herself behind the gate as he swept in. As usual, he made straight for the stairs to the basement. The colonel felt his daughter looking at him and noticed that she had by now shut the gate and was running her palms softly down over her face and down her chin to her neck and throat. The last that the colonel remembered seeing of Khezr Javid that night was of his hands shoved deep in the pockets of his parka, and of his epaulettes and the diamond shaped crease in the top of his woollen cap disappearing down the stairs.

Parvaneh had come into her father's room and was drying her face and hair with a towel that she had brought in with her. The colonel stubbed out his cigarette in the ashtray without looking at his daughter. She stood by the stove and lifted the lid off the teapot to smell the tea, to make sure that it had not stewed. She checked the kettle and poured two glasses, one for her father and one for herself, put them on the table and sat down.

"Papa, would you like some tea?"

Why didn't I have some? Life for an old man is made up of small kindnesses like this. Didn't she know that? ...but of course she did.

"I'll put some more paraffin in the stove for you presently."

I knew it. Parvaneh did this for me every night. The kindness in my daughter's voice breathed new life into that simple act of topping up the paraffin stove. I wanted to show willing, so I said if she was busy I could do it myself, but she ignored me and asked if she could take some tea down to her brother and his visitor and give Amir his night-time pills before she got her hands all paraffiny.

"Should I give them some tea?"

"Yes… do you know how many pills your brother is meant to take, and when?"

She knew. She put the teapot, sugar bowl and two glasses on a tray and, before leaving the room, pulled her scarf over her head and put a towel over the teapot to keep it warm. When she got to the basement, Khezr Javid was just taking off his parka and hanging it on a clothes hook. Parvaneh could see his shoulder holster, which more than satisfied her curiosity. Khezr was evidently taken by surprise for, as the door opened and he saw the girl putting the tray down on the stool, he started, then quickly composed himself and shot a sideways glance at Parvaneh. She could see from her brother's face that she should not have come in without asking. Mortified, she had to get away from her brother and his strange visitor as fast as she could. She fled up the stairs but, before she reached the yard, she heard Khezr Javid's voice, as if for the first time:

"She's still very young and weak. You really shouldn't have got her involved in the revolution and all this activism. It's dangerous for her, very dangerous."

Parvaneh realised she was standing on one leg. Khezr's voice had made her stop stock still, balancing herself with her other foot on the top step. She only noticed it when Khezr stopped speaking. She had been holding her breath while they had been talking about her and, when she realised that Khezr had finished, she breathed again. Putting her weight on both feet she stood, listening, with her ear to the wall, trying to make out her brother's reply to Khezr over the sound of the rain. Amir said something along the lines that Parvaneh just had a youthful zeal for revolution, and that she had only been selling a few newspapers on the street. Besides, no-one in particular had forced her to get involved. His voice was pleading, as if he was begging Khezr to cut him some slack and not be too harsh on his little sister:

"…But she's very fragile. She's really just the colonel's nurse and carer. You know very well that there is the world of difference between her and Mohammad-Taqi, and you've already beaten him up. Frankly… I beg of you…"

You would have thought there was nobody in the basement with Amir, since Khezr Javid made no reply. Amir could just as well have been talking to himself. A few moments later he fell silent and Parvaneh heard loud, irregular snoring from Khezr. He must have fallen asleep. She didn't like the idea of her brother's companion dropping off like that in the middle of his sentence – wasn't that deeply insulting both to her and her brother? When she went into the colonel's room, she felt as if a bucket of cold water had been poured over her. She realised immediately that, instead of going to her father, she should have gone straight to her room, buried her face in a pillow and cried herself to sleep.

Parvaneh had even forgotten she'd said she'd fill up the stove. Clean forgotten! As if she'd never said it in the first place and as if she never used to do my stove for me every night and plump up my pillows as I like them. All that I could see on her face that night was death and dishonour. Her cheeks were scarlet with shame and her lips were grey with the fear of death and her eyes – well, I never saw her eyes that night, as she never looked at me.

The next morning, at about the time of the call to prayer, Khezr Javid got up and got ready to go. From the expression on his face, he did not want to hear another peep out of Amir.

And when Amir did try to speak to him, Khezr ignored him and went upstairs to wash, leaving him there, sitting on a mattress on the floor. It was as if Immortal Khezr had cast a spell on him and struck him dumb. Speechless and filled with a terrible sense of foreboding, he guessed that Parvaneh had already got up to say her morning prayers. He knew that she always came down to see him before going out in the morning, but he could not summon up the strength to go upstairs and warn her that, just for today, just this once, she should stay at home. It was all he could do to haul himself up, sit on the edge of the bed and, ignoring the acid taste in his mouth, light the first cigarette of the day and clutch his head which, from long lack of sleep, weighed half a ton. And there he sat.

Watched by her father, who was sitting watching the rain through the window, Parvaneh ran down the steps into the yard. Crossing to the steps, she went down to the basement, just in time to snatch out of Amir's hand his second cigarette, which he was about to light, and stub it out. She was wearing a grey school smock, with a dark blue satchel slung over her shoulder. Amir could guess what sort of pamphlets and newspapers she had stuffed into it, and Khezr Javid would obviously soon find out.

Why on earth had Parvaneh come down to the basement again after the night she had just gone through? This question really bothered the colonel. The fact was that the girl, after a night of agonising, had got a grip on herself and conquered her fear of death. She had got it into her head to confront her brother and this scowling, arrogant guest, who had never been accepted into this house anyway, and try to correct the false impression that her brother had formed of her. She especially wanted to face down Khezr Javid, and so she waited in the basement until he came down. Not deigning to glance at him, she looked at her brother:

"Isn't your friend going to have breakfast?"

"No, and I don't want any either."

Without looking at her, Khezr went straight to get his parka off the coat hook while Parvaneh, boldly curious, stared pointedly at his shoulder holster. But Amir was looking down, too weak to watch his sister's self-possessed performance. He was turning over in his mind what Khezr had said the night before: "It's dangerous for her, very dangerous."

Khezr's voice was still ringing in Amir's skull as Parvaneh stepped lightly up the stairs. He heard the swish of her blue plastic satchel as it rubbed against her coat. He could also hear that Khezr was ready to go and, hard as it was, he lifted his head to see the Immortal One doing up his shoelaces on the step.

The sound of the front door slamming told Amir that Parvaneh had left. Propping both hands against the side of the bed, he got up. Khezr zipped up his parka and went upstairs. Amir slipped his raincoat over his shoulders and followed him into the yard to hold the gate open for him. Khezr went out and Amir peered out into the alleyway. He imagined Parvaneh's quick, light footsteps. Amir put the chain back on the door and was about to go back to the basement when he was seized by a strange spasm of fear, of a fear that he had been struck dumb. The rain, which he thought might have stopped for a while, had started again and he stood there, hunched up, mortified and soaking wet. He had no idea how long for. He could sense the colonel standing by the window of his room, looking at him and following the receding footsteps of his daughter. The window had steamed up, blurring the colonel, just in the same way that Amir had been in a blur as he watched the colonel, after he had killed his mother, standing out there in the rain with blood dripping from his sabre. But the difference was that the colonel had not been hunched up like his pathetic son. He was ashamed of nothing and was not going to hide his crime from anyone. Amir was not ashamed either, for he knew that only a healthy mind could feel shame, and he felt no shame. No, the reason why he could not lift his head was fear of meeting the colonel's gaze. For he would have found reflected in those eyes the thousand nightmares that were whirling round in his own head. He was terrified that Parvaneh would not come home again.

Nor did she.

I could have done something, could have put my foot down... I had not just the right, but a duty to put my foot down. After all, they were my own flesh and blood. Granted, they were all grown up, but so what? Now, let me check again... Shroud, shovel, pick, shroud... On my way now. Yes, this is the way to the cemetery. How are we doing for time? Not to worry, there's still been no morning call to prayer from the minaret yet. But this rain, this never-ending rain...

It was still pouring and the colonel had to watch his step at the end of the alleyway. He had to pick his way carefully down the slope at the end, round a big muddy puddle, and then up a steep bit. He stopped for a breather before carrying on towards the cemetery and mortuary, where the two policemen were still waiting for him, probably fed up by now. He rehearsed what he would say in case Ali Seif and his colleague had a go at him for taking so long: "Look, my friend, my dear young friend, I'm so sorry. I'm an old man now, it's a long way and it's a rough track and…" He would impress on them how much effort it had been for an old man like him to get all his bits and pieces together, *but I won't breathe a word to them about Amir, not a word! Though, it's not actually risky talking about him nowadays, now that he's inactive politically and a complete irrelevance. But fear is now invading my soul – has invaded my soul – fear and a wish to hide myself away from wagging tongues and knowing looks.*

Repressed, hidden fear: the image of Amir. Fear eats away at the soul worse than leprosy; it hollows a man out and takes him over. The mere fact that he was alive and breathing was enough to convince him that he stood accused, guilty and condemned. Even though he had withdrawn from life and become completely passive, the colonel considered him to be inherently guilty. Amir himself felt guilty of the crime that must have been committed because of him. After all, he had never set foot on any of those conveyor belts that had been set up to take the likes of him to their deaths or, if he had, he had quickly jumped off. Albeit at the cost of his own gradual self-destruction in his father's damp and mouldy basement. In any case, he was guilty and a "corrupting influence on the people" and, at some point in the future, he would have to give palpable shape and form to his unmentioned crime, if only by killing himself.

The colonel felt guilty, too – guilty for the very existence of his children, or lack of it, as the case may be. He bore the burden of the offences of each one of his offspring on his shoulders. As for Amir, apart from having fathered him, he was guilty of harbouring him and allowing him to just sit there in a corner. Although he had done his duty as a father, he could not rid himself of the leprotic grip of a feeling that he was somehow his accomplice, and he passively awaited the day of his punishment. He did not hide from himself that maybe one day, out of sheer exhaustion and confusion, he would lose his grip and would bring this day forward, perhaps by strangling his son and rushing out naked into the street and running to the only hospital in town – the one which had just been opened, and the only psychiatrist had been accused of treason and committed to the central mad-house in Tehran for 'treatment and re-education.'

Up to now he had managed to live with Amir and his problems. Whenever he ran into other people, however unimportant, he behaved as if Amir did not exist, and tried to pretend that he was estranged from his son. He would sometimes even go so far as to believe it himself. But on the other hand, after such encounters he would always reproach himself, telling himself that what he had done had been sheer egotism and selfishness. He asked himself what he was hoping to achieve by such egotism. And in response he came up with the following dictum: people who are drowning in a sea of problems and have lost all sense of self-worth often grasp at egotism and alienation from everything outside themselves as their only point of fixity, and this can help anchor and fortify them – if only to the point of madness. This is what it can come to, then, if you live in a hostile environment and have lost all your dignity.

I'm capable of anything when the world treats me as nothing. I'll become like the ant which fell in the water and, thrashing about wildly, shouted: "The whole world has been washed away!" And, insofar as I have become nothing, all things are therefore permitted unto me, even unto strangling my son and running about naked in the street all the way to the madhouse... No, I'll never, ever lose my nerve. I'll stand by my children through thick or thin. I'll keep a stiff upper lip and never forget that I'm a soldier...

"But, Sir, I am just a simple soldier..."

"We are all soldiers, colonel. Haven't I made myself clear?"

* * *

Amir was still awake when the colonel got home. His wife was still out. They were all well used to Forouz's late-night absences by now. As he had got older, even the colonel had got used to them. Perhaps the sense that he was in danger of eventually just taking everything in his stride played a part in his next decision. So he sat up and waited for her. When Forouz turned up well after midnight, drunk as usual, she flopped like a corpse into bed without more ado. She knew very well that her husband knew exactly what she got up to at night. Sometimes the colonel was aware of her hand sliding under her pillow to pull out a small bottle of sleeping pills.

That rainy night was the last time that the colonel had drunk himself senseless. Amir was sitting at a little table doing his homework and the colonel was sitting on the edge of his single bed, knocking back glass after glass of vodka, not knowing what he was doing or, rather, he knew exactly what he was doing and was drinking to forget. He persuaded himself that he didn't know what he was doing, using a thousand and one tricks to convince himself that he had lost all power of rational choice. And that was the state of mind he was in when he put the final touch to the plan that he had been toying with for some time.

The colonel was weeping. He did not know how long ago it had started. All he could feel was that his eyes were burning with alcohol and – probably – red with his tears. Everything round him was swimming and he could not make out whether it was his own Amir sitting at his little table by the window, or someone else. Nor could he make out whether Amir was looking at him or was staring at the pages in front of him with his ears pricked up to listen to what his father was saying, to the incoherent, crazed ramblings, welling up from deep inside him, as if from some other person. He thought, he hoped that Amir could see what a state he was in. He was sure that Amir had recognised his mother for what she was and could see the fix that his father was in, and that he had no choice but to do what he was about to do. For it seemed only natural to the colonel that the convulsions and spasms that were shaking his whole being should be transmitted to the closest person to him, to his son, who was right there in front of him. And why shouldn't Amir be part of the tragedy?

The colonel sensed that the hairs on his son's neck were standing on end with horror, but his instinct also told him that Amir was at one with his father in what he intended to do, and would help him, for he saw that all the powers of the earth, visible and invisible, were behind him in the crime that he was about to commit. Without allowing himself a second's doubt as to Amir's ideas on the matter, his one thought was to make him his accomplice in the deed.

Yet at the same time he could not involve Amir in the crime. The colonel thought himself a fair man and, however much Amir might sympathise with him, he could not be so selfish as to expect his boy to turn his hand to murdering his mother. After all, he knew that to kill someone, let alone kill one's own mother, was not an easy thing to do and even to think about it was upsetting. It was unthinkable. So the colonel thought it best to leave his son sitting awkwardly on his chair while matters took their course. Amir's silence could mean only one thing: that he wished to stand aside from what was about to happen and let his father sort his problem out by himself.

Eventually, when he staggered up from the bed, he was barely able to keep his balance. Something – probably an empty glass – dropped on the floor and smashed. The colonel stamped on it. He swayed back and forth and everything seemed to go black in front of him. He wiped the sweat off his brow and, in one stride, hauled himself over to the stove, steadied himself on the mantelpiece and began bawling like a stubborn and angry baby. He felt that he did not even have the courage to look The Colonel in the eye. For the black eyes of The Colonel in the photograph were staring at him from under his bushy black eyebrows, behind the glass on which dust never settled and, from the reproach in that look, he felt not just shame, but terror. All he could do was lean his forehead against The Colonel's field boots and, weeping, call out his name over and over again. *Colonel… Colonel…*

Later – he did not know how much later – he pulled himself together, picked his officer's cap off the bed and set it squarely on his head, drew his sabre from its scabbard, took one step back and looked The Colonel straight and firm in his unyielding eyes:

"I'll kill her, I'll kill her tonight!"

I can't remember, but in all likelihood that was the night *when Amir began to change into a completely different person. It was that night that opened the wound that never healed. It must have been after that that Amir went off, got engaged, joined some revolutionary groups, lost his wife, went to prison and put himself through ordeals of fire and water* in order to be born again and get his life back on track. But it didn't happen, in fact things got even worse – he lost his wife first and then himself. A man can cope with only so much in this life. It must have been after this that my son and I came across each other in prison.*

* * *

It was only in the final year, before all the prisons were opened anyway and the inmates released, that Amir and the colonel found themselves thrown together. Amir was a political prisoner, accused of "endangering national security," while the colonel had been found guilty of a string of offences, both political and criminal. His case had been investigated by military counter-intelligence. Only after he had been stripped of his rank, sentenced and automatically cashiered from the army did they transfer him to a political prison. It was there that the colonel found himself next to Amir and got to know his son in a new way, in which Amir was not merely his son, but first and foremost an independent man in his own right, with his own future in front of him.

The colonel had always let his children find their own way in life. He had not even prevented Parvaneh, the youngest of his children, from ploughing her own furrow. But now he could not help but wonder whether the dreadful fate that had overtaken every one of his children was in fact due to his *laissez-faire* approach. But no, this did not really provide the old man with an easy answer, either. He firmly believed that he had bequeathed to his children only the most natural of rights, namely the right to determine what they wanted to do with their lives. But that did not mean by a long chalk that he had been guilty of teaching them to be irresponsible – none of them could ever be accused of being irresponsible. No, he had done his best to bring up his children and had, perhaps, at times even gone to extremes to control them.

In the end, perhaps the colonel's wish that his children lead independent lives was a reaction on his part against a life which he felt had been imposed upon him. He felt that he had been short-changed by never having had the freedom to live his own life. This made him feel like some sort of cripple. He felt himself a lesser man for having being forced to live a life under duress and that, until a man takes charge of his own life, he cannot truly know himself. Such a half-baked creature, whether in life or in death, cannot be judged for what he is or was, for he might have become something that he could never even have imagined. The colonel's firm views on this score made him convinced that he was not the person whom others thought him to be, whom others presumed to pass judgement on. Given this verdict on himself, he certainly was not about to accept other people's judgements of him without demur. And he would probably never discover who he really was, now that he had burdened himself with a weight of guilt that it would take him thousands of years to wash away.

At least one of you should look out for himself. It's not as though you were carrying the weight of all history on your shoulders! I'm not as strong as you think I am. That's what he really wanted to tell his children.

* * *

They came and told him that Amir was in prison as well, and showed him a file containing a bloodstained knife.

"A knife? With blood on it? Do you mean Amir has killed someone with it?"

"Yes, colonel. Do you find that hard to believe?"

* * *

"Do you recognise this knife?"

Yes, Amir did recognise it. The knife still had blood on it and it had been put right under his nose on a grey metal table. On the opposite side of the table stood not Khezr Javid, but another man, twice the size of a normal man, who kept playing with his false teeth and swaying back and forth. He was tall and square-shouldered, with a slight stoop. He had a big, block head and short grey hair. His eyes were narrow, lifeless and glassy. To Amir, in his fever, he looked like a monster.

Maybe the monster did not intend to frighten Amir but, with his rolled up sleeves, massive scarred and filthy hands, low brow and glassy eyes, and his colossal frame, which almost scraped the ceiling, and the way he kept pushing his false teeth in and out, he was threatening enough. His shoulders were so broad that they seemed to fill the whole room. His whole appearance was quite fearsome enough, to the point of being a joke. Amir felt the man was playing with him. There was no cable whip in his hand; he didn't need one. But Amir could see one hanging coiled, serpent-like, on the wall. He could hardly breathe and his stomach, swollen and heavy, was pressing up on his chest. He wanted to get a look out of a window or even a skylight, just to get a breath of air and see what time of day it was. But there was no window; the room didn't seem to have a door, either. It must have had one, but Amir could not make it out. There was just a small shaded lamp, which lit the bench that he had collapsed onto. The monster was in shadow, while the lamp was trained on the bloodstained knife on the metal table, so that Amir could see every detail of it. He thought he could see Mansour Salaami's fingerprints on its bone handle, but that was probably a figment of his fevered imagination, brought on by torture and terror.

"The knife… I'm asking you, do you recognise it?"

"Yes… I've seen it before."

"When? Was it night-time or daytime? What time was it?"

"I don't know. I don't know. I just remember seeing it… That's all."

"Where did you see it? Who had it?"

"One of the people working with me. Just a boy."

"What's the name of this person working with you?"

The monster seemed to want to give Amir some respite, for he took out a pack of long Winston Golds, lit one, stuck it in the corner of his mouth, sat down on the metal chair next to the table and began to puff away at it. Between each drag, he clicked his false teeth in and out, without averting his obscene, glassy gaze from Amir's face for even an instant. Amir longed for him to offer him a cigarette. It would have been the best smoke of his life. But it didn't happen. Amir later understood that an interrogator only offers his victim a cigarette when his subject has cracked and starts talking, and he can start a file. Amir had been broken long since, of course, but he had not had any information to give. The man, that horrifying monster, had smoked his cigarette only halfway down and could easily have offered the rest of it to Amir, to satisfy his killing need for a smoke, but instead he crushed it under his massive foot and started again:

"What's the name of this person working with you? Give me his name."

"Mansour Salaami."

Amir had told him. Without stopping, he went on: "Khamami, Nur-Aqdas Khamami... my wife... why did you arrest her? Just tell me that."

The monster gave no reply. Amir had thought that if he gave Mansour Salaami away they would reward him by telling him what had happened to his wife, but he got no answer and the man showed no anger. He found out later that the accused is not supposed to ask questions; he is just required to give answers. The reason why the man had not got angry was that he could not make up his mind as to what to do about what he had just heard. He was worried about the person who would see his report on the interrogation, and the executive decision that would follow it. Amir could see the man thinking. The furrows on his low forehead grew deeper and his eyes narrowed so far that they almost disappeared. Clearly, thinking was quite an effort for him and Amir, in spite of his fever, his weakness, his pain and exhaustion, had a shrewd idea what this sluggish brain was struggling to grasp: Why, after claiming to be unable to recall anything for so long, was the accused now suddenly singing? The answer clearly eluded him. He took another cigarette out of the pack, turned on his heel and left the room without a word.

If I hadn't heard the door shut, I'd probably have assumed that he'd just gone into some dark corner to watch me as I lay like a paraplegic on that wire bed. I'd lost all sense of direction, you see. But when I heard the same noise again a few minutes later, I knew that this room wasn't some hermetically sealed chamber, but was connected by a door with the world outside. It was nothing but madness, sheer madness, it was like living in a bubble of insanity. How else could I have imagined a room without a door?

Now the two of them, Khezr Javid and the monster whom Amir had so disconcerted, were standing there in the pool of light near the wire bed, facing Amir. It turned out that the monster did have a name after all. The two of them were very different in appearance and stature. They were both in the light, but Khezr's face showed up more than ex-sergeant Ramazani's, as he towered high above the lampshade. To Amir's unsteady vision, their bodies appeared to be warping and twisting and turning. Amir now understood why Ramazani had gone out to fetch Khezr the Immortal, and that Khezr was very angry with him, for he picked up the bloodstained knife from the metal table and thrust the point at his throat:

"I'm going to kill you right here and now, you little son of a bitch. You've given me the name of a corpse, you creep, you son of a whore."

It wasn't my fault that they had murdered Mansour Salaami, or someone else of that name, eleven months before. I just told them everything I knew. But what Amir knew clearly did not satisfy the Immortal Prophet Khezr, who responded with a stream of oaths before handing him back to Ramazani to get him to talk. He then stormed out, in a foul mood.

How naïve I must have been to think that I could get them to tell me about my wife's arrest by giving Salaami away. Ramazani was getting to work once more; I saw that he had rolled his sleeves a fold higher and, much more agilely than you'd expect from such a giant, walloped me in the face with his great big ham fist. My eyes closed and I just had time to think "here we go again," when he shouted to two others torturers standing outside to come in. Over the noise of Ramazani's oaths I heard them rush in. Then I heard him tell them: "Put the son of a whore in the clamp."

Amir had no chance to think what else he could tell them, as they hauled him off the wire bed like a piece of meat and put him in the clamp, which he had heard vaguely about from the other prisoners who had been through it. Now he saw that it was quite a sophisticated apparatus, brand new, designed to bring concentrated pressure to bear on different parts of the body. It gripped you so tightly that you could not move.

Before they clamped on the steel helmet, which came right down to my chin, I heard the monster once more: "The knife, the knife…" Then silence. I could just see from the movement of his lips that he was still talking about the bloody knife, while beating the soles of my feet with a length of wire cable. I was screaming… screaming. My screams went round and round inside my head, getting louder and louder, deafening me. And the worst of it was that, apart from screaming until my eardrums burst, I couldn't react in any way to those savage blows from the cable. Both my forearms were fixed immovably to the clamp and both legs were screwed down to two metal bars, so that the slightest movement increased the pressure on my shin or funny bone. Leather straps held my arms and chest tightly against the back of the clamp and I could hardly budge an inch. Every blow from the cable made me jump and all I could do was scream. What else could I do?

"The knife… the knife… this bloody knife!"

The words echoed in the pit of Amir's mind. He was incapable of thought, as every cell in his brain was focused on enduring the blows to the soles of his feet and the rest of his body. He was thirsty and his mouth was dry. He had no idea what time of day or night it was, what day it was, or where on earth he could be, so totally isolated, alone and exposed. He was giddy, dizzy, as if he had had a shot of morphine against this never-ending pain. His whole brain felt paralysed. Then suddenly, as if in his death agony, he heard a different sound, one that didn't seem to come from him, like the dull thud of a stick on a bale of wool.

It was like the end of a party, or a wedding or a wake, I don't know which. I didn't have a watch on. Or did I? Maybe I did, but if so it had stopped, and I can only guess that it was around midnight. I was taking good care of my new blue suit, which I was wearing for the first time. This may have been why I had come to Tehran, to see my wife Nur-Aqdas – or were we still just engaged? She was still at university, renting a room with a tiny kitchen in an aunt's house. As usual, I was a bit confused, and I was standing at the top step of the hallway in an old house. There was a cheap carpet runner on the floor and I saw Mansour Salaami who had, apparently, just come into the hall. He had the bloody knife in his hand and he was pointing it at my throat. It didn't strike me then how odd it was that he still managed to stab me, right in the throat, even though I was standing with my back glued to the wall in terror, and he was on the bottom step. The distorted perspective seemed perfectly normal to me. Nor was I surprised when I saw not one but two Salaâmis. One of them grabbed the other's hand and forced him to drop the bloodstained knife at my feet, right on the top step. Mansour Salaami seemed drunk. With his jacket slung casually over his shoulder like any Jack the Lad, he went past me. My face must have been as white as the whitewash on the wall. The other Mansour Salaami was right behind him, as if he were controlling him. As he brushed past my chest he looked at me. There was a complicit expression on his face as he pointed at the other one, who was just about to hide behind an old folding screen:

"Anyway, it was a good thing. He nailed the bastard right in the heart and got his sister, too."

"Whose sister?"

"The chief of police's."

Rooted to the spot, Amir watched Mansour Salaami disappear behind the screen. In a blind panic, he ran down the stairs two at a time to get away from the scene and get to Nur-Aqdas's house. He was worried that he would not find transport. He knew that the buses stopped running at eleven and he might not find a taxi at that hour either. He came out of the narrow alley in Amirieh, got to the end of the pavement, crossed the gutter and the kerb into the main road and kept running up it to the bus station in Sepah Square, looking back all the time to see if he could catch a taxi coming up. *I was going uphill with my feet and looking back with my eyes. You could say I was going to a bus that wasn't there and looking for a taxi that wasn't coming.* The car that Amir eventually flagged down turned out not to be a taxi. He realised his mistake as it came to a halt just behind him; it was an old banger, painted a strange mix of green and rusty blue, a combination of colours that Amir had never seen in his life. The back door opened. The interior light went on and Amir could make out a woman. She got out and he saw her go down the same alley he had just come out of. There were four young men in the car, tittering lasciviously. Amir didn't want to miss his chance. He went up to the car to give them the address of where he wanted to go – he didn't know where it was – to see if they could take him there. But just as he was about to open his mouth, there was another burst of raucous laughter from the rowdy young men. As if trying to take the piss, they started driving past him really slowly and made off. Amir looked round to see where the woman had gone. She was just turning into the alleyway. Not young, she was plumpish and was wearing a cream-coloured scarf on her head and carrying a blue bag in her hand. She seemed to be heading for the house that he had come out of. She didn't look anything like Nur-Aqdas.

Anyone else would have thought that those four lads had picked the woman up for a gang bang and were now dropping her off near her home. But, in spite of their dirty laughs, such a thought never crossed my mind for a fraction of a second. Yes, a fraction of a second, that's all it takes for the brain to cover a lot of ground and process a whole load of random impressions. But believe me, when I say that not for an instant did I entertain a single dirty thought about that woman. I was completely distraught and paranoid and, for some stupid reason, all I could think of – though it was nothing to do with me – was how the taxi system could be better organised, so that one could get one at any time of day or night. At the same time I knew Nur-Aqdas must be worrying about how late I was.

Amir had only had one brush with the security police

before, and he had got off with a warning that time. It was the stories he kept on hearing about them from other people that made him permanently afraid of them. The empty streets that night, the strange goings-on at that party, and that inexplicable bloodstained knife – it all conspired to reawaken his dread of the police. He began to feel guilty for a crime that he had not committed.

A police motorcyclist suddenly appeared out of the darkness. In a show of innocence, Amir flagged him down and asked him the way to the bus station, even though he knew it was just a short way up the road. He grumbled about the lack of taxis, which seemed to pack up early for a big city. Then he saw that the policeman was just a traffic cop. No matter – the police were the police and fright was fright. The young policeman, who clearly came from the sticks himself, told the small-town lad, lost late at night in the big city, that he had better get a move on if he wanted to catch the last bus, which was leaving from the stop outside the National Park in a few minutes, as he would have trouble finding a taxi at that hour. Amir realised that he didn't have a bus ticket on him. The policeman pulled a sheaf of tickets out of his pocket, and the small-town lad bought half a dozen off him and raced off.

From a distance he could see the bus, just under the archway into the National Park, with the last few passengers getting on. Then he lost all sense of direction. The archway faced north-south, but now in his mind it seemed to face east-west. He was pretty sure the bus was going in the direction he wanted, towards Sepah Avenue, Salsabil and Jey.* *I didn't care where it was going, but it was bound to be somewhere beautiful and heavenly.* Even if it was the wrong bus, he would run for it anyway. He just had to get away from there as fast as he could. But before he could reach the step and swing himself on board, the bus pulled away and left him standing. For the first time in his life, he was overcome by a feeling of utter despair.

He stood there, stiff now and confused, until he pulled himself together. Wandering off, he found himself going up the steps of the central post office, with its pre-war German architecture. He leant against the wall; all of a sudden, as though they had simply boiled up out of the ground, a great flood of people came spilling out. Amir realised that some sort of celebration was going on in the main hall of the post office and that there was no room for them all inside.

They were all bazaar folk, and some of them seemed to know me and came up to shake my hand, or gave me a nod. They were such ordinary folk that my clothes looked very new against theirs and I felt embarrassed. They were all dressed alike, in a forties or fifties style. Later, I saw television footage of street demonstrations from that period where people were dressed like that, with double-breasted jackets, hair parted on the left and pencil moustaches.*

He was dazed, tired and thirsty and had forgotten that he had to get to Nur-Aqdas's house, wherever it was. He just wanted to find a quiet corner to sit down, but there wasn't room to swing a cat in that crowd, and no way of getting a glass of tea, or even a glass of water. He felt unsafe in a crowd. His tight collar was suffocating him, and he twisted his neck this way and that to get some relief. It had not occurred to him to undo his collar button. In the middle of his contortions, he suddenly saw a police vehicle pull up by the kerb. It was a paddy wagon, with a side door that could be opened to snatch people off the street. A bunch of armed policemen jumped out, looking agitated. Some of them were talking into pocket radios. Amir could not hear what they were saying, but he guessed that all this kerfuffle had to do with something that had happened, or some ceremony that was about to take place, that he had not heard about.

I had guessed right. In no time at all a group of men in smart new dark suits, shiny black shoes, clean-shaven and with neatly combed hair, gathered round the police van. Their numbers grew as they went up the steps in front of the building next to the post office, which led to the front of the senate house.

The throng was now pushing its way up to the senate building, forcing Amir back down the steps. He was being pushed back towards the entrance by the crowd, which seemed intent on forcing its way in. As he struggled to keep upright, he caught sight of the old banger again, with its strange combination of green and rusty blue paint, parked at an angle on the south side of the road. It was on the kerb, tipped over onto its left side. The passenger-side doors were flung open and the roof appeared to have been blown open by a grenade or a small bomb. It was riddled with bullet holes and the dust of a hundred years of death appeared to have settled on the seats. There was no sign of the four young men who had been in it before, just a trickle of blood and engine oil dripping from the back seat onto the road.

Water... water... just a sip of water... My tongue feels as dry as a brick. My mouth's on fire. A sip of water, just a drop...

He had to think hard to find a way out of this bizarre adventure, out of this story that had started with Mansour Salaami's bloodstained knife and had led on to Nur-Aqdas's room on the second floor of her aunt's house, squeezing the juice out of Amir's heart as it went on its simple way. Against his will, he was being thrown from one frying pan into one fire after another, each one hotter than the last. He was being passed from the jaws of one defeat to another, which could end only in his death. But what was killing him now was his thirst, which he could not do anything about. The crowd that kept pushing him into the building was not interested in the raging thirst of a young small-town boy.

The senate building was a glorious architectural mish-mash of vernacular and foreign styles from unrelated periods. The ceiling was supported by thick, round pillars finely carved in the Greek, Roman and Persian styles. It was reminiscent of the Reichstag in the way it conveyed a sense of might and majesty. It had the same kind of showy opulence that Reza Shah, who had built it, had once seen, or thought he had seen, in the Christian churches he had visited in Isfahan and Rezaiyeh,* but it also called to mind the proportions of the Vakil Mosque in Shiraz. The floor of the entrance hall was covered with red carpeting that was clearly not the work of Persian weavers. It was completely plain, with none of the wonderful workmanship of Kashan, Tabriz or Isfahan to be seen anywhere. Amir could not work out where it might have been made. At the end of the hall he could just make out what looked like a kind of huge prayer-niche. It looked nothing like his idea of Zoroastrian or even Buddhist architecture. He had never seen a synagogue either, not even in films, so he could not tell if it looked like one or not. With its tall, massive carved pillars, the place was unlike anything he had ever seen. It was not like a church, either, which would be all draped in purple, with dark bare benches, he thought, not like the bright and shiny furniture here. And yet, despite the fact that this hall was like nothing he had ever seen, it seemed somehow familiar to him, perhaps because it oozed power from every detail, like the winter prayer hall of a mosque, or a church, a synagogue, a fire temple or even the Reichstag.

Amir was intimidated by the sense of power that he felt all around him, among those grand people who had nothing in common with him. He was alone and lost, a stranger among strangers. He looked dejectedly around in the hope of finding someone he knew, a pretty futile exercise. All he saw was a procession of men dressed in black coming in through the four entrances. To escape from this dangerous and frightening isolation, all he could do was dart from one pillar to another. So as not to excite suspicion by making it seem as if he was trying to hide, he leaned casually against each one as he reached it. He felt safe there and could see what was going on.

This was pure hell. How could he get out of it? On either side of the doors stood invisible sentries, while more and more dark-suited men streamed into the hall. They all seemed to know each other, as if they had been summoned here at this late hour for some extraordinary meeting. Was it something to do with the assassination of the police chief, which had taken place that very night, just before midnight?

Monsters, ghouls!

The new arrivals looked like demons, their size nigh surpassing the pillars in height and girth. Out of the four of them, three wore long cloaks, with sweatbands wound around their heads. Their faces were round and chubby, boneless, like pink balloons with eyes and noses painted onto them. Seen from below, they looked like minarets, small, medium and large. The littlest one was the size of a Scud missile and Amir could now see why the ceiling was so high. The fourth one was a Slav, the same size as the others, wearing a traditional Russian long white shirt with embroidered hem, and tight trousers tucked into a pair of tall brown boots. The Slav's square, bony face was endowed with a bushy moustache and long curly hair that fell over his forehead. The biggest of the new arrivals acknowledged the respects of the black-suited crowd with a proud nod of his head and carried on, looking neither to his right nor his left, to the end of the hall, which looked to Amir like the prayer niche of a mosque, as the crowd parted to make way for him and his entourage. The Slav put his hand to his chest, bowing humbly to the crowd, and followed the other three monsters, half a step behind them. As they came level with Amir's gaping eyes, he could not help looking up at them, as if at the shaking minarets of Isfahan,* for the knot of the sweatband round the fez of the biggest one almost touched the ceiling and his painted eyes were like the eggs of a goose, staring straight ahead without expression, paying no attention to the prostrations of the rows of respectful, silent onlookers. The three of them made a smooth and practised progress through the crowd as if rolling on invisible rails, while the Slav praised and lauded them to the people.

They said that a bereaved family was coming in. Amir looked up and saw five or six people: a couple with a young boy and a girl and a smartly dressed youth who seemed to have oiled his hair in mourning for his father. The Slav, with no glimmer of human kindness on his face, appeared carrying a tea boy's gold-plated round tray. On it were glasses of tea, and one cup half full of tea, and he stood in front of the small-town youth. Amir remembered how thirsty he was. He tried to take a glass of tea, but the Slav turned the tray round, forcing the cup onto him.* Amir had forgotten all about his thirst by now, but he took the cup all the same. He would use it as an excuse for finding a corner to drink it. A cup of tea in his hand would make him part of the scene and explain his presence to the crowd, who seemed to be eyeing him up and down. It allowed him to wander along the eastern end of the prayer hall.

In the north corner he found a low door that opened into a neat little room. Amir felt that divine intervention had led him to this hiding place and he was drawn in. On the threshold he was stopped short by what he saw. The room was like the pantry of the Safi mosque in Rasht. Six or seven middle aged men, smartly dressed, were sitting on brown bentwood chairs. This was something that Amir did not want to see, particularly as one of them seemed to be Khezr Javid, who was looking at him askance, as if they had met somewhere three generations back. There was nothing Amir could do, except stand there, just inside the ancient door. If he retreated, he thought, he would only arouse more suspicion. *So I greeted him, as if it was the most natural thing in the world, and drank the rest of the tea.*

He ran his eye over the other men, who were busy chatting away and pretending not to be looking at him or to have even noticed him, except for the Prophet Khezr, who was now staring at him more obviously. He looked like a man whom he had seen a thousand times on the back of the *Women's Weekly* magazine. Khezr Javid was sitting, staring at Amir, in the same pose that he had adopted at his interrogation, three incarnations ago, and a shiver ran down his spine at the memory of it. Why wouldn't Khezr give some sign that he had recognised him? That way he would be sure that at least one person in the room knew him for who he really was, and who better than a secret policeman. He just wanted to find someone he knew in this bizarre place, and explain how he had come to find himself there. He had to avoid giving the wrong impression. But Khezr Javid showed no sign of acknowledging him. Amir was convinced that they were all secret policemen on high alert, which made him even more frightened. His head was whirling with all the accusations that might be levelled against him, and tears welled up in his eyes at the thought of what a dangerous mess he had got himself into. He wanted to beg the men for mercy and get them to understand that he knew nothing at all about the business of Mansour Salaami's bloodstained knife.

Looking silently into their unblinking eyes, he begged that they would get on with it and start asking him questions, so that he could clear the air with them, but it seemed that they were not interested in investigating anything, or perhaps were just pretending not to be interested.

Amir began to weep openly until, one after the other, they looked up and regarded him with a mixture of suspicion and mockery. One of them pointed at him:

"Just look at the young gentleman now!" He turned to Amir: "What are you crying for, then?"

"For ... for the late General..."

There was a fusillade of laughter at this and Amir, mortified, dissolved into floods of tears. His sobs grew ever more violent until they reached a crescendo of loud and uncontrollable wailing. Suddenly a bullet whizzed through the air. The policemen immediately reached to their shoulder holsters for their guns, pushed Amir out of the way and ran out. He followed them out into the hall and looked out onto the street, where a pitched battle had broken out. The south side of the building, which gave onto the street, had turned into a single panel of glass. Through it he could follow the battle outside. The people who had been at the party in the post office building were now out on the street. Amir found himself in a scene from the late 1940s, watching the railway workers at Abbasi Square laying into a crowd in smart black suits.

As the august gathering in the hall dissolved into chaos, Amir saw a chance to get away. He forgot his tears and began running from column to column of the prayer hall. He did not know where he was going or what he could do, except use the general confusion to find his way out of that horrible place unnoticed. He found himself in a place where there was no sign of the monstrous creatures, facing a wide staircase that seemed to lead down to a basement; he ran down it. But as he went down, he heard a din of clashing swords and knives. His way was blocked by a thicket of flailing weapons. As he rushed back and forth looking for a way through, he ran up against two sword blades thrust directly at him. They were wielded by two young lads wearing the black shirts worn by flagellants, with Arab keffiyahs wound round their heads.* With a forthrightness that belied their age, they glared at Amir as if about to lynch him:

"Where do you think you're running off to, then?"

I was tongue-tied. I wanted to say that I wasn't running anywhere, and what was this all about, anyway? But not a word came out.

But the young men were not looking for an answer. They seized hold of him and marched him down the broad staircase, into a dark basement containing a small cistern. There they handed him over to two innocent-faced, virginal boys of about fifteen or sixteen with newly sprouting beards and scrubbed faces, dressed in olive camouflage jackets. They in turn escorted him to a dingy side-room to hand him over to their supervisor. It was there that Amir caught sight of Khezr Javid once more, who was looking on as a sergeant strapped someone to a clamp. There were more people lined up along the basement wall, shrouded in darkness, for the only light in the room was positioned so that it shone only onto the rack and the sweat-soaked face of the prisoner strapped into it. Beaming as if they had just solved some complicated riddle, the two fresh-faced youths now dragged Amir towards the clamp. One of them, who appeared to be the son of Ramazan Kolahi, began: "So, you use whistles to signal to each other in the streets at night!" and, expertly releasing the prisoner from the clamp, strapped Amir onto it in his place. Then he attached two wires to Amir's knees and switched the current on and off, inducing a terrifying shuddering all over his body. Although he remained conscious, Amir was unable to speak. He remembered that one of the effects of an electric shock is loss of speech. He wanted to say something or scream, but he could not produce a sound of any kind. His throat, tongue and chest had all seized up. The only sound that emerged from his throat was a pathetic croak, a mousey squeak. Khezr Javid and his minions were unmoved. Perhaps they could not even hear him. Every time Amir blinked, he saw a hand in the darkness holding the bloodied knife under his nose. He was suffocating and could not speak. At one point, he thought that he had gone deaf as well, for he could not hear a thing, not even his own squeaks. Things got to such a pitch that his torturers decided that their victim was resisting and refusing to talk. It never occurred to them that he simply could not speak.

The man standing in front of him, that terrifying giant, kept waving the knife under his nose and screaming: "This knife, so what's this bloody knife, then? So whose are the fingerprints on it? Are you going to talk or not?"

He could not tell them that he could not speak. He could not tell them that he was thirsty. He could not even produce the word "water."

Khezr Javid was standing over Amir on the wooden bed where they had left him, holding a glass of water in his hand and smiling. In the course of his nightmares, Amir had undergone such comical convulsions that Khezr had been popping in and out to watch him, with a big grin all over his snout. Amir's head ached and his mouth was as dry as a mud brick. The glass of water was like the offer of a new hope of life. Half sitting up, he reached out, took it from Khezr Javid's hand and gulped it down in before lapsing into a sort of trance, staring blankly into space. The nightmare had left him utterly drained, but at the same time he wanted it to continue, to see how it would end. For, little by little, these dreams had come to occupy all of his thoughts. And so he waited until he could sense Khezr Javid's presence in the gloomy cellar once again. Amir lifted his head up to look at him.

Khezr was sitting on a stool, looking at Amir. His nose was as big as ever; he evidently had not pursued the idea of having a job done on it, then. He looked no happier than when they had last met. If anything, he had got thinner, but his eyes shone with a new confidence. He seemed to have got less talkative, and now measured his words with care. Amir found it all the more surprising, then, when Khezr, without any preamble, took a puff at his cigarette and said:

"They put me in prison."

"Prison, you?"

He laughed. "Does that surprise you?" Amir said nothing, since there was an alarmingly triumphant tone to Khezr's words. It reminded him of those nights when Khezr came into the prison wing, drunk and swaggering. The clang of the bolt and chain on the steel door made everyone, even those who had gone to sleep, immediately adopt the required position, squatting on their heels, as they waited to see which cell Khezr would go into and what he would say. Depending on what he was up to that evening, or whose ear he was going to whisper a sly word into, he would unlock a cell door and step inside. With his hands on his hips, or leaning against the wall, he would say whatever he had to say, in whatever tone of voice suited his mood, and then throw a couple of cigarettes at the prisoner's feet. He would then leave and make his way down the wing, chucking a cigarette or two through the inspection hatch of each cell and chanting, in his adenoidal voice, "*Zar... zar... khar... zar-ra khar mike-sheh!* – Golds, Golds, only an ass smokes Golds!*" When he had finished, he would crush the empty pack in his fist and go back to the steel door, swearing drunkenly and making snide remarks at the prisoners on the wing until his voice faded away and he left. His exit was followed by the drumming of knuckles on the hatch covers, demanding matches, which roused the sleepy guard, who grumbled and cursed at them to shut up. The warder went down the line of cells, lighting each cigarette in turn as the prisoners poked them through the hatches and drew on them until they lit. No one ever wondered why Khezr chose that time of night to wander down the cells dishing out cigarettes. Was it just a show of power? Or was he fearful of the future? Or wracked by a sense of contrition and guilt? Might it even be that Khezr, in the dead of night, suddenly felt the urge to make pets of his sacrificial lambs, some of whom he had tortured to the point of death, if only by giving them some fags and visiting them without hitting them for once. No, none of this occurred to any of them, for such thoughts were too much of a luxury.

* * *

"You tortured me for no reason. I had nothing whatever to do with that business."

Khezr Javid just looked at Amir and calmly drank the water in the glass that he had just poured for himself. He took out his cigarette case and held it out to Amir. Hardly daring to refuse, Amir took one, and Khezr lit it for him. Amir exhaled the smoke and asked:

"Nur-Aqdas. Nur-Aqdas Khamami. I want to know what happened to her."

It just came out. A fleeting smile crossed Khezr's face as he half closed his eyes and stared into the bottom of his glass. Amir thought he was trying to find a way to change the subject. Khezr carried on looking into the glass for a while, then looked up and stared so intently, as he often did, into Amir's eyes that Amir was forced to take a drag on his cigarette to avoid his gaze. He realised that Khezr would not be drawn on the subject of his wife. He was far more concerned about his own future and had no wish to stir up the past; the man had never felt regret for his past.

Even on that last occasion when Khezr had visited Amir in the cellar, he had displayed remarkable self-confidence. Despite the fact that wounded people were still lying on the streets, Khezr, whether on purpose or just through habit, still walked with his old swagger, showing not a flicker of apprehension; his only concern was how to adapt to the new order. It was then, through one or two things that he let slip, that Amir realised that Khezr had been one of the organisers of the demonstration by the security police in front of the office of the Prime Minister in the revolutionary government.* This shocked him, and he began to think that Khezr Javid, "the immortal one," might have good reason for feeling so confident about the future. So he gave up asking him direct questions, even about the fate of his wife, and settled instead for slipping him the odd surreptitious, seemingly casual question. So during that last visit, as he always did, he got out the open drum of home brew and put it down beside Khezr with a dish of olives, emptied the ashtray into the waste bin and put it back next to the tray that was perched on his bedside table. As usual, Khezr poured himself a glass but, before downing it, he felt in his pocket and took out a leaflet. Passing it to Amir, he sneered:

"This is the handiwork of your commie chums! They demanded that we publish a list of SAVAK informers!"†

Without waiting for a response from Amir, he continued in a mocking tone: "So *we* published them, more than nine thousand names!"

Amir could not lift his head up. This humiliation, deeper than ever, was more than he could bear. Khezr's show of power and his withering contempt had not just made a fool of him, it had made a complete fool of a whole nation. At moments like this, Amir felt defiled, as if a freezing lake of mud had been poured over him.*

Etched on Amir's mind were the countless occasions in his life when Khezr, with his big nose and pea-like eyes, had played a role. He thought of the man who, imitating that poet with the reedy capon voice, had stood on a stool outside the prison gates and sung the praises of the revolution. And he thought of the fisherman who smoked cheap Oshnu Specials† on an empty stomach for breakfast, and the glint in the eye of the forty-year-old party leader as he sent young men off to the slaughterhouse of war and despair. And finally his thoughts turned to himself, to the shadow of himself and his fellow men. He made an effort to wipe all the disturbing thoughts from his memory and concentrate instead on the great, important moments… Like when the prison gates were flung open. Where exactly was Khezr, and what had he been doing, when that happened? He now called to mind that Khezr was hardly ever to be seen during the troubles, but that he had reappeared in another form the minute it seemed expedient to do so. Just as he was doing now…

* * *

"Won't you take even one step towards the cemetery? After all, your sister's about to be buried…"

"I'm tired and I need to sleep for an hour or two…"

"Will you really not come? I would if I were you. Damn it, how many brothers and sisters does a man have?"

No, this man, in his shabby raincoat, this skinny fellow with long, wet hair wandering among the gravestones can't be our Amir. Anyway, he was curled up in his blanket; he couldn't have got here by now. No, this man mooning about the rainy cemetery at dead of night, prowling about looking for something that he can't find, couldn't be our Amir – or could he? No, it's not him. Funny, though, he does look like Amir. It must be Amir's nightmare who's turned up here. Perhaps I'm seeing my son in his own nightmare. Perhaps... I'm going crazy. No that can't be it, because what I'm seeing is real, it's got nothing to do with madness. Otherwise I wouldn't even be aware that I'm going off my head, would I? There's no getting round it; that man skulking about the cemetery looks more like Amir than anyone else. It's got to be Amir. "Amir!"

* * *

One rainy evening, at dusk, Amir's sister Farzaneh had come to see him, bringing modelling clay and plaster and other bits and pieces for his sculpting. The colonel was standing at the window of his room, smoking and staring out at the rain. He could catch the odd word of what they were saying. *I don't think Amir had asked her for any materials.* As far as the colonel knew, Amir did not work in the traditional materials that most sculptors used. No, this solicitous gesture must have been Farzaneh's idea, *probably some excuse to come and see the brother she's closest to and have a chat with him...*

This time Farzaneh had behaved quite sensibly. For once, she wasn't crying, and she had not brought her children with her. And the way Amir spoke to her gave her no opportunity to lapse into her usual gloom.

"You've really gone from us, sis. As for me... well, I'm lost. Those who try to find their true role in life are always hit the hardest. Take our father, for instance; in his effort to be true to himself and keep up his standards, he communed with the photograph of The Colonel until his hair went white. And the only reason I'm working on this bust is to get involved with something permanent. I'm in a bad way, little sister. I'm a stranger in my own home! The tragedy of our whole country is the same: we are all alienated, strangers in our own land. It's tragic. The odd thing is that we have never got used to it. Yet, woe betide us if we do. The irony is that, if you really want to be seen as a good Iranian, and especially if you aspire to high office in this country, you first have to be a foreigner, someone who wasn't born here at all. On the other hand, if you were born and bred here and try to remain true to yourself, your country and your people, then alienation is the most lenient punishment you can expect. It's only through being a mouth-piece of foreigners and becoming a foreigner yourself that you'll be accepted as a native and be honoured and respected. My little sister, I wanted to speak up for my country. I love my country more than anything, but since I no longer speak with the voice of my party I've become a non-person, a stranger in my own land. That's the whole wretched story of our country. I have not been true to myself, my sister, so I am corrupted. That's why I am thinking of ending it all. But… but not in the way that others have said we shall all end. No, I won't allow myself to be killed by one of my brothers, although I could certainly bring myself to have their blood on my hands. I already have. No, I shall kill myself and, by doing so, will bequeath them a handicap like a horn on their heads. This may be absurd, but it is the only independent act I am capable of, since we are all done for, or soon will be.

"Oh yes, we'd just begun to find our feet when they came down on us like a ton of bricks – oh, they really made us pay dearly for that. They kept trying to convince us that our real problem was the enemy within, the snakes in our bosoms, they called them. 'Kill them, wipe them out,' they said – 'they could be your children, your brothers, your neighbours, your friends. Exterminate them. Exterminate them all. Kill your offspring, stamp out life, stamp out resistance. Can't you see they're dangerous?' This wave of vengeance just makes one want to weep. I know that my sister will die, I know that they will cast my brother's corpse at my feet, and that my father will finally lose his mind. And you will end up being ground up between the yellow, stinking teeth of al-Hajjaj ibn Yusuf. And I know that I shall kill myself, for I have read every line in the book of death, but I shall not weep. I'm not prepared to play the court jester any more, either, putting on a mask of scornful jollity and cracking jokes about the impending catastrophe. No, silence is the only answer... It is with the white blade of silence that I can purify a world that accepts the ruin of an entire people and does nothing. What a price we have to pay, sister, what a terrible retribution!"

The colonel could not hear Farzaneh's reply. Or had she been struck dumb by surprise and disbelief at her brother's outburst? But what could she possibly have said in response anyway? Nothing. With her brother in that state, all she could do was shed tears of silent misery.

About an hour passed before he heard her coming up the basement stairs. When she emerged, the colonel was still standing by the window. He saw her sit down by the pond in the yard to wash away her tears. The colonel turned away from the window and paced up and down the room. Expecting Farzaneh to come in and see him, he turned on the light, sat on the chair by the desk and lit another cigarette. He knew that his daughter would not leave without seeing him, however upset she might be by what Amir had said. He also knew that she could expect a stream of abuse, insults and mudslinging from Qorbani Hajjaj, that husband of hers, whenever she went to see her father, but that she took it all in her stride. And he knew that she would probably have brought some tranquillisers for him. The colonel, of course, just threw them away in the pond. But not when she was there – there was no point in upsetting his own daughter.

* * *

No, this man lost in his shabby raincoat, this gaunt, skinny man with long, wet hair wandering among the graves can't be Amir… Why am I so obsessed with this delusion? I need to get on with the job, and I've got a deadline. I mustn't waste time on irrelevancies. Now, where's the mortuary got to?

The mortuary was a bit over to the right from where the colonel was heading. Earlier, it had struck the colonel as a chamber of horrors, worse than the graveyard. The thought of entering it, especially at night, made his hair stand on end. One often heard of people wandering into a mortuary in the middle of the night and being literally frightened to death.

How come, then, that I now feel not the slightest twinge of fear? It was more likely, the colonel thought, that the two young men he had left behind would be far more unnerved than he was by being surrounded by dead bodies all that time. It is only professional body washers who have no fear of bodies and the darkness of the mortuary. The minds of these young men had been unsettled by the daily toll of blood, bodies and slaughter on the streets. The fact was, the colonel thought, that however much the youth of today had got used to blood and guts in the street, they still had a long way to go before they attained the detachment of a real body washer. The young still had white teeth. Their teeth had not gone yellow, wolf-like, grotesque and misshapen, *like I imagine old fashioned body washers' teeth get from a lifetime of bone cracking*. Even wolves would be frightened by darkness, corpses and mortuaries, though perhaps they would not show it.

He could hear them now. As he got closer, he could see them walking up and down. Without taking his eyes off the mortuary, he leaned against the wet trunk of a leafless tree to take another breather. All the while, he was watching the young policemen, their faces in the shadow, as they tramped nervously back and forth, shoulder to shoulder. They did not even appear to be talking to each other, just pacing incessantly this way and that, trying to kill time.

Maybe they're frightened of the skinny corpse of my daughter, by the ghost of an innocent child. Or perhaps they're angry at me for taking so long. That's fair enough, it's no job for them really. Instead of being given a proper job to do, they've been sent out on a rainy night to keep guard over my daughter's dead body. What sort of job is that? All this hanging about has given them too much time to think about their lives.

Yet, judging by the anxious and aimless way they were roaming around, they were not much given to thoughtful reflection. They did not appear to be smokers, otherwise they could have found a sheltered corner under the mortuary eaves and, like most old prison warders, have had a cigarette or two to pass the night away.

I could really do with a smoke now, if only this wretched rain would let up. No, he had to go and finish the night's work.

He could light up after that, just as he had after Mohammad-Taqi's funeral, when the cup of coffee and cheap Homa cigarette he had had when he got home had really hit the spot. It had tasted as wonderful as his very first cigarette. That day was the first time he had really noticed Amir's squint, and the way his eyes stared at a point in the middle distance. And it was on that day that the thought had flashed across his mind: "My children... oh, how I wish I had never had you!"

Now I really must get going and put those lads' minds at ease.

A short distance away, The Colonel was standing on a gravestone, which made him look a lot taller. His black field boots were dazzling, unsullied by the mud, rain and dirt of the graveyard. *Thank goodness they can't see him, otherwise his terrifying appearance would give them heart attacks on the spot. I must not look at The Colonel, or these young fellows are going to think that the old man is off his rocker.* The colonel walked up to the policemen, propped his pick and shovel against the wall of the mortuary and wiped the sweat and rain off his face. He greeted the young men briefly and apologised to them for his lateness:

"I'm so sorry, gentlemen, but you can see what one has to cope with."

Now I have got to make peace with Forouz.

The colonel's wife was standing by the door of the mortuary awaiting his return, as if she had already heard that Qorbani would not allow Farzaneh to go and wash her sister, as if to say that it would be grossly unfair and offend her deeply if the colonel blocked her way and stopped her doing her job. She had come to lay out her daughter, but before starting she wanted to be sure that the colonel would not stand in her way. He certainly ought not to prevent his wife from doing this good deed; it would be very heavy-handed of him not to let Forouz wash her own daughter's body. Such meanness, particularly in the presence of The Colonel, would seem impertinent, *and on no account would I want any impertinence on my part to upset The Colonel.* So, as if nothing had ever happened between them, he showed his wife into the mortuary.

Forouz's face was shining like a moonbeam, her hair was all white and her lips were as white as the cotton shroud she was wearing. Only her eyes, caught in the light of a tallow lamp that stood on a plaster column in the mortuary, glowed red, like two bowls of blood. Apart from her red eyes, in her long white shroud she looked like a silken wing, floating gracefully over the earth. She did not speak or glance around. As at the most submissive moment of her life – *this was indeed a rare event* – she kept her head dutifully bowed and, walking in step with her husband, glided towards the slab where Parvaneh lay. Her demeanour was so calm and pure. *She must want my blessing, that her soul might be purified. What a way to get her own back on me!*

* * *

"I'll kill her. I'll kill her before I go off on this sordid posting!"

The colonel had risen from his chair, and Amir was staring at him in astonishment. He could not believe it of the colonel, of his father, that he could murder his mother and, what is more, announce his intention for all to hear. *He might have wanted to give me a helping hand, but how… No, he couldn't alter my decision.* Nor could Amir help him, other than by standing aside and looking on as his father sorted his own mess out. *I started crying again and I broke down.* This might have given Amir some brief hope that the colonel would change his mind about murdering his mother but, *to put a stop to any such hope*, the colonel stood up, threw off his army cap, strode bare-headed out of the room, crossed the courtyard and went out of the front gate to stand in the rain and wait for his wife to return.

* * *

"You see how hard it is on a man, don't you, gentlemen? Now I am at your service."

He had given the bundled-up shroud to Forouz. Now he had to go and fetch the pick and shovel, which he had left at the bottom of the crumbling wall of the mortuary. When he got there, he started grumbling out loud:

"What kind of mortuary is this, anyway? It hasn't even got electricity. This sort of town needs more and more of it, what with all the migrants, refugees, and war wounded, not to mention all the executions that are taking place, and all those young comrades on the run…"

The rain, lack of sleep and the long wait had knocked the stuffing out of the young policemen. Even so, one of them tried to cheer the colonel up by telling him that the city had plans for a brand-new mortuary to meet the needs of the community. It had been approved by the city councillors and had been put out to tender, and work had even started on it. The other policeman chipped in morosely, "Why did those bastards in the Shah's day never think to build a decent mortuary anywhere outside of Tehran?"

The colonel felt his coat tails flapping round his legs as he walked, as if the coat had grown too big for him and he was getting lost inside it. Perhaps he had shrunk without noticing it. Or maybe his knees had doubled up with exhaustion and he was turning into a hunchback. He tried to ignore it, not wanting to show the slightest sign of weakness. He still had an old soldier's sense of pride, and he was determined to keep a stiff upper lip. Strange, but there it was. And so, when they found the place where they had to dig, he stuck the shovel into the mud like a seasoned peasant and, rubbing his hands together, grasped the pick and set to work.

"Not bad for an old man, eh? I dug a lot of training trenches as a young man."

Ali Seif just grinned, but the other one, Abdullah, seemed to take pity on the sweat-drenched old man and decided to pitch in. He passed Ali Seif his weapon, took the shovel and started digging. The colonel stood at the foot of the grave. Wiping the sweat from his brow with his left sleeve, with his right hand he groped in his coat pocket for his brass cigarette case. Then he turned up his collar, pulled his hat down and turned his back to the rain so that he could light his cigarette without getting it wet. Before it had a chance to get soaked, he lit one up and sank into a daydream.

Who am I trying to fool? I'm well aware that at every stage of history there have been crimes against humanity, and they couldn't have happened without humans to commit them. The crimes that have been visited on my children have been committed, and still are being committed, by young people just like them, by people stirring up their delusions, giving them delusions of grandeur. So why do I imagine that people might improve? Everything going on around us seems to indicate that the values our forebears passed down to us no longer apply. Instead, we have sown the seeds of mistrust, scepticism and resignation, which will grow into a jungle of nihilism and cynicism, a jungle in which you will never find the courage to even mention the names of goodness, truth and common humanity, a crop that is now bearing fruit with remarkable speed. We're obliged to dig our own children's graves, but what's even more shocking is that these crimes are creating a future in which there is no place for truth and human decency. Nobody dares to speak the truth any more. Oh, my poor children… we're burying you, but you should realise that we are also digging a grave for our future. Can you hear me?

Abdullah had shovelled all the loose earth out of the hole. The colonel took up the pick to carry on digging the grave: "Wouldn't things go a bit quicker if they dug these graves in advance, gentlemen?"

Clearly touched by the colonel's plight and frustrated by the slow pace of his digging, Abdullah took him gently by the arm and helped him respectfully out of the grave. The colonel was grateful for this, as he was utterly exhausted and demoralised. If he had to do it all by himself, the sun would be well up before he was finished. He knew that he should show his gratitude to the young man for helping him, *but The Colonel's dazzling boots had completely distracted me, and were drawing me towards him, as if to say that it was not my duty to dig my daughter's grave; it had never been up to me to do that.*

You see my difficulty, don't you, Colonel? But why have you put yourself to so much trouble, coming here on this dark rainy night? I thought you'd gone back long since. Of course, I meant to pay my respects to you earlier. But with my wife right there outside the mortuary, I didn't want to embarrass her by *acknowledging you. I thought you were just going to look in for a moment and then go. Oh, my dear Colonel... the blood is still dripping from your throat!* I'm so ashamed. I wish you'd stayed at home. I could have sorted everything out and given you a report. It's a wretched and sickening business, but it'll soon be over. I think I'll be on my own soon, as none of my children are left now. They'll be bringing Kuchik back from the front for us to bury him. He'll be less trouble, because they'll take care of most of the arrangements. You probably heard about Mohammad-Taqi's funeral... and Parvaneh will be buried tonight. That leaves Amir and Farzaneh, and she has already buried herself in Qorbani's house, while Amir, as you know, won't last more than another day or two. He dies ten times a day; he only comes alive to die again. He can't take much more. He'll be gone soon. His death will hardly leave a ripple. Tonight is the worst bit, and perhaps tomorrow night as well. As you can see, it's hard work in all this mud and muck and rain. Shall we take a look inside the mortuary? It's not a very nice place, Colonel, but... Our Parvaneh was going to be fourteen this year. The blood on your throat, Colonel... the blood on your throat... I wish you'd brought your head with you. For how many years, how many hundreds of years, must that dear, strange head stay on my mantelpiece? I know the true worth of that head, Colonel.*

* * *

Forouz, with her white hair and red eyes, was leaning over Parvaneh's corpse on the concrete laying-out slab. The colonel could see that her arms were smeared with blood up to the elbows. The mother seemed to be washing Parvaneh's thin, frail body with tears of blood. The colonel saw his daughter's whole body covered in blood, and blood had dripped down all four sides of the slab into the channel below and was now licking at the toes of The Colonel's shiny black boots. The colonel went and stood next to his wife to get a better look at Parvaneh's face, and saw her skinny arms and hands, drenched in translucent blood, moving over the newly ripening body of their daughter. He bent down and looked at Parvaneh's face, more intently than he had ever done before. Her eyes opened, and she looked at him briefly with a cheerful smile, before slowly closing them again. He could not believe it; leaning over the slab, he stooped to look at her open eyes once more, but it was too late... For his wife was laying her long bony hands on Parvaneh's forehead and drawing them gently down from her hairline to below the girl's delicate little chin, ending in a kind of tired shrug that signalled that her work was now done. And when she took her hands away, Parvaneh's eyes were closed, her lips were closed and her face seemed mummified in blood... The colonel felt suddenly giddy.

The Colonel's black field boots were on the march, heavy and hard as stone, crashing in the silence of the mortuary and keeping time with the beat of the old man's heart as, stiff and frozen, he stood by the concrete table, staring at them. Their soles and polished toes were now red and, with each stride, they left a bloody trail behind them. Presently, the boots came to a halt by the table and he found himself saying, "You need more than your heart to see with, Colonel; it's a pity you didn't bring your head with you." His voice echoed round the mortuary and, as it echoed back, it sounded as if someone else had been speaking. But then normality returned. Continuing with her task, the colonel's wife had taken hold of Parvaneh's hand and was busy lifting her down off the concrete table, handling her as carefully as if she were a mirror, a full-length dressing mirror. Parvaneh was being careful, too, putting her dainty little feet down softly on the cold floor of the mortuary. Looking as if she was wearing a shirt of blood and earrings of red dewdrops, she strode off and away, hand in hand with her mother, who floated along like a white cloud beside her. The colonel stood gazing at the trail of blood left by their feet as they crossed the cold, wet floor, as if he had forgotten for a moment that he should be going along with his daughter and his wife.

At the door Forouz, soft and translucent, turned her head and glanced at the colonel with her bloodshot eyes, as if she were about to call him. The colonel quickly pulled himself together, plodded towards his wife and stood beside her *as if ready for anything that she might suggest*. Forouz turned to him and whispered reproachfully into his ear:

"I expected you to invite me to Parvaneh's wedding; you should have come to pick me up!"

The colonel stood transfixed, his mouth gaping in astonishment. He did not know what was going on or what his wife was talking about. With the fingers of her left hand, she pushed back a loose strand of white hair that had fallen over her cheek and was dangling beside her nose. Then, carefully lifting the hem of her shroud with her fingertips, she left the mortuary. As she receded into the distance, her figure seemed to grow in stature, like a tall white cloud, hand-in-hand with Parvaneh, who was glowing like a bright red tulip. The colonel stood in the doorway, watching the vanishing cloud and the moth-like wings of his Parvaneh and muttered: "Did you hear that, Colonel? She was talking about a wedding,

Parvaneh's wedding, Colonel!" But he could not sense The Colonel's presence there any longer. His polished black boots, which seemed to be made of steel, had marched out of the mortuary in a huff, away from the rain, the night and the mud. So there he stood, a broken old man, abandoned in a mortuary and drained of all emotion. He felt paralysed, his head felt swollen and odd voices were buzzing round inside it. All he could remember was that, if he did not get a move on, he would not be able to find the grave and would have to spend the whole night wandering about in the mud looking for it. He had to find a way out of this dead end of congealing death before he got caught in it.

* * *

I could feel the rain, which was still pouring down. Drunk and seething with rage, I was standing in the alleyway, bare-headed and with my collar undone, and staring at the drawn sabre in my hand, which I was about to plunge into my wife's heart.

That night was the first and last time that the colonel would drink himself nearly to death. While Amir was at his little table by the window reading his lecture notes, the colonel sat on the edge of the bed, tossing back glass after glass of arack. He did not know what he was doing, or more accurately: *I knew exactly what I was doing and I was drinking myself into oblivion.*

The sabre glinted in the dim glow cast by the streetlight. There was no-one in the alleyway save the colonel and a soggy stray dog with its tail between its legs. The colonel listens to the cars, as they roar past the entrance to his street on the wet main road. He is waiting for one to stop at the road end and drop off Forouz. She will open her little umbrella and head towards her house, and the car will move off.

I never thought about the man behind the wheel, what he looked like. I'd always thought the man who brought her home was just a driver, and that, from where she was sitting on the back seat, Forouz probably couldn't, or didn't want to, see the driver's face properly in the rear-view mirror. But I remember that she always got out of the car left foot first. And then she would hug the wall as she came down the street towards the door, over a little road that bisects the street north–south, and then down our little cul-de-sac. On those nights her head was always held low, she never looked right or left. Even though she was drunk, she could always find her way and… then I thought about what was in my wife's mind and I supposed that she must be dying a thousand deaths as she made her way home. But who can say? I have no other choice. I wait as she approaches, thinking whatever she is thinking. I won't say anything stupid or insulting to her, I'll just thrust my sabre straight between her left ribs and drive it right into her heart. I'd done this in my thoughts at least a thousand times before, so my mind and hand were steady and I didn't miss, I got my wife bang in the heart. To make sure she was finished, I gave the sabre a full twist round in her chest and, as she fell back, I thrust at her once more, and once more after that. At the last blow it was as if I was trying to skewer her to the wall, like Shaghad.

* * *

"As well as hurting other people, you have also ruined your own life, colonel."

"I was aware of that, Your Honour."

* * *

He could feel it still raining and he realised that he should not have taken so long. His wife was standing in the grave. All he could see was her white hair tumbling over her shoulders. Parvaneh was standing awkwardly at the graveside, waiting. Forouz lifted up her skinny arms towards her daughter. The colonel stood next to Parvaneh in case she needed help, but there was no need. Holding her in her bony arms, like a full-length mirror, her mother carefully took her down into the bottom of the grave and very gently laid her down and stretched out beside her, her arms encircling her neck and cradling the little girl's head on her chest, and merged into her. She gently closed her eyes and waited, peacefully, to be consigned to the earth.

The colonel stood by the graveside as Abdullah finished his good deed by shovelling the earth back into the grave. Just as his bleary eyes saw it was now filled in, the colonel heard the *Allah-u Akbar* of the morning call to prayer and realised that it was all over and he could at last relax. Abdullah smoothed out the earth with the back of the shovel. Ali Seif stepped onto the now-level ground to hand the colonel back his pick and slung his weapon back on his shoulder:

"See you again, Colonel. You know that you aren't allowed to put anything on the gravestone, don't you?

"Yes, I know."

They went off, and the colonel felt dreadfully alone once they had gone. He had better go home now, he thought, but then he thought of the long-haired man who was presumably still wandering about the graveyard in the rain. Was he glad that he was now free of the great weight that had been taken off his back?

I'll go home, but I'm tired and done for. It's all been very strange… it really was just like a graveyard!

What could I do? Just what? My feet were my feet, my home was my home, my problem was my problem and nobody else's, and getting back was up to me. My head is hurting!

A feeling of faintness had overcome him once again. The false dawn added to his dizziness. Everything around him was blurring into fuzzy infinity – *and the rain!* He had to get moving. He had no fear of losing his way. He just had to keep calm and head for home the same way as he had come.

* * *

"That way, Colonel. You look like a drowned rat!"

"No, Colonel, it's this way!"

Well, which way is it, my children? But nobody answered. All he heard, coming from every door and window in the city, was the news that the great trial was about to take place. The great trial of the past. The one they had been promising for ages. It would be remarkable. The whole of history would be in the dock. It was possible that the funerals of the war casualties, including the colonel's Little Masoud, the news of whose return had been broken to the colonel by Qorbani, would all take place in the full, naked light of history. It was not unlikely that, for greater effect, the two performances would be combined into one, but this was all beyond the colonel's comprehension. He would just have to put up with whatever came. He was not surprised by anything any more, since people are only surprised by things that fall outside their everyday lives. But when chaos and disorder become part of the very warp and weft of life, as they had done for him, there is nothing surprising about being surprised. If you want to retain your sanity, the only thing you can do is look on without letting go of your mind. So that is what the colonel did, sure in the knowledge that he was in full control of his faculties and that his brain was in full working order, whatever people might be saying about him behind his back.

* * *

He wasn't going to Qorbani's house for two reasons. Firstly because, as one of those responsible for staging the great forthcoming event, Qorbani would have his work cut out with all the preparations, and a visit from his father-in-law would be even more unwelcome than usual. Secondly, Qorbani's pick and shovel – *that family have been grave diggers for generations* – would come in more handy at the colonel's house. So he should go straight home, and dry his clothes, dry his whole body and dry his bones. He felt that even the brain in his head had got soaked and that, if he did not dry it out, it might rot.

When he got home, he saw Amir squinting at him through the sitting-room window, his wide eyes looking like those of a sick owl. But the colonel's most pressing need was to get rid of the pick and shovel and find the lavatory; he was bursting. Hopping round in circles holding his hands tight over his privates like an old buffoon, he recalled that most houses had their lavatories at the end of the yard, so why should his be any different? He ducked under the low roof in the corner of the yard and presently came out, feeling greatly relieved. The only thing weighing him down now was his clothing, which seemed to have absorbed a vast load of rainwater. He was chilled to the bone and felt that he had shrunk to the size of a rat. What a treat it would be if the paraffin had not run out and the stove were still burning. He then fell to speculating that, if Amir could only snap out of his nightmare for a moment, just this once, and if he could be bothered to do so, he would witness this absurd and ridiculous spectacle of his father. He would then be able to compare it with that other, similarly rainy night when he had been staring out of the same window into the courtyard, and the colonel had marched back in with his drawn sword still dripping with the warm blood of his wife's heart, as if returning as a conquering hero from a great battle. His blood-charged sabre glinted in the dancing light of the never-ending rain, and the thought struck him that, by having been put to use on his wife, this weapon, which he had only ever worn on parades, had finally lost its historical pointlessness and found some real purpose. He was victorious; with his head erect and his shoulders back he marched up the steps into the room and, as he laid the sabre, still loaded with warm blood, down on the mantelpiece, right in front of The Colonel's photograph, he stood to attention and declared, to no-one in particular: "I'm a soldier, a soldier am I, and let the whole world know it!"

But now, as he climbed the stairs, he looked like nothing so much as a condemned man. As he walked into the room, he could not bring himself to look at his son. Amir would not look at him either; his face looked as though it was framed behind the glass in the window. The colonel wanted nothing to do with him and dragged himself like a whipped dog to the stove, which still had a glimmer of heat in it, and began unbuttoning his clothes, which were all covered in muck and smelt of death and rotting flesh. As he did so, one baneful thought kept nagging at him, buzzing round his head like a fly: he wanted to ask Amir whether he had ever thought about his own death.

Amir's finally emerging from his basement appeared to signal some change in his state of mind. Everything and anything seemed possible to the colonel, except that his son's mental state might have improved. *It meant he could only be heading for his death.* It could also have been that the pressure of his never-ending nightmares had forced Amir out of his basement. The colonel remembered that Amir had once wanted to become an architect and had been fascinated by history.

Youth, youth… the fleeting moment of youth is like a school exercise book overwritten with correction marks; the forces that keep a young man going are his hope and his ambition. Sometimes a young man realises he cannot fulfil all his aspirations, but he won't let that get him down. For instance, a young man who has decided to become a doctor or an engineer can go one of two ways: he can become a vague idealist who believes that he can go and eliminate hookworm from the south of the country, with its hot, foul climate or, if he can get through a course of road engineering, he might believe that he will be able to produce a comprehensive plan to improve the country's road infrastructure. On the other hand, it is only those realists sitting on the benches in the university lecture halls who, right from the word go, imagine themselves actually owning a lucrative medical practice or running a construction company.

But no-one has the right to undermine or obstruct the hopes and aspirations of the young on the basis of one's own experience. It is quite wrong to be a doom-monger. No, one should keep one's peace and just nod one's head in agreement. To launch young people on their way, one should provide them with all the space and opportunities that one can and then leave the rest up to them and up to luck. That is what I did for my children.

But when I ran into Amir in prison I saw that his views on life, on his education, on his course of studies and on his future and so forth had completely changed from what they had been a few years before. Without any logic, he had grown more embittered and yet at the same time more hopeful. Embittered by what he had had to go through in prison, yet still hopeful for the future of his country.

This may have been some sort of realism appearing in him, but his new realism was just as embittered as his old hopefulness had been so delightfully energetic, so when they let him out I was surprised by the sudden naïve, over-hasty optimism that had seized him, as if he were starting with a clean slate. Had he been swept along by the sudden wave of unrest, which had taken everyone by surprise? Yes, that must have been it. By the time he had come to his senses, the universities had been closed down and he found himself teaching history and design in a secondary school. I remember clearly that he showed no sign of concern when they closed the universities, and I even heard him say that this was the only way to root out the opposition groups!* I can't remember much in particular about him getting his first job, but I remember exactly the day when he lost it, as if it were engraved on my mind.

It was raining that day and it was exactly seventeen minutes past nine, and the colonel was sitting behind the steamed-up windows of Noqli's teahouse, gazing out at the muddy pavement, when he saw Amir coming back from the school. Amir was walking along the pavement with his rain-coat collar turned up and holding his old umbrella over his head. He slowed down in front of the teahouse and stopped. The colonel could see him, but through the steamed-up windows Amir could scarcely make out any of the customers in the smoke-filled room. "Perhaps he wanted to come in for tea and a cigarette," thought the colonel, but Amir changed his mind and carried on. The colonel decided that it was the thought of facing his father that had changed Amir's mind, for of course Amir knew that Noqli's teahouse was his father's regular haunt. He even knew some of the regulars: one of the longest-standing was Kerbela'i* Ramazan Kolahi, who was already losing his sight. He was usually to be found keeping warm beside Noqli's big samovar, peering through his spectacles, which were as thick as the bottom of his tea glass.

It was not only the thought of finding his father in the teahouse that had made Amir change his mind. It was more likely to have been that, in his present mistrustful and listless state, he did not want to meet anyone at all. Whatever it might have been, Amir carried on past the teahouse and went home.

Thereafter, though, what seemed odd to the colonel was that, unlike the other teachers who had been sacked and wore their dismissal as a badge of honour and who, for a while at least, had exploited it to boost their egos, Amir cut himself off from everyone and retired to the basement. He lost all interest in life, and made no secret of it. He did not always show it in public, but he did not force it on anyone, either. Most people, including his sister Farzaneh, judged his silent introspection by normal standards, but the colonel saw it in a different light: *I saw that Amir had arrived at a new certainty. He had realised that this was a way of isolating him and his ilk from society as a whole.* For the colonel could not believe that being sacked, on its own, could have had such a demoralising effect on Amir. He knew his son; coming as it did after he had been prevented from continuing his university studies, his subsequent dismissal from his teaching post would have taken on far greater significance than just one of those disappointments that happens now and again at work. *I could see from the way my son reacted that he felt deeply humiliated. Perhaps I can't explain exactly what I mean, but I'll try to find the right words. Yes, my son believed he had been rejected and ostracised by society, something that he had never envisaged for himself. Maybe this had speeded up the process of his disintegration, which was why he was now turning all his energies to shutting others out of his life.* From that day on Amir never wound his watch again, and did not read a newspaper or listen to the radio. The colonel never saw him buy another book, or begin reading a new one. *Amir never even left the house.*

Meanwhile, the colonel had slowly undressed and was trying to wrap his freezing bones in a tattered old sheet to keep warm. He was thinking that, if he could see himself in a mirror, he would look like a harmless little goblin. Then, forgetting all about Amir for a moment, he suddenly realised that his clothes were still wet – but he needed them today, this very day, which had followed on from yesterday and would slide into tomorrow without stopping. Today, he would have to put his suit on once more and go out into this wretched rain again, this time for the funeral of his Little Masoud. It was enough to make you weep – except that he felt no self-pity and could not cry. In this situation, where absolutely nothing seemed to be normal, and indeed nothing was normal, the colonel simply felt unclean and disgusting and that there was nothing human about him. All he wanted to do at that moment was to be able to purge himself of all the filth and misfortune, to slough his skin, his whole body, his entire being, and so free himself from the dirt, death and humiliation that surrounded him. He had to accept all these wounds, all this pain and corruption, as just a disease, a disease that he wanted to get away from and shake the filth of it off his back. He wanted to scrub off the dirt and filth; he wanted to scrape the scrofula off himself, but he was incapable of recognising the baneful truth that its cold abscesses had already invaded the stinking fabric of his being and had taken it over.

Knowing what he did about the state Amir was in, how could he possibly demand that he come with him to Masoud's funeral? On the other hand, if he did not tell him, it might well later come back to haunt him that he had kept quiet about his brother's death at the front.

He was shivering; the dwindling warmth of the stove and the tatty sheet did nothing to dispel the cold that had penetrated to the marrow of his bones. The teapot and kettle were still sitting on top of the stove and the tea glasses were on the table in their saucers, with the remains of yesterday's tea still in them. The colonel took the sugar bowl down from the shelf above the fire, glancing as he did so at Amir's watch on the mantelpiece, which had been sitting there, unwound, for more than a year. He did not know what time of day it was, or whether it was yesterday or tomorrow. He knew that its hands had stopped, frozen in one long, leaden moment of time. He would have to drink this tepid tea and think about getting the stove going again. He felt that all the last few days had been compressed into one, and all the past seasons into one long cold season, a season that was as cold and lifeless as lead.*

On a whim, he asked Amir: "What do you know about the days and the seasons? Can you remember anything about spring and autumn, summer and winter?" Amir gave no answer and the colonel expected no answer to such a pointless question. He did not exactly expect Amir to burst into speech and tell him, or anyone else for that matter, what was on his mind. For some time now, he had realised that Amir had lost his past, and he had even heard him saying it: "I feel as though my past, all the lines my past is written on, have been wiped out with a rubber." And the colonel wondered how a man without his past could live. And how could a man without a past have a future? The colonel's son, Amir had become aware of his loss of identity, of his lack of identity, and believed in it and had accepted it. *The tragedy of my eldest son's life is that he has lost his belief, and his nightmare might be that he knows he had a hand in the killing of his sister and brothers.* The colonel's view was that such a creature, if he exerted all his hidden, innermost strength, would only destroy himself. His masterpiece would be to bury his own corpse.

"I don't exist, I'm nobody's child, I belong nowhere. I exist only to deny my existence. My final trick will be to choose the manner and time of my own death, so that others will have to take to their graves their wish to kill me. This is the only way that I can take my revenge on the horror that has engulfed us. It'll also be my revenge against myself. For I worked for the glory of the revolution, committing all kinds of crimes in its name. In fact, the only crime I had nothing to do with was the one involving that bloodstained knife!"

At first the colonel could not take Amir seriously, and he ascribed the boy's ravings to his fragile mental condition. But in a strange way he gradually began to grasp their meaning. He would never have believed that the day would come when, as a father, he would accept his son's judgement without demur. Revenge… Amir was always emphasising the word "revenge," a word whose proper meaning, at least from Amir's point of view, was a long way from the colonel's view of it.

"Father, the tragedy is this! They say that the servants whom the Almighty loves, he kills. And I see that our country kills those who love it the most. Is this country committing suicide? They get under your skin, they use you to speak for them and, in your name, they then kill you. Crying "salvation and welfare" they drive you to destruction. Your servants – people like you were once – are destroying you. First they denounce you with their eyes, then they falsify your identity with their tongues and, finally, they shred you with their teeth. And then you hear a terrible cry coming from the herd of gullible fellow-travellers, which sends a shiver down your spine, a chant that has been dinned into them: 'Kill them! Tear them apart! Your number one enemy is the brother who shared your mother's milk. There is a snake in your bosom, smash its head in! Your own children are snakes, your sister and your mother, your own kith and kin, the whole generation of your youth, even your friends! If anyone dares to laugh, smash his teeth in!' Laughing is counted as treason, mourning and lamentation are now the order of the day. You are allowed to lament your own innocence, your stupidity and your perfidy and join in the general chorus of wailing. This pantomime delights the seekers after vengeance, it gives them the chance to laugh at their victims. All that remains are hollow creatures who have capitulated and who accept the most lethal sicknesses as normal. When those after us come to judge us, they will say: 'Our forebears were people who lied to themselves, who believed their own lies and sacrificed themselves to them. And if they ever doubted their beliefs, they were lined up and it was off with their heads!'"

The colonel listened in silence to Amir's monologue. In his father's presence, Amir was doing his best to speak in a measured and reasonable way. He seemed to be concentrating and trying hard not to get angry in front of the colonel. And for his part, despite the fact that Amir was not looking at him, the colonel was trying to look as though he was listening to him. He did not want to patronise his son. Whether he agreed with him or not, he was not going to allow the veil of their relationship to conceal the facts. On the face of it, he had no grounds for being proud of Amir, but inside he felt a glow of satisfaction that at least his son was at last thinking deeply about the problems of his country and his people. As a youth, like all the others of his age, Amir had been infatuated with muddled notions of changing the world.

And had the Party had a hand in all this? While Amir was being tortured in prison, he had been forced to think about the realities of life and, when the prison gates were thrown open at the beginning of the revolution, he had tried to maintain a balance in his mind between revolutionary fervour and cool calculation. When the revolution happened, however, everything suddenly changed and, in spite of his utter sense of doubt and disbelief, he had fallen for the arguments of those willing Party fellow-travellers who had volunteered to join forces with the new Islamic regime, and had allowed himself to be sucked into their ranks, until the revolution began to take knives to his comrades' throats. Then Amir,

knowing full well that he had had some part in the sharp-
ening of those knives, had suddenly fallen into silence and
brooding, and had begun to disintegrate.

From then on his whole being had been dominated by
doubt and the wish to be allowed to think for himself – but
it was a bit late for that now. There was no room in his head
for all the questions whirling around in it, nor could he hope
to resolve even the least of them on his own. The more he
thought about it, the more he hated himself. He was disgusted at the way he had been taken in: hook, line, sinker
and all. He did not know what to do. He had nowhere to go.
He could not join those who had been executed, informed
on, or who had become refugees, nor could he join those
who had gone over to the new régime, which was only going
to bring about a new era of refugees, informers and executions. No, he was one of those who chose to sit on the fence,
ashamed of themselves, perpetual refugees from themselves,
gradually immolating themselves. He tore himself apart,
crying: "No, I shall not weep for the death of my friends, I
shall not submit to the executioner's sword, I shall not give
myself up to lies and slavery. No, I will kill myself, for this is
the only thing I can do, and I will do it."

What he was saying these days was radically different from
what he used to say. There was a lot of sense in what he
said now. But it could not last. Before long Amir had lapsed
into hatred and resignation and had retreated into his shell.
Rather than speak, he stayed silent and instead of thinking,
he lost himself in his nightmares once more.

His hands, which were big to start with, had grown bigger,
larger than all the other parts of his body, and his fingers were
even longer than his palms. When he opened his fists and showed

the palms of his hands, his whole body disappeared behind them and his face looked like a battered coin. All you could see of him between his fingers were his hate-filled eyes.

"He thrust those same fists, those same long fingers, into my mother's body, twisted his fist and forearm inside her and pulled out her womb. His fist was covered in blood and torn, slashed afterbirth and we – me and Parvaneh and Masoud and Taqi – were all left struggling like newly hatched chicks in his fist, which had turned into a vulture's talons. With his malevolent and vengeful claw he pulled us out of the afterbirth and I saw that long scrawny, seemingly mummified arm, with his sleeves rolled up to the elbow, dripping with blood, and we did not know which of us would be the first to die. We were screaming, but there was no sound. We flapped our wings, but our unfledged little wings were scrunched up in those bony fists. There was a gale blowing and we were caught up in flying branches and dead leaves and we were in the clutches of a wild eagle. There was a storm, and our screams were lost in the air and there were devils as big and black as the night sky as those claws dragged us down and down... Then I was aware of nothing until I felt his member in my throat, warm and filled with hot blood, and I heard the sharp blow of the old gravestone on my head, at the back of my neck, on my cheeks, on my shoulder blades, on my shins and arms and on my tongue, and I felt numb with pain and chewed up, like a piece of meat that has been through the mincer. He keeps beating his member – me, and all of us. He has laid his member over a lump of black stone in the hallway of that old house in Khorasan and is pissing blood, which flows down my throat and out into the street, spraying all those who pass by."

When he had his epileptic fit in the hall, the midday summer sun was shining, it was August. It was unbearably hot.

"Trapped between his legs, I am beginning to smell, I am rotting and flies are crawling over me. My wounds gradually turn into pus-filled scabs, which grow larger and larger and spread to him, covering first his legs, then his thighs, and stomach and chest and head and shoulders and arms and lips and teeth and mouth and his tongue so that we can stink together, and be corrupted. And then a unit arrives from the Point Four office to disinfect us all.* But the putrescence has gone far beyond any normal bounds, so they have to use scissors and kitchen knives and a bow saw to remove the rotting flesh from our bones and, since we are rotten to the marrow, they decide to amputate our bones and they cut off our hands, that this corrupt body might be dismembered and then, in a manner of their own prior devising, reassembled. Once more I was lying on the concrete slab in the mortuary, and all I could hear was the rasping of the saw cutting through my leg and the roar of bulldozers outside digging a trench to bury our rottenness. I could also hear numberless graves being opened, and I imagined that they were exhuming bodies, dressing them in shining raiment and putting jewelled walking sticks in their hands. Led by a band of minstrels, the dead are to form a procession, to be honoured and glorified. And they are saying that there will soon be a big-screen showing of a sad film about the latest round of dead, a common occurrence these days. And I am still on that concrete platform, and my ligaments are being sawn through, and I hear that they are going to cremate my rottenness in the trench behind the mortuary and I shudder at the thought of the smell of burning bones and flesh and of the damp body washing house, and I am retching, but can vomit nothing up."

"Amir... Amir, my boy... don't do this to your father!"

But Amir was not there, and the colonel's voice echoed back to him. A moment before, Amir had been sitting cross-legged on the floor the other side of the window. How had he managed to leave without the colonel noticing? Maybe he had not been there at all, and the colonel had just imagined him to be there? *But no, he was sitting right there, just as he had been on that night when his mother was killed!* The colonel could still hear him shouting:

"Hate and loathing! How long can I go on living with all this hate inside me?"

"Where are you, Amir, my boy? Speak to me, let me see you. We're just two human beings. We used to talk to each other. I'm your father!"

"I don't recognise anyone. I don't know anyone and I can't understand anything. I can't remember my past and I don't want to remember. I'm afraid, afraid and disgusted, that's all."

Where is he? I can't believe I am here. No, I am not imagining things! Here is the kettle and... and here is the teapot, these are the table and chairs, and there is The Colonel's portrait on the mantelpiece by the stove, and that's me, wrapped up in a sheet and shivering, and that's the noise of the same rain as always, battering on the tin roof... My God, what time is it now? What time is it? And these old clothes of mine aren't dry yet. Haven't I got to go to a funeral? And the canary, why isn't it singing?

There was no sound from the canary, but the colonel was in such an abject state that he found himself searching for an excuse to forget whether the bird existed or not. He was shivering so violently from the cold that he could not bring himself to go out onto the verandah and down the corridor to take a look at the bird. His putting off going to see the canary had nothing to do with the fact that the canary was called "Parvaneh" and that, having buried his daughter, he did not want to be reminded of her. No, it was just that he was cold. But the fact that he could not hear it singing made him aware that time had cracked on, since the canary always started singing at dawn, and continued warbling until the sun was well up. Then it stopped for an hour or so, and started again at about nine. So, if the canary had not retreated into its shell, it must now be about nine in the morning, the interval between its two performances. But why should the colonel have imagined that the canary had not withdrawn into its shell as of today?

"Amir… what are you doing? Are you coming with me to your brother's funeral?"

"No, I haven't got a brother to get up and go to a funeral for."

Amir did not need to be in the room for the colonel to put such a question to him and to get such an answer. No, absolutely not. The colonel was sure that even if Amir had been in the room, he would have got the same reply. There was no need for this kind of conversation between them any longer. The day that Amir came out to escort Mohammad-Taqi's body home was, in the colonel's view, unlikely to be repeated again in his lifetime, any more than was the atmosphere that prevailed on that day. In those days of easily won victories, people were happy to make the most precious sacrifice of all, the blood of youth, in the cause of supposed freedom. The blood of the masses flowed so freely that there seemed to be no end to it. Even the donating of blood seemed to serve the people's lust for ecstasy.

To share in this collective ecstasy, even I, who had long since lost the courage to face up to bullets, went to the hospital, rolled up my sleeve and told the nurse: "Take my blood, as much as you need!" In truth, in such circumstances, if you hadn't done your bit, you would have felt so guilty that you could not have slept at night. So it was when one of our boys was killed in battle; soul-destroyingly painful as it was for us, we were given no chance to grieve. After all, you told yourself, there was a revolution going on, and our country was on the threshold of momentous historic change, and this change could only come about through the sacrifice of the blood of the people, of which we were a part. In such circumstances, how could we complain about the loss of one of our sons? But, in the upheavals of the revolution, families who had sacrificed their children were caught in the grip of conflicting feelings. On the one hand were internal and deeply personal feelings, which overcame you in quiet corners at home, while on the other hand you were required to put on a public face and show other feelings, feelings for which you had to search deep inside yourself to give them legitimacy. This led to a soul-destroying conflict between the outward and the inward, the private and the public.

Bent under the weight of grief and misfortune in the privacy of your own home, you are like a broken-winged bird, but in front of other people, who are shouting for joy, you become another person entirely – an invincible hero! But the fact is that this conflict is exhausting. You can take refuge from yourself in the company of others, or you can avoid others and withdraw into your shell. This unrelentingly schizophrenic existence sometimes becomes so exhausting that it makes you ill. *That is exactly what happened to me, but what could I do? At that time, I never found a chance to be by myself. They never gave me the time to stop and taste the pure pleasure of grief and misery...*

The feverish, frenzied atmosphere of those days swept us all up like a fire. When they laid Mohammad-Taqi's blood-soaked body down in our courtyard, it was as if a haystack had been set alight. When Mohammad-Taqi was killed, it was not just ourselves and our immediate neighbours, but the whole city that went up in flames. Even Amir was caught up in the blaze. He knelt down beside his brother's corpse and kissed his bloody shirt. When he got up I saw that tongues of fire were licking out of my son's eyes and his cheeks were aflame. I wasted no time thinking about Khezr Javid or reproaching my son, as I could see how the fire had taken hold of all of my children.

Farzaneh was aflame and her wailing melted everyone's hearts. Parvaneh had lost control of herself and was flapping madly around her brother, while Masoud got up off his knees beside his brother, clenched his fists, like two balls of fire, to his head and screamed: "I'll kill them, I'll kill the bastards who killed my brother..." His rallying cry was taken up by the crowd, and from that point on Mohammad-Taqi's corpse was no longer ours – it had become public property.

And what a crowd of people there was. They seemed to have boiled up out of the ground to gather round the coffin, which they were now holding high up above their heads. Their hands formed circles that opened and closed, as they tried to touch the coffin, but it was too high, far up above all the hands, and getting higher all the time. The colonel did not notice when or how the coffin had become bedecked with flowers or when he and his family had got swallowed up by the throng, nor did anyone know what his children were really feeling inside.

I can honestly say that, in the face of all that adulation, with all the hands stretching out trying to reach the coffin, I felt truly small and humbled. Before long I was feeling completely out of place, a stranger utterly divorced from the hands that were bearing my son to the cemetery. The masses had commandeered my son from me and were carrying him off where they wanted and how they wanted and were shouting out whatever they wanted about "the killing of my son" and chanting a slogan which my hearing was too weak to make out. I was just an onlooker. It now seemed to me that the corpse that was being carried off in procession had nothing to do with me and that I didn't even know him!

* * *

It is as though time and existence have been compressed and that it was only last night when that stranger came to the house for the first time. The colonel was standing smoking behind the cracked window, listening to the rain falling heavily on the pool in the yard, when there was a knock at the courtyard gate. The colonel waited to see which of his sons would go to open it, and who it was that had turned up at that hour of the night. At the second knock, the colonel saw Mohammad-Taqi with his jacket over his head running down the verandah steps. He opened one half of the gate. At the sight of the new arrival he seemed to start for a moment, but then he stepped aside to let the visitor in. The newcomer had the air of someone who would have come in anyway, even without permission.

He was short, sporting a fedora and an overcoat, with a briefcase in one hand and a walking-stick in the other. The pince-nez spectacles he was wearing made it hard for the colonel to make out his face. The man paused for a moment and seemed to be asking Mohammad-Taqi a question. Mohammad-Taqi shut the courtyard gate and showed his guest the way to the basement. As if he already knew the way, the little fellow made straight for the basement steps and began to go down. Assuming he was one of Amir's comrades from the party, Mohammad-Taqi called down from the top of the steps: "There's someone here to see you, brother!" Then he came back up on to the verandah, without noticing that his father was watching him and observing the change that had come over him.

Amir's untimely afternoon sleep, the sleep of one permanently exhausted by the struggle, the mayhem, the speeches and arguments and the endless to-ing and fro-ing, might have lasted until the following morning if the knocking on the door had not shaken him out of bed, with an even grumpier face than usual. Now, shattered and only half-awake, he thought how much better it would have been if nobody had knocked at the door and Mohammad-Taqi had not called him and… But it was too late and things had gone too far. He had to get up, switch on the light and wait for his visitor to come in. The switch was on the pillar beside the door. All he had to do to turn on the light was to reach out his hand for it.

"Brother, there's someone here to see you!"

The light was now on. Amir's gaze fell on the stairs, on a

pair of shiny, pointed shoes, spattered with mud, and a pair of trouser legs with knife-like creases above them. "Please come on down," he called, as if his visitor would not have come down if he had not said it and, as the legs came down the stairs, Amir recognised the tails of Khezr Javid's dark overcoat. His heart missed a beat. Taking his time, Khezr descended and, as he did so, more of him became visible to Amir: his coat buttons, chest and shoulders, and finally his face, his glasses and the fedora on his head. This was something new for Amir.

Amir stood up quickly from where he had been sitting on the edge of the bed, not out of respect for his visitor but driven involuntarily by some innate fear. He found himself standing respectfully before Khezr Javid, with a greeting on his lips. Khezr took his glasses off his nose, rubbed his eyes with the back of his hand, smiled and propped his stick in the corner against the wall as if it were a nuisance. It suddenly dawned on Amir that the walking-stick and glasses were a disguise. In all the time that Khezr had interrogated him, he had never seen him with a fedora, or a walking-stick or spectacles for that matter.

The smile on Khezr's face was odder than ever, so odd that it forced Amir to offer him his hand and show him a place to sit. The best place he could find for him was the edge of the bed. Before sitting down, Khezr Javid unbuttoned his coat and took off his hat. Not sure what to do next, Amir pulled up the stool he used for sculpting and sat down in front of him. Then he thought he should get him some tea.

"Brother... can I bring you anything down to drink?"

Amir shouted up to Mohammed-Taqi to bring some tea and then thought he ought to offer to take Khezr's hat. As he was hanging it on the hook, Khezr got up and took off his elegant dark brown overcoat. Amir took that as well and hung it on the coat rack.

Now, apart from the long moustache drooping over his lips, Khezr Javid was the same person that Amir had first encountered. Khezr put his briefcase down on the bed, dipped into his pocket and pulled out a packet of cigarettes, offering one to Amir. With his gold-plated lighter he lit Amir's cigarette first, and then his own. He studied the flame over the end of his cigarette:

"You've made this place into a studio, then?"

Amir was about to say that he had not yet started seriously, but that he was thinking of taking up sculpture, when he was suddenly reminded of Khezr coming down the prison wing in the middle of the night, pushing a cigarette or two through the cell hatches and saying: "Golds... only an ass smokes Golds."

"Sculpture... that's a good idea."

"Yes, if I can manage it," Amir replied, far away.

"I gather you've been having some exciting meetings?"

"I expect they've entertained you."

"No, why?"

Amir shut up. He had realised that he had forgotten who Khezr was and what he did for a living. He had started talking to Khezr as a friend, sounding like someone worried about what others thought of him, and wanting their approval. If he had not quickly stopped himself, Khezr would have stopped him anyway. Khezr – ever the professional – quickly changed the subject:

"Haven't you got a telephone here?"

This could have been taken any number of ways, for it

was not hard to find out whether the colonel had a telephone in his house or not. Even so, Amir's first thought was that Khezr just wanted to make a call, but then he thought that perhaps he wanted to be absolutely sure whether there was a telephone in the house or not. Faced with Amir's silence, Khezr turned to sarcasm:

"What, not even a cordless phone? You'd be amazed at the things people have in their houses these days!"

Amir laughed. "No." He was sure that, before he had come to the house, Khezr had investigated all the security angles and already knew most of the answers to his questions.

Mohammad-Taqi was now outside his room with a tray of tea; following Khezr's glance, Amir could see a sliver of Mohammad-Taqi through the half-open door. He got up, went to the door and took the tray off him. Once Mohammad-Taqi had gone, he offered Khezr a glass.

"Was he listening at the door?"

Amir said he did not think Mohammad-Taqi did such things, but without thinking he got up and pushed the basement door to, feeling Khezr's eyes on him all the way. Khezr turned almost bashful:

"I'd heard Mohammad-Taqi was in Tehran. I'd rather it hadn't been him that opened the door to me. He's the only one here I'm worried about."

Amir was silent, probably preoccupied despite himself with the difference between himself and his brother. He put a lump of sugar in his tea and listened as Khezr went on:

"It's true that he escaped arrest, but I had seen reports about him and I recognised him. It was because of Mohammad-Taqi that I was in two minds about coming here. Now I don't want him to know who I am, although I am sure he could find out through his friends, if he really wanted to. But I don't want him or anyone else to know. Got that?"

Amir kept his eyes glued to the floor, but Khezr Javid was clever enough to know what he was thinking. He had no doubt prepared himself before the meeting for all possible reactions on Amir's part. He knew all too well what a bind he had put Amir in. Even so, he probably did not expect Amir to start singing like a canary there and then. After all, Amir's situation was now quite different to when he had been under arrest and was being interrogated.

Khezr took a sip of his tea. Amir had his head down, but he was sure that Khezr was looking at him all the time, drilling into his forehead with his gimlet eyes. His being sunk in silent thought was presumably annoying Khezr. Amir did not want to be brooding like this, either. He might lose control of himself and start kicking up a fuss about this security policeman being in his house. Who knows what consequences that might have? There were still plenty of people out there who were baying for the blood of hundreds of the likes of Khezr. Khezr, who imagined Amir might be thinking along these lines as well, broke the silence:

"I remembered your address from your file."

Amir just nodded. But Khezr, trying to break his concentration, went on: "So I came straight here. I thought you'd be surprised to see me, but you haven't reacted at all. Why not?"

Still with his head down, Amir seemed to be talking to himself: "It's amazing, really bizarre. After I was freed I always imagined we might meet again some time, and in a situation just like this. Bizarre, isn't it?"

"You mean right here, in your house, in this basement?"

"Not here particularly, but in circumstances like this. I always thought so. Isn't it odd?"

"It's interesting, not odd. And it's interesting that I chose your house... Why you? It's not as though I haven't got friends in this country. I had over a thousand prisoners to interrogate, and quite a few of them turned. But we didn't ask you to come over. So why did I choose here, why did I choose you?"

"Maybe because of my weakness, my weakness and vacillation and my lack of certainty about anything."

"No, I don't think so. No. My decision was in response to my need, and what I need now is to be rescued by my enemies. There has been a revolution, you see. So far, they have strung up seven of our people from the trees along the street, more than seven of our local officers... It's just my good luck that nobody knows me here. But maybe that's precisely why I came to this town, to your house."

Perhaps hoping to stop the conversation right there, Amir simply nodded again and said, "Right." He still couldn't look Khezr in the eye. With his professional agility, Khezr now adopted a practised conciliatory tone:

"But some of our people were real bastards, it's true... particularly the high-ranking ones, who were just looking out for themselves and trying to save their own skins. Lots of them got the hell out of here while there was still time. Then I was arrested. I learned later that some of them had packed their families off abroad a full six months before the prison doors were thrown open. Then they followed them, and hung the rest of us out to dry, leaving us behind as scapegoats for everything that had happened. They sacrificed us to a people who all seemed to have gone mad. It's obvious now that the higher-ups knew a full year ahead that the game was up, maybe even longer than that!"

Amir was now able to look at Khezr: "Have you resigned?"

It was not in Khezr's nature to answer questions, and his response was silence. His silence may have emboldened Amir to press him: "Why? Do you still imagine you are protecting something?"

Khezr did not look at Amir: "I don't know… perhaps I just don't know any other life. Perhaps because I've spent all my life doing this; it's what I believe in. Perhaps I am just saving myself."

He looked up, looked Amir straight in the eye. There was an implicit threat in his voice: "Are you certain no one is listening to us?"

Amir nodded, though he was not at all certain: "Apart from Mohammad-Taqi, the only other people living here are Masoud, the colonel and Parvaneh, right?"

"Yes."

"And Farzaneh lives with her husband Qorbani, doesn't she?"

"Yes."

"I know Qorbani well. He knew quite a lot of our informers here. But I don't trust him. He just waits to see which way the wind is blowing. He's a pompous idiot. At the beginning, he probably hung around you quite a lot, didn't he? Yeah… and he thought that your lot would end up on top. As if our lot were already dead and buried!"

"You say what you think, don't you, Khezr Javid? I noticed that about you when I was your prisoner. Don't think I'm flattering you, but I have to say that you've got some nerve. You're a brave man. But what I still don't understand is how anyone could put such qualities at the service of a hellish system like that. What made you do it? What was it all for?"

Javid finished the rest of his tea and reflected for a moment: "My face didn't fit. My nose was too big."

"No, I'm serious."

"And I gave you a serious answer. My nose was too big. It made me want to worship something, so I worshipped the Shah, so my nose made me enter the service of the Shah."* But as for a 'hellish system,' I have to say that you intellectuals really do exaggerate. You use the most overworked terms for everything, don't you? Hellish system, indeed. No, if you ask me, that was only purgatory. The real hell is yet to come."

There was nothing more to be said. They both fell silent. Khezr tucked a cushion under his elbow and leaned back on it. He lit another cigarette and, so that Amir could not see what he was thinking, closed his eyes as if he were having a nap. Amir felt the air around him becoming suddenly heavy, and the dead end to their conversation felt unbearably oppressive. He decided now was the time to confront Khezr, and ask him why he, a security policeman and his former interrogator, had come to his home – when the whole city was alive with rumours, counter-rumours and misunderstandings, which could destroy not just individuals but whole families as well? Did he not think that that might be asking too much? Amir was still weighing his words when Khezr spoke, without parting one eyelid from the other:

"Not all revolutions get off the ground these days, you know. The fate of small nations is in the hands of the superpowers, comrade. So I haven't given up all hope. You don't remember the days between 15th and 18th August of '53, but I do. I was a young man then, counting the minutes for the order to come out into the streets. But then the tables were turned and we saw with our own eyes that Sha'ban the Brainless was sitting there instead of Mossadeq and Khosrow Rouzbeh!"* With his eyes still closed, he continued:

"Tell them to bring us something to eat, anything. And find a way to tell your family I'm here, without letting on who I am."

"Where will you sleep? Do you want to spend the night here?"

Khezr did not answer, but just stared back at him. Amir looked down, just as he did when he was being interrogated and had dared to ask a question, only to have Khezr bark back at him: "I ask the questions here. You just answer them." To escape Khezr's vice-like hold over him, Amir got up, stuck his head out into the stairway and called up for someone to make them some supper and bring it down. He hoped that Mohammad-Taqi would answer. He guessed that Parvaneh had not yet come home and he knew that, as usual, Masoud would be late back from the mosque because after the mourning ceremonies and prayers he would stay behind to sweep the prayer hall and clean up the pantry and only come home if there was nothing else to do. It was not unusual for Masoud to sleep in the mosque. Which was why, whatever Mr Immortal Prophet Khezr might have preferred, there was nobody except Mohammad-Taqi in the house to serve them. All that Amir could do was to go back and talk to Khezr and distract him from thoughts of Mohammad-Taqi.

I had never got over my wife being taken away by the police and, although I was still in a state of shock at seeing Khezr in the house, I was strangely tempted to take it up with him. I was sure that he must know what her file said about her arrest and interrogation; he must know all about what had happened to Nur-Aqdas Khamami. It seemed perfectly natural that, now that Khezr had taken refuge with me, I should ask him to tell me what had happened to my wife, who had disappeared without trace. But what was it that held me back from mentioning her? I don't know, but a powerful force was preventing me from uttering my wife's name. Maybe it was my oriental mentality that made me want to draw a veil over anything that reflected on my honour. All the dreadful images that I had had of what might be happening to Nur-Aqdas had destroyed my mind and left me in a state of terror. I wanted to shut her, and anything that was to do with her, out of my mind. I did not want to see or hear of her again. Nevertheless, my curiosity would not let go of me. It was impelling me to keep digging to find out what had happened to my wife. If the security police had executed her, there had to be some trace of her grave, or of the common pit they had thrown her into. But there wasn't. So what had happened to Nur-Aqdas? I don't know. So I don't see why I shouldn't put Mr Immortal Javid on the spot and get him to answer me. Wasn't he now a criminal hiding in my house? So why didn't I quiz him? Was it that I didn't dare? That was it. I didn't have the courage to ask the policeman personally responsible for her file what had become of Nur-Aqdas. I was hesitant, and maybe this shyness came from a sense of shame. This was nothing new; when other people behaved totally disgracefully, it was me that went red with embarrassment. What was holding me back was perhaps this overweening sense of shame. I just sat there on the stool, staring at the floor, and started thinking about Nur-Aqdas. I remembered the first time I saw her, with her eyes blindfolded, her feet swollen and bandaged, sitting on an old blood-soaked chair in one of those deformed, twisted prison cells. She was leaning backwards and I wanted to be able to see her eyes under the black blindfold once more. They had probably lost all their brightness, and I wanted to be able to look out through the half-closed door of that warped interrogation room, to see what hour it was of that night that seemed to have had no beginning. Then suddenly, I don't know how, I was no longer tongue-tied but, instead of asking Khezr what had happened to Nur-Aqdas, all I could manage to say to him was, 'What's the time?'

"Supper's ready, bro!"

At the sound of Mohammad-Taqi's voice, Khezr blinked and sat up on the edge of the bed. Before his brother could come down, Amir shot up and grabbed the tray from him and was about to turn round and come down with it when Mohammad-Taqi said, rather louder than he should have:

"Father wants to see you, bro!"

Amir went weak at the knees, but, toughing it out and giving no sign of his alarm, he went back down into the cellar, set the tray down on the rush mat and made a place for Khezr to sit down next to it, while watching for Khezr's reaction to what Mohammad-Taqi had said. Khezr gave no sign that he had heard anything and began to chew quietly on his food. Amir now seemed to have lost interest in inquiring about Nur-Aqdas. He was more interested in where Khezr was going to sleep after his supper, and why Mohammad-Taqi had used their father as an excuse to get him away from Khezr. How was he going to find an excuse for leaving his guest alone?

"Is there any hooch around the place?"

There was. He put the plastic petrol can of arack down in front of Khezr, with a glass and a bowl of olives. When he got stuck in, Amir had an excuse to leave the room. He put on his slippers and went upstairs to the sitting-room, where his father was waiting for him. He was sitting on a chair next to the stove, beneath the portrait of The Colonel, reading the *Shahnameh*, the story of Manuchehr, most likely.*

Mohammad-Taqi was sitting on the bentwood chair, oiling his pistol in the light of the lamp hanging from the ceiling. When he caught sight of Amir, he looked up from his task for a moment. Amir waited patiently to find out what the colonel wanted, but the old man's head was buried in the *Shahnameh* and showed not the slightest interest in his son, even though he had heard Mohammad-Taqi calling him up from the basement. Amir was worried that he should not have left Khezr alone. The long silence forced on him by his father and brother made him feel small. Finally, he broke it himself.

"Father, what was it you wanted to see me about?"

The colonel peered at Amir over the top of his glasses, shook his head in irritation and buried himself once more in the *Shahnameh*, handing Amir over to his brother. Mohammad-Taqi did not give Amir a chance to speak. As he finished reassembling his weapon he adopted an abrupt tone that Amir had never heard him use before:

"Who is he, bro?"

Amir did not answer. He decided to stand on his dignity as the elder brother and shut Mohammad-Taqi up. Without a word, he turned round and headed for the door. But, before he reached the verandah, he was brought up short by a bark from Mohammad-Taqi. He stopped, then turned to face his brother, who was casually examining the weapon in his hand.

"What does it matter to you who he is?"

Mohammad-Taqi looked him straight in the face: "I know what sort of person he is."

"What sort of person is he, then?"

"Police."

"How do you know?"

"I've seen him, I recognise him."

"Where from?"

"Around the prison, before they stopped visits from brothers and sisters."

Mohammad-Taqi did not need to add that he had actually seen Khezr Javid face to face, on one of his visits to Amir. Amir was shocked into silence and his knees began to shake. It seemed that they now took him for an accomplice of Khezr. Struck dumb by this realisation, he stood awkwardly in front of his brother. His tongue felt as dry as a brick and he could not swallow his saliva. The colonel had looked up from his *Shahnameh* and was peering at him in astonishment over his spectacles. There was nothing for it; he had to come clean, before things got out of hand. And so, steadying himself on the table with his hands, he leaned over to Mohammad-Taqi and said:

"He's a guest. He's staying with us tonight. He didn't treat me so badly when he was interrogating me. Anyway, I want to get something out of him about the disappearance of my wife. So don't go kicking up a fuss about this – understood? I'm being completely above board with you."

The colonel had sunk back into his book. Amir had not noticed that, while he had been talking to Mohammad-Taqi, his father had lit a cigarette. He saw that he had put his half-empty tea glass down in front of him. Amir turned round and looked at his brother once more. Mohammad-Taqi avoided his glance, got up and went over to the far end of the room, where there was an old wooden bed. Amir watched him go in silence. Not wanting to dilute the force of his words by saying anything else, he slipped out of the room, went out onto the verandah and crept down the stairs to the basement, making an effort not to let on to Khezr that anything to do with him had been going on upstairs.

But Khezr was no fool; Amir knew from experience that he was always suspicious of his own shadow. As he lifted his glass to his lips he looked at Amir and, for as long as it took him to drink half of it down, he kept his eyes firmly fixed on Amir, piercing his very soul, so that he felt all the hairs on his body stand up on end like kebab skewers. He felt dried out. He could not move. It felt like being back in the interrogation room. His heart was thumping. He looked around for the card on the wall with the verse from the Qur'an that read, "Salvation comes to the honest." He stood waiting, like a scarecrow, for Khezr to give him permission to sit down.

"Sit down!"

Amir sat down. *I sat down. I did just as I was told.* Sitting down is a perfectly normal thing for a human being to do; if one hears of someone that he has sat down, one can have only one thing in mind. But in that instant it struck Amir that there were as many ways of sitting down as there were people in the world, in all their diversity. On the face of it, Amir sat down politely, but he was aware that, beneath the surface, his mind was seething with that sense of subjugation and fear which occasionally shows itself as "good manners," and that there is not a clear line between the two… It suddenly seemed vitally important to him to prove his utter obedience to Khezr Javid. His bearing, his expression and everything about him had to signal to Khezr that he was prepared to meet his every wish and do whatever he wanted. Meanwhile, as if to underline Amir's utter humiliation, Khezr Javid was not even deigning to look at him, but was glaring round every corner of the room instead. Amir hoped that Khezr would accept with magnanimity his signs of humility and surrender. *Observe my subservience, Your Excellency Dr Javid!*

* * *

Nobody had told Amir how to behave under interrogation. He assumed from the layout of the place and his general position that he was required to keep looking straight ahead, even though right next to him the screams of Nur-Aqdas Khamami were rending the air, as she was being savagely beaten by one of Khezr's lieutenants. A braver soul than him might have dared to lift his eyes up a little, as far as the portrait on the wall of the Shah with his medal-bedecked chest, but even that would have been to break the unwritten rules of the interrogation room. Rules which, like minute airborne particles, from the first moment of your arrest, work their way out of the air into your very soul. When they made you change out of your clothes in the guardhouse and put on a pair of scruffy grey overalls, which made you look like a scarecrow, you felt those unwritten rules becoming engraved on your heart.

"Hand him the form!"

It was the charge sheet.

"Sign here."

Both the basic principles of human rights and the written law require that a suspect must be informed of the nature of the charges against him within twenty-four hours of his arrest. Within that time he must be formally charged and he has to sign the charge sheet. If sufficient evidence is not produced within twenty-four hours, the prosecution is not entitled to pursue the case against the accused. Amir only found this all out later. He had never felt the need to think about the whys and wherefores of having such a clearly spelt out law. What earthly reason would any Iranian have to trouble himself about the law or try to keep to it? Here, the law had always been delivered at the blunt end of a cosh, hadn't it? All Amir wanted to find out, law or no law, was why he had been arrested, for he still had no idea. *Desperate to know what I was accused of, I had high hopes of Khezr Javid*, who was now standing by his desk.

"We beat people's feet till they're black as boots here!"

With the end of his cable whip he forced Amir's head round to the left, to face the two blindfolded women who had collapsed onto old chairs and, before Amir could fix in his mind the lines on the face of the woman he thought might be Nur-Aqdas, Khezr took a step towards her. Amir looked away. As the sharp toe of Khezr's shiny shoe connected with the bruised and bandaged legs of the nearest woman on the bloodstained couch, she let out a terrible scream and then fell silent. Khezr Javid now returned to the desk. He waved his whip at five of the prisoners in the room to indicate that they should be led back to the cells, then pointed at the sixth:

"The one with a moustache goes to administration."

He looked round at the woman on the couch: "You... pissy old woman, have a think about it tonight. Tomorrow you either talk, or I send you off to join your two boys in Behesht-e Zahra.* Take her to her cell, soldier!"

As the soldier led her away, leaving only the echo of her feeble whimpers in that dark and sinister room, the old woman looked as fragile as a blade of straw. Khezr sat down at his desk without looking at Amir or saying a word to him, lit himself a cigarette and began smoking it. After a long, frightening silence, Amir heard the sound of dragging foot-steps coming to the interrogation room. He had no idea how much time had passed, or even what time of night it was. Khezr got up, came forward and twisted Amir's head round, forcing him to look at his wife, who had been made to sit on the blood-soaked old couch by the door. A black blindfold covered her eyes and they had made "black boots" of her feet. Khezr turned Amir's head back again and moved back into the light. All of a sudden, Amir seemed to hear the screaming and wailing of all the women of the world spinning round the prison and reverberating in his skull until, as abruptly as if his spinal cord had been severed, he passed out. He remembered nothing until he came to on the wire bed and saw, on the lead-coloured steel table, a blood-stained knife in the pool of light under the anglepoise lamp.

* * *

"Here, have one of these cigarettes."

Khezr's eyes were bloodshot. Amir saw this, not in the feeble light of the ceiling lamp, but in his mind, which was still filled with the thought of those long, endless nights of interrogation. He could even remember every detail of Khezr Javid's yawns. Tired and exhausted after a long day's interro-gation and getting over his drunkenness, Khezr would read through the response to the final question once more, and Amir would see him yawn and hear the gurgling noise in his throat. The Immortal Khezr did not seem to the colonel's son

Amir to be the same man as the one who was now sitting on the bed, spitting out olive stones and putting them on the edge of the plate. For that Khezr, the one in prison, had long since etched himself indelibly on Amir's memory. Amir knew all his habits and foibles inside out. He knew that when he wanted to sleep, his drunken snores would not last more than an hour. There had been many occasions when he had set him a question and, stretching out on the camp-bed in a nook against the wall, had promptly had forty winks while Amir wrote down his answer. He would then get up, bright-eyed and bushy-tailed, and sit on the bedside, without even needing to splash water on his face to wake himself up. So now Amir was certain that Khezr was going to lie down on his bed for a short nap, but he could not be sure that he would sleep until morning. He did not dare ask him again about where he planned to sleep because, in all likelihood, he must have heard his conversation with Mohammad-Taqi and may have got the wrong idea about him. When Amir had come back down to the basement, he had seen a brief flash of suspicion cross Khezr's beady eyes. That naked, ruthless look, which contained the whole burden of Khezr's past, had stopped Amir dead in his tracks. His real personality – his brutal, overbearing nature – came flooding back. *Khezr hasn't changed; behind the friendly mask, he's just the same as he always was, however much he tries to hide it.* Amir would have to wait before Khezr would tell him what he wanted to know.

Khezr put down his empty glass, crossed his right leg over his left, undid his shoelaces and took off one of his shoes. Amir took it from him and put it in a corner, leaving Khezr's hands free to undo the other one. As Amir placed it beside the other, he realised that Khezr was intending to stay the night.

His heart sank, not least at the thought of Mohammad-Taqi's pistol in the sitting room. The pistol on its own was cause enough for horror but, added to it, was Mohammad-Taqi's alarming curiosity about Khezr, a curiosity blended with a suspicion that had turned into a certainty. Given what Amir knew about his brother's state of mind, and in particular his belief that the revolution had to be brought about through violence, he was worried that Mohammad-Taqi would take out his pent-up feelings of hatred on an enemy who, in his view, was a well known agent of the destruction of a whole generation of his countrymen. There was bound to be a bloody outcome. Nowadays, there were any number of people, ordinary people on the street or bazaar folk, all looking for revenge, either on personal grounds or simply because it had become a national pastime. From every other tree lining the streets they were busy stringing up dozens of known police informers like Khezr the Immortal. To a hot-headed, vengeful young man like Mohammad-Taqi, who had lost so many of his comrades over the years, it would seem only natural, after more than half a century of oppression, to drag a police torturer out of his house and sacrifice him to the mad juggernaut of the revolution.

...But what am I supposed to do in this situation? The ancient tribal customs of our country still more or less obtain, albeit they may have faded somewhat, and one of them is the sacrosanct duty of a host to protect his guest — even if he is a sworn enemy. The pressures of city life may have made it harder to observe these customs, but one does not forget them.

Why was I inclined to take these laws of hospitality so seriously, as if it were some sacred duty to look after Khezr Javid? Didn't I have every right to throw him out? Not one hair of my body is happy to have him in the house. I'm terrified of the consequences of having him here, but just as terrified of driving him away. If I have invoked custom and tradition, it is only because I was afraid. I have no doubt that if I saw Khezr in the street, I would just cross over to the other side. But now it is a different situation and I am trapped in a corner and I can't see a way out of this fix.

"Penny for your thoughts, comrade?"

He had used the word "comrade" ironically, of course. Amir had no idea where on earth his mind was wandering to. He turned round to look at Khezr. He was lying on the bed, half leaning on the pillows and half propped up on his right elbow. He was looking at the tumbler in his hand, which he had filled without offering any to Amir. He was swirling the arack gently round in the glass as Amir stammered back that he had not been thinking about anything.

"I'll be sleeping here tonight."

Khezr said this in a bullying, aggressive tone, boasting his self-confidence. With a smile dripping with artifice, Amir replied that there was a bed and that he would change the sheets.

Khezr said nothing and Amir realised that he was pretending that it did not matter. Khezr seemed to be feeling hot, for he got up to take off his jacket. When he reached up to hang it on the coat rack, Amir saw his shoulder holster with his side arm in it. Just as in the interrogation room, it hung off his left shoulder and was slightly angled so that he could easily reach the butt with his right hand and draw it. As Khezr sat down again, Amir could see the holster more clearly, with the black pistol butt sticking out of it. Khezr picked up the glass and, raising it to his lips, he grinned:

"Would you believe that in all the mayhem of the revolution I still walked right through the middle of town, just like that? Would you believe that?"

Amir said that he believed it. He knew that the arack had gone to Khezr's head, but had not made him drunk. He remembered that, some nights when things were not busy in the interrogation block, Khezr would sit in his room after a glass or two and talk about himself and brag about his deeds of derring-do, how he had been in Dhofar and been on dangerous missions in the marshes along the Iraqi border, which had all ended in success. And indeed, his swift rise in the security services did seem to indicate that there was some substance to his boasts.

"It must have been towards the end of February, in fact ten days after February 11th, the day the Shah left, that I saw three of your comrades. Two of them had been my prisoners and I knew the other one. What do you think happened? They went white as chalk. They knew very well that, one squeak out of any one of them, they were all dead meat. So what do you think happened then? Everything went off nice and peacefully, as it turned out. Except that, the very next morning, on the front page of your newspaper, there was a lead article asking what sort of revolution this was that allowed former executioners to walk freely in the streets. And this, of course, was under a big headline announcing that you were publishing a list of all SAVAK informers. The comrades had pointed out the lion tracks. So what was your politbureau up to, then? Why aren't you drinking?"

There was no doubt in Amir's mind that Khezr was telling this story because of Mohammad-Taqi. Khezr was clearly both suspicious and afraid of Amir's wild and hot-headed brother, but he wanted to give the impression that he was not in the least worried by what he might do. Perhaps he had decided to spend the night here precisely in order to dispel any impression that he was going to creep around in fear of Mohammad-Taqi. As it happened, his reasons for doing so were quite different, but Amir would only learn about this later.

"You said you don't want a drink. Why not?"

Amir said he didn't like it; it damaged his brain. Khezr had already asked him this question. Now he was asking again. This showed that he liked repeating himself. Amir knew Khezr well enough to know that this was not a sign that he was unexpectedly drunk. Khezr drained his glass and told Amir he could put the stopper back on the can, and keep it for tomorrow evening. Then, not fussing about creasing his trousers, he stretched out on the bed and closed his eyes.

Amir knew that Khezr always slept with one eye open and never went into a deep sleep. But at least he was in bed now, and the evening was at an end, which meant that Amir, too, could think about sleeping at last. He could have gone upstairs to get a mattress and blanket for himself, but decided against it, firstly because he didn't want to run into Mohammad-Taqi and, secondly because he did not want to stoke up Khezr's suspicions any more. Instead, he made a makeshift bed on the rush mat on the floor, but he entertained no hopes of sleeping. He got up once to collect the glasses and other bits and pieces on a tray, which he did not want to take upstairs, then again to turn off the light and switch it back on again. Then he lay awake for a long time wondering whether Khezr wanted the basement door shut or left half-open. Every time he got up he noticed that Khezr's right eye was half open. He also took in that Khezr was lying so as to face into the room. Amir usually slept with his face glued to the wall. Finally, leaving the light on and the door half-open, he lit a cigarette and lay back. With one arm flung over his forehead, he tried to calm himself down by watching the smoke curling upwards between his fingers. Sleep was out of the question, not because he had been sleeping all afternoon, but because he kept turning over in his mind what to do about Khezr – the enemy within – as Mohammad-Taqi would have put it. He wanted to treat it as a perfectly ordinary matter, but even that was impossible. He could only hope that Mohammad-Taqi had got off his high horse and had gone to bed. It was even more important that Masoud should spend at least tonight either in the mosque or at the neighbourhood Komité* and not show his face at home. He also hoped that Parvaneh would not get to hear of his little problem. For it was quite possible that she, the last person one would expect to do such a thing, would let the cat out of the bag and bring disaster down on the family. Amir felt as if the evil eye had struck him through his brothers and sister, with all their crazy carryings-on in the revolution, and he was frightened by it. *They were all in it, up to their necks, for heaven's sake!*

"I think I'll go and get a nose job!"

There was a change in tone from Khezr now, from his previous sickly-sweet, drunken and sleepy utterings. Thinking he ought to show that he was listening, Amir propped himself up and turned towards Khezr to face him. There, standing in the doorway, was his brother Mohammad-Taqi holding a mattress and quilt under his arm:

"I thought the floor might be damp, bro. I'll take the tray up as well."

Amir sprang awkwardly to his feet. He did not know which to do first, take the quilt and mattress, or pass his brother the tray. To his utter bafflement Khezr who, through his half-open eye must have seen Mohammad-Taqi standing there in the doorway, began to speak, in a perfectly flat, even voice:

"My father said… my father wished to be buried… in the highest part out in the country… on the highest hill outside the town… he had seen a little place and bought it."

"Er… yes… er… God rest his s…"

"Brother!" Mohammad-Taqi's shout drew Amir up sharp and made up his mind to take the mattress first and then pass over the tray. His brother had already spread out the bedding on the mat and was waiting with arms outstretched to take the tray. This helped him. Like a sleep-walker, he picked up the tray of dirty plates and handed it to his brother. "I'll get you some water."

"My father wanted to be buried in the open air, he wanted a cool breeze coming down the mountain to blow over him. You know, he believed that fresh air was good for the soul… I don't know why I'm thinking about your father's death, the colonel's death… damn it!"

"Mr Javid, would you like me to make you up some lemonade?"

"I'm going for a nose job… And, when I get back, you will see that this lumpy monstrosity on my face will have gone… My father was always saying that a man needs fresh air for the good of his soul… Damn you… Damn all of you!

Damn you all, you useless bunch! Couldn't you have

blown him sky high? Didn't you have even a Kalashnikov or an RPG-7?* Did none of you have any balls between your legs? Oh no, you stupid airheads went out waving silk handkerchiefs to welcome him, waiting for him to come and stick a hot poker up your arses, and forced me to submit my honourable nose to the indignity of the surgeon's knife… and to glue a fuzz of beard onto my immaculate face, which I have been shaving religiously every morning for the last thirty years… and made me drink this revolting hooch out of an old petrol can, instead of the sublime Johnnie Walker, and wake up half-blind from it in the morning… couldn't you, couldn't you have just blown him out of the bloody sky?† No, you couldn't… Damn the lot of you! And now you want to go and start a revolution in Turkmen country, do you! I'll kill the lot you, you whoresons!"‡

"Would you like me to light you a cigarette?"

The only response was Khezr's snoring. Amir calmed down a little and, hoping that his guest would fall into a deep sleep, he rested his head on his arm once more and stared up at the damp, bulging ceiling of the basement. But he was far from certain that Khezr would fall into a deep sleep, or even a drunken slumber. In prison, they had called Khezr "The Dog," because dogs are both awake and asleep at the same time.

From near and far came the sound of occasional shots, as if to remind Amir what a risk he was taking by sheltering Khezr Javid. It was precisely the likes of Khezr they were shooting. The odd thing was that Khezr remained completely oblivious to all the goings-on outside, or at least pretended to be. To all outward appearances, he seemed to regard everything that was taking place as completely normal and natural.

Amir, however, knew that Khezr was no slouch and that this detached and carefree attitude of his, even if he had nerves of steel, could not be real. He must have been driven by some inner sense of security and self-confidence that underlay all this show of coolness. After all, he was not some unknown, nameless policeman. It was a sign of his thrusting ambition but also of his raging inferiority complex that he had once declared, "Did you know that I was the only one in the office not to have a cover name?" Amir saw no reason not to believe his story about the three ex-prisoners of his, presumably revolutionaries, whom he had come across in the street. Amir knew Khezr well enough to suspect that, aside from his sheer bravado, he must have some other trump card up his sleeve. Had he not once said himself that he had been one of the organisers of the demonstration of jobless security policemen protesting outside the prime minister's office in the Revolutionary Government? During his time in prison, Amir had come to the conclusion that SAVAK was the most solid and tightly structured of all the secret services. But did its members really believe in what they were doing? It was fair to assume that the people's revolutionary uprising must have had some effect even on people like Khezr, and made them reflect, if only briefly, on the lives that they had led. For sure, with all the courage of his profession, Khezr was not going to admit to his own fear of the revolution. Otherwise, why was it that his incoherent mutterings when he was in his cups, whether uttered consciously or subconsciously, all had to do with the revolution?

"Couldn't you – or weren't you allowed – to do anything without permission? It could have been done, I know it could have been done, because even we had had a plan to shoot

Khomeini, but we weren't allowed to do it. What about you? You had orders from on high not to do anything! Oh yes... you lot assassinate people when you are supposed not to be terrorists, and when you arc supposed not to be democratic, you become democrats all of a sudden. You're nothing but hired mercenaries, traitors to your country!"*

I was looking up at the bulging basement ceiling, with half a smile on my face and thinking how interesting this all was. Because there was no doubt that, no matter what we did, we were traitors and were to blame. The men who ran State Security held the whip hand over the country's oil, the police, the SAM-7 anti-aircraft missiles and the army. All we needed was a nod and a wink to blast the Leader of the Revolution out of the sky and into eternity! No, it's our fault, whatever we did or didn't do. The worst of it is that, whatever we might or might not have done, the end result is that we are to blame, and we are traitors to our country as well.

"It's you who claim to be carrying history forward, not me, not us!"

"But, even if we could have done it, we couldn't have blown up someone who was supposed to be the saviour of the nation."

"Was supposed to be, or you supposed him to be?"

Khezr was sitting up now, confused, looking at Amir. Out of respect for him, Amir was obliged to reciprocate and prop himself up on his elbow so that he could look back at him. He was expecting Khezr to lay into him with renewed vigour, but instead, he pulled the can of arack towards him, poured himself half a glass, downed it in one and settled back on two pillows without a word. This silence may have prompted Amir to ask him, out of sheer curiosity:

"What difference, just what difference would it have made to you if the revolution had turned out differently?"

This time, without blinking an eye, Khezr answered him: "In that case I would have worked for you lot, I'd have been able to have my whisky again, I'd have carried on investigating people and I wouldn't have had to get a nose job, or stick a floor-brush of a beard on my face in order to work for this bloody bunch."

"What makes you think we'd have given people like you a job? How come you're so sure we wouldn't have just rubbed you out?"

With a quiet smile, Khezr puffed on the cigarette that Amir had lit for him and, with disconcerting certainty, replied: "Listen, boy. Political police are like a religion. Has anyone ever heard of a religion being overthrown?" He paused and went on: "A new gang may take over, but they don't go and overthrow the very basis of the old régime. I grant you that some of us were strung up by a few of your hot-headed brethren, but that's not the end of the story. Not by any means. We're the very base and foundation of everything, we are the underpinning of the state, my engineer friend!"

The cigarette ash was dropping into Amir's hand, so he fetched an ashtray, and held it under Khezr's waving hand, catching the ash as it dropped. As Khezr started talking, it was not clear whether he was awake or asleep; he sounded drowsy and he appeared not to be talking to anyone in particular; he was rambling to himself, going over his old life:

"...so I said that I'd come to serve the Shah and my country. I thought that the colonel was staring at my nose. I looked down, so that he couldn't see my nose, and I asked him to put in a good word for me. I had been recommended to him before. I was fed up with the Thursday evening local teach-ers' book club meetings.* I'd only joined it out of boredom; in fact I had set it up, and I was fed up with it. Fed up with those evenings, and fed up with the teachers who only went along so as not to become opium addicts. And I was fed up with my rickety old bicycle, which always got a puncture on the rocky tracks, and I always had to hump it on my back all the way home to mend the puncture and then go back to the village in the morning to give lessons to those shaven headed, lice-ridden, snotty-faced children about the battles of Xerxes the Great… You were a history teacher, too, weren't you?

"Yes."

"Then there was the bloody heat. I was sweating non-stop out of all my seven orifices. Everything was dust, date palms and despair. There was an occasional tall, gangly Arab and some water buffaloes… So I told the colonel that I was tired of teaching, of the bicycle, the humidity, the dust and the children… the filth on their faces would feed seven hungry dogs. I said that I wanted to serve my country. The colonel said he was always delighted to hear from ambitious young men wanting to serve their country. He said that a young man should advance himself and secure himself a bright future, and he said that I appeared to be a deserving young chap. And I was; I was capable and deserving, and this was the first time that anyone had acknowledged me. I was sick of nobody paying any attention to me. I was suffocating from being ignored. If anyone did look at me, all they saw was that I was short and had a big nose. Was that all there was to me – just a shortarse with a big nose, eh? Oh no, I knew I was more than that, I knew I was worth something, not like those teachers who got together on Thursday nights and poked fun at me, in front of me and behind my back, because I didn't understand the poetry of Nima Yushij* as well as they did. But I proved, in those first six months, I proved to the colonel that he had not got me wrong."

"Are you awake?"

"Yes, and I'm listening to you."

"Don't imagine I had some sort of illness. No, I was fed up with being humiliated. I wanted recognition. I wanted a sniff of power, because there was nobody who knew how good I was, how deserving I was and how strong I was. I was going to prove this, at any price. So I went and knocked on the colonel's front door and I told him that I wanted to serve my country, because I had had enough of all the flies buzzing round the filthy heads of my children and I was fed up with the classroom that stank of goodness knows what. But power... real power... that was what I wanted.

"The colonel told me to show him how deserving I was. I said to him, 'give me forty-eight hours, colonel,' and he gave me till the end of the week. On the Saturday morning I produced full reports on all the six teachers who were doing commentaries on Nima Yushij and George Politzer† and put them on his desk, to show him what sort of man I was. Six months later they were behind bars. That showed them. I wanted to get their attention, and I certainly did. I wanted to show them that they shouldn't judge people by their lack of inches and excess of nose, and I did. Then I ordered a pair of shoes with built-up heels and decided to get a nose job. But the office wouldn't let me have one. They said that if I had one, I wouldn't look intimidating enough. Then I realised that everything in this world has a place and that I had the most perfect nose for my chosen job. But this revolution has made me worry about it now, and I need to get it done. So, if I live long enough, the next time I come back here you won't see this surplus lump of meat and cartilage squatting on my face, because I'm thinking of having more than half of it cut off."

"Your cigarette butt, Khezr Javid, let me take it."

"I've made myself pretty clear, haven't I? Here, put it out."

"Yes, crystal clear. When you used to interrogate me, I always thought you were very straight, and even very courageous. But why did you turn those qualities of yours against the people? You must be afraid now, surely?"

"You're a bloody fool." Getting no answer from Amir, he went on: "I've killed a lot of people."

He was silent for a while, staring obliquely into Amir's face, waiting for his words to flow like toxin through his veins. He continued:

"...But a coward cannot kill in cold blood. A coward usually talks about humanity and morals, to hide his fear behind such waffle. Such people are just chicken. But me... I've got courage. I've only been frightened once in my life, when I began to worry that those teachers' fear might take root in me and suck me in.* That's when I went to see the colonel. So, I overcame my fear of the secret police by becoming one myself. You see, by surrendering to my fear before it got the better of me, I ended up beating it. After that I was never afraid again, only excited. When I knocked on the colonel's door I knew what I was doing; I was giving myself up to the vocation of torture and death, so I had to be brave.

"Are you asking me why I'm still carrying on? You're so naïve, you've got no idea. What should I do, then: give myself up? Make a public confession and repent of my sins?

Where, who to, and when exactly? And you expect me not to be brave? If I'm not brave, I'll be killed all the sooner. If I'm afraid, I'll die a hundred deaths before they kill me! Quite a few of the lads lost their nerve when they heard the first clarion call of the revolution and then cocked everything up for themselves for lack of balls. Chickenshit cowards! So I have to be brave, because I want to stay alive and I don't want to get my throat cut. No, if you were me you wouldn't want to get killed and you – as I well know – would definitely not want to be in my shoes! Do you hear all that racket outside?"

Yes, he could hear it all right. Had Masoud come back home? Or had Mohammad-Taqi gone out into the street? Would he smell blood, lose his nerve and charge down into the basement and shoot Khezr?

He could not help looking at Khezr's holster resting on the left side of his stomach, and then he looked at the revolver. At that very moment, Khezr's right eyelid twitched open and shut in his mask-like face, and his hand moved to grip the butt of his revolver. Amir decided to lie down, have a cigarette and stare up again at the bulging ceiling, so as not to have to look at the revolver.

"If I'd passed the entrance exam for the officer training school, then maybe everything would have been different. But I failed. You had to be over five foot seven. It was fourteen years before I faced that selecting officer again, who meanwhile had become a brigadier-general. That was the day I went personally to staff headquarters to arrest one of his sub-alterns, a young second-lieutenant. I twisted his little finger and dragged him off to the general's office, hurled him to the floor, looked the general straight in the eye and then kicked that second-lieutenant, who was over five foot seven, hard on the shins, and told the useless lanky bastard to get up!"

They are banging on the basement door and Khezr and I can hear heavy footsteps coming down the stairs. We sit up together and I can feel his hand shaking on his pistol holster. I am sure it is only Mohammad-Taqi at the door and my heart is exploding in my chest. I glance at Khezr and he has gone white as chalk, as if he has just walked into a trap. His face has gone purple from all the arack. I can feel him struggling to control himself.

"Brother!"

I am getting up – now – and I am putting on my shoes and going out. Mohammad-Taqi is standing at the top of the stairs and, as I am pulling the door shut behind me, two or three volleys of shots shatter the silence in the alleyway outside, and I think I can see the colonel's face through the window. I am stunned by Mohammad-Taqi's confusion. He is about to say something, which I know Khezr is going to hear too:

"Did you hear that?"

I did hear it, but Mohammad-Taqi wanted a reply. What needed to be said had not been said. I take him by the elbow and steer him up the stairs to Parvaneh's room. She has come in without my noticing it and is tearing up sheets for bandages. I see a cardboard box beside her bed full of medicines and… I sit Mohammad-Taqi down on a chair beside the bed and I can see that the vein across the middle of his forehead has swollen up and that he is looking down so that I can't see his bloodshot eyes. I pace up back and forth for a bit and then stand in front of Mohammad-Taqi: "I beg you to…" *but Taqi does not let me finish. He looks up, and this is the first time that he looks into my eyes like this and he says,* "Masoud is out on the street, he is in trouble and your guest's partners in crime are shooting people; can't you hear them?"

"Yes, I can. And I get your point!"

"My point doesn't matter. You need to know what the people on the street are saying."

Amir didn't respond. He knew that was the only way to calm his brother down. And it worked; Mohammad-Taqi became more mollifying:

"I'm sorry I shouted at you, brother. I was angry."

"I know, it's all right. But please try and see my position and put up with it just for tonight."

But Mohammad-Taqi had already dashed out of the room in response to a frantic banging on the outside gate. Parvaneh appeared, clutching her makeshift bandage strips. She was so bound up in her work that she seemed not to notice Amir. Amir ran out onto the verandah to see if his young brother Kuchik Masoud had come home. Yet it was not little Masoud who ran into the yard, but Abdullah, Habib Kolahi's son. Mohammad-Taqi shut the gate behind the young man and pressed him for news of Masoud: "Kuchik, Kuchik... do you know what's happened to him?"

"They went off into the forest.* Kuchik and his lot followed them. I'm slightly..."

"Have you been wounded?"

He had been. Mohammad-Taqi led him past the pond towards the verandah steps. Meanwhile, Amir had disappeared into the basement, aware all the time of the colonel looking at him through the window. He seemed to be exultant:

"My children... ah, my children!"

Khezr Javid was sitting on the bed, smoking. He had got some colour back into his cheeks. Amir was beginning to understand that he was not as brave as he made himself out to be. His courage was the courage of men who know they have got the backing of a system behind them. Amir sat down, without drawing attention to the upside down turn of the events happening outside. Khezr was too clever to be easily led up the garden path, but he had not faced up to the facts of the situation. He either couldn't, or wouldn't face it. Stubbing out his cigarette, he simply remarked:

"I've put you in a bit of a spot, haven't I?"

"No, no, not at all."

"You know, If I had passed into officer training school, things might have turned out very differently, but I failed. I've no regrets. I'm not going to whine like a child the others won't play with."

"You still think you have a future, then?"

"I can see my future very clearly, rather more clearly than you can, with your crazy distorted view of life."

Amir heard Mohammad-Taqi and Abdullah Kolahi going back down the verandah steps and hurrying to the main gate. Their footsteps were fast and light; Amir guessed they must be wearing trainers. He could take no more of it and ran up the stairs, just in time to see them going out into the alleyway with the boxes of medicines and bandages that Parvaneh had made. She peered out of the half-open gate and watched them go, then closed it and headed back to her room. Before she came in, Amir slipped down to the basement, closed the door softly behind him and waited until he was sure that his sister had gone upstairs. Then he went and sat down again. Khezr Javid was still lying there, with his arm over his forehead and his eyes closed. Sarcasm had got the better of him:

"So, the lads are out doing their bit for the movement,

are they?" Then, as if talking to himself: "I suppose I shall just have to go out and sort something out with them in the morning."

Two shots, one after the other. Amir's heart missed a beat, and he forgot what he was going to say to Khezr. Khezr did not press him but instead, as if a great calm had come over him, began to snore loudly. As one eye was half-open, Amir assumed that he had gone to sleep, and lit himself a cigarette.

I know Khezr hadn't want Mohammad-Taqi to open the door to him, but he had, and I could have done something about it. Khezr is deeply worried, I know, but he won't face it. I know that Khezr is not unhappy that I went up and spoke to Mohammad-Taqi, and I'm damn sure Khezr is well aware of what Mohammad-Taqi thinks of him. I did my best not to let things get out of hand with Mohammad-Taqi and end in a fight, and they didn't, but it was only about him letting Khezr stay just for one night, and not for ever. I tried to go straight back down to Khezr, which I did, and he didn't say a word directly about what had happened, but… I'm still worried. I'm worried about my brothers, and I could see the same worry in the colonel's eyes. Mohammad-Taqi has gone out, if only to take Abdullah home. Little Kuchik is still out there and, according to Abdullah, the trouble has spread beyond the city, out into the forest.

I was in a cold sweat. My eyelids felt like dried bricks rubbing together. One cigarette, then another…

Just as the morning call to prayer was called, I heard someone at the gate. I slipped out, dodging the watchful half-open eye of Khezr Javid, and went upstairs. Mohammad-Taqi was in the courtyard, squatting by the pond and washing his hands and face to freshen up after his long night. What on earth had he been getting up to all that time?

"Where's little Kuchik? Did he spend all night at the mosque? Why hasn't he come home?

"He's just fine."

"I was worried."

"It came off all right this time."

And with that, Mohammad-Taqi got up and went up the verandah steps. Amir thought he might as well have a wash too. He sat down on the edge of the pool and sluiced the grime and tiredness of the night off his face. But he was still worried. He waited to see what Mohammad-Taqi was going to do. He felt in his bones that his brother was not going to stay in. And nor did he. A minute later, he came back out on the verandah with a bag slung over his shoulder. Amir wanted to ask him if he was going out by himself or with someone else, then realised there could be no more pointless a question. So he kept quiet, waiting for Mohammad-Taqi to come down the steps towards the gate. He could feel his heart beating, worrying that, in his huff, Mohammad-Taqi might leave without a word, without even saying goodbye. But Mohammad-Taqi reined in his bad temper. Stopping by the gate, he turned round and, as if not knowing why, stroked his index finger over his thin, golden moustache and looked at Amir:

"Forgive me, but I am not setting foot in this house again as long as there's a policeman in it. Parvaneh's asleep. Say goodbye for me to her, and to Father and little Kuchik."

Amir had no answer to that, and Mohammad-Taqi did not expect one. As he went out, he braced his foot against the wall to do up the laces of one of his trainers, which must have been loose. Amir stood there until his brother had gone and then turned round to go back inside. As he did so, he caught sight of the colonel, who had been watching Mohammad-Taqi's departure through the window.

My son... my son... oh, my children...

Amir could not meet his father's gaze, and carried on down the steps to the cellar. Khezr opened the door in his face before he reached it. He was astonished to see that Khezr was all ready to go out and was just bending over to do his shoe up.

"What about some breakfast?"

Khezr did not answer. Amir could hardly ask him where he was off to at this hour of the morning so, like a lizard, he darted after him into the yard, as far as the gate. As he opened it, he remembered that Khezr had left his walking-stick behind.

"Your stick, Doctor."

Khezr did not answer, but just muttered something about being back soon. Amir shut the gate after him, but it was a while before he was conscious of having done so. As the sound penetrated to his brain, he felt as if he had been shot. Everything went black...

Why has he gone out straight after Mohammad-Taqi?

Amir was overwhelmed by a dreadful sense of foreboding. He felt that he was losing his mind. This was worse than any of his nightmares.

My children, oh my poor children...

He had no idea how long he stayed there behind the gate, in the rain, endlessly turning over in his mind the last thing that Khezr had said to him: "I suppose I shall just have to go and sort something out with them in the morning." The words "sort something out" hammered over and over again in his head, but he was unable – or maybe he just did not have the courage – to grasp the ominous meaning behind the words. Only now was it beginning to dawn on him how much he detested both himself and Khezr Javid. In his mind he saw only his own wretched, morbid self and the savage visage of Khezr Javid during those terrifying interrogations in the small hours of the night. Grilling after grilling, and *that damned bloodstained knife…*

And he also felt ashamed at the sight of the colonel, who was still standing there by his sitting room window, just where he himself had been standing, watching the colonel crossing the courtyard having killed his mother and standing in the pouring rain with his bloodied sword, shouting: "I've killed her! I've killed her at last!"

He dared not look up to meet the colonel's eyes. Parvaneh's canary was going berserk: its trilling had turned into one long scream. It just would not shut up. A thousand nightmares were wheeling inside Amir's brain now, all hammering at him the same thing: that Mohammad-Taqi would not be coming home alive.

And neither did he.

* * *

"Amir… Amir… Amir… what are you up to? Are you going to come with me to your brother's funeral or not…"

"No, no! I am a brother to nobody and a son to no-one. I am nobody and I don't know anybody, anybody at all!"

Maybe the boy is right. It's not easy; dying peacefully is no easy matter. Now I'm over sixty, I've realised people don't know how lucky they are to have a quiet and peaceful death. One gets fed up with the headache of dying; the weariness of it sticks to one like a layer of grime. Just thinking about it infects one with a clammy feeling of lethargy. It even makes one feel ill. Even my most unsympathetic listeners know that I don't normally bang on about death. It's simply that here I am, drenched and rotting away under this never ending morbid rain. If I have a fault, it is just that I am trying to give a simple, unbiased account of dying. I feel that the last trace of my own human vigour is this rather inadequate account of dying. It is the only thing I can do; I'm not banging on about dying, not at all. What else can I do? Didn't I want to spend the rest of my life sitting on my verandah in a beautiful sunset, with a bubbling samovar, the charcoal set alight by the wife sitting beside me – my companion through all the ups and downs of my life – as I work my way through a glass of vodka with a bowl of yogurt and cucumber, and I'm playing a gentle mahur *on the* setar *on my knee, safe in the knowledge that my children are all doing well in good jobs in different parts of the country?*

Oh yes, I did want that, and I believed I deserved it. It was not an unreasonable expectation, after all. But now there is a thick layer of greasy brown dust on my setar, *the dust of death. As for the other broken old bits and pieces lying around my house, I don't even know what they are now. The paraffin in the heater has run out and my clothes never get dry in this damp; I'm like a stiff, rolled up in this dirty, clammy old sheet; I can't be bothered to go and keep an eye on my daughter's canary in its cage, and the voices I hear echoing from every brick and every door in every street just add to the sum total of my misery, and this deathly rain never stops and it never will stop.*

So, there's nothing to do but wait for Masoud's funeral. How can I think about anything else, or look at anything else, while death surrounds me on all sides and I feel as if I have been swallowed up to my chest in a swamp? I know the answer. There will come a time when my lips and eyes will close in the face of death, and at that point I won't be able to talk about death or see it any more. That will be when death will rise up from my heart and finally take me by the throat. That time can't be far off now. But… why aren't these bloody clothes dry yet? I've got a funeral to go to, haven't I?

"Amir… Amir… I need your help, son…"

"No, no, no!"

The gate. There's someone at the gate. Thinking that Qorbani has come to fetch him, the colonel goes up to the window, but as Amir opens the gate, he sees that it is not Qorbani but the two young men who had helped him bury Parvaneh. Abdullah Kolahi and Ali Seif are standing by the door, looking Amir up and down. Amir does not know what to do, and is cowering in the door of the outside privy. Under the colonel's watchful eye, Abdullah walks up to the veran-dah steps. The colonel loses sight of him for a moment, then he sees him coming into the room.

The colonel is standing by the window and is clutching the sheet round his body. Abdullah offers a humble greeting and the colonel turns round to respond. Abdullah waits for a moment by the door with his head bowed and politely asks permission to come in. When it is given, he approaches the table timidly and respectfully, takes a small packet of sugar plums from under his parka and puts it on the table. Then he puts his hand into the pocket of his leopard camouflage trousers and pulls out a few banknotes and lays them on top of the packet of sugar plums.* He stands there perfectly politely, with his hands folded deferentially over his privates. Silent under the colonel's stare, he studies his toecaps until, his hands trembling with reverence, he breaks into speech:

"Allow me to be your humble servant, colonel. I am your servant… what am I to do? They told me to say this. But… I swear to you, I treated your daughter as a sister… But even so… I'm so ashamed, colonel, that I've decided go and join Masoud at the front in the next draft of reinforcements. To be honest, I don't intend to come back. I've told my wife. I've come to ask for your blessing. Give me your blessing, colonel."

Abdullah disappeared, vanishing in a cloud of black smoke that washed over the colonel's eyes. His head felt as heavy as a millstone and his heart felt as if it had been uprooted and was crashing around inside his ribcage like a demented canary. When he came to, he found himself gripping the back of the chair. The old sheet had slipped off and was lying on the floor in a heap, and he was standing there, stark naked and shivering like a dog. His mind was a blank. But he could still feel, and he felt cold. He picked up the sheet under his feet and wrapped it round him, but did not know what to do next. The canary was huddled in its cage. *All I thought was that it was just a canary that had stopped singing.*

Wondering whether canaries liked sugar plums, he took one out of the packet, walked down the passage, stood in front of the cage, pushed it through the bars of the cage and offered it to the canary. But the canary did not move, or even look up. The colonel looked at the rain and decided not to let the canary out. *Even if it hadn't been raining, letting the canary free would have been to pass a death sentence on it. It's not used to life outside its cage. One flap of its wings and it's on the floor, and the first cat…* That black cat skulking round the pond would go for it.

Mind you, if it hadn't been raining, I probably would have let it go. After all, since it'll just pine away and die in its cage after we're all gone, I might as well let it die free, outside its cage.

But Parvaneh's canary was already pining away, wasn't it?

He did not know, nor did he know how long he had been standing there by the cage, silently studying the bird. He walked out on to the edge of the verandah and stood there, on his usual spot, looking out at the rain. The courtyard gate was half-open, and there was no sign of the pick and shovel.

I do hope Amir hasn't gone out and taken them with him.

There was no certainty about anything. The colonel felt a terrible pang of loneliness. There was nothing but the rain, drumming on the rusty old tin roof. The colonel could not recall that once, at least once a long time ago, he had seen the ochre colour of the roof in the sunset after a rainstorm. His mind was a blank. Was it sunset, or wasn't it? It was night, or wasn't it? What time of day was it, anyway?

What is it? Qorbani must be along soon to take me to the cemetery. And my clothes are still wet. What shall I do if they come to tell me that they've brought Masoud in? But they won't bring him, they won't. No, they haven't brought back my Kuchik now for forty days, forty winters, forty times forty days and forty nights in the wilderness.

Gentlemen of the cloth! You gentlemen who want history not to be written down, to keep history hidden under a heap of shit, I have told you before that I have lost count of the days and of the nights and of the seasons, and it is now forty days, forty times forty days and forty nights that I have been wandering in the rain, and I feel my bones to be damp and hollow and that I have drained myself out… All I can see now are grotesque crea-tures. Stranger still, those ghosts are coming back to tell me that my sight is fading, because I can't distinguish my Masoud from anyone else, while I… It's bizarre, outlandish… I am telling them that this severed head that has been stuck onto a body is not my son's head. But do they believe it? No, they don't. It's just not possible that I should have forgotten what my son looks like. It's true that a bullet took one eye and half his face off, but what's left of this face cries out to me that it does not belong to my Masoud. But the body, the body could well be my son's. Why would I want to tell a lie, and say that this dishevelled head stuck on to Masoud's body isn't his? I know my son's shoulders, his arms and even his hands. Even though one of his arms is missing from the elbow down, I can still identify him. And let's not mention that his guts are spilling all over the place and one of his knees has been practically severed and… but nobody is listening to me, which is very odd, very odd. Because, every time I try to speak, before I can get more than one word out, the hired mourners start their lamentations and flagellations and drown my voice out. I want to say, "Gentlemen, my brothers, my sons… believe me, this severed head does not belong to my Kuchik." That is all I want to say, nothing more, but they won't let me. They are filling the mortuary with the noise of their wailing and howling and their chest-beating. They are forcing me into silence.

I suppose I could suggest that they go and fetch the father or mother of this head so they can put it back where it belongs, but then it occurs to me that this head might belong to a Kurd. This dishevelled half a face is not Masoud's, I am sure of that. From what's left of it – the nose and chin and a bit of the forehead – I'm guessing that the owner of this head must have been Kurdish. I've seen it in a book, The Faces of Iran *I think it was called, which had photos showing the physiognomy and skull structure of the Kurds, which are quite distinctive. Quite apart from that, I've seen a few Kurds and have had a bit to do with them. It's a problem, and not just because I can't get anyone to listen to me; the problem is that it's a forbidden subject and I'm sure I daren't mention it to Qorbani, who seems to be in charge of the funeral arrangements and has implicitly made himself the guardian and owner of the martyr – that is to say, the owner of my son Masoud.*

The colonel was quite astounded at the efficient way Qorbani was setting things up and organizing the funeral. One would think his family had been body washers, grave-diggers and carrion eaters for generations. There was nothing he could do about it. This was his fate and it was plainer to him than the lines on the palms of his hands that if he did not accept his lot, *they would ram it up my arse* and then his problems would be a hundred times worse. He would just have to accept it and agree that that head, *a head that does not belong to my Masoud!* did belong to him and that it would have to be stuck on to Masoud's headless body and be buried. That was it.

* * *

The colonel had served in the army of the dictator* (who was nothing but an invisible, white-kid glove covering a bludgeon up the sleeve of an ancient nation) and he had learned that power was exercised through the business end of that bludgeon, but he had never imagined that a time would come when coercion would come from both ends of the bludgeon.† But, thought the colonel, he would just have to put up with it. If only he had been better prepared for such times, *but they don't tell you anything! They take you unawares and thoroughly brainwash you until you really believe everything they say.*

"Now, young man, will you tell me how to get from here to where everyone else is going?"

"Oh, for heaven's sake! What kind of question is that? Just follow everyone else. Can't you see which way the coffins are heading? Are you blind? Just follow the stiffs."

"No, I'm not blind. I can also hear people's voices, rattling together like the links of a chain, so I'm not deaf, either."

But the fact of the matter was that the colonel was feeling a bit dizzy. He thought it was the feebleness of old age, but he could not mention it to anyone in that crowd. What really mattered to him was that he should not be losing his mind. It was no fun getting old. *You need to be in my shoes to understand what I'm talking about, what it feels like to be old.*

In the procession of biers, he could make out Masoud's, draped in a silk embroidered cloth, provided through the kind intervention of Mr Qorbani Hajjaj. All forty-one coffins, including Masoud's, were swathed with black and green bands bearing quotations from the Qoran. They had stacked the bits and pieces of his body and the severed head, like the remains of a crashed car, into a coffin, covered it with an embroidered cloth and stapled black and green bands round the sides. They had raised it up on high and were carrying it in the cortège through the wailing, howling throng. In the rain it looked darker than the others. The colonel tried to remember his son's coffin so that he could recognise it when it was committed to the earth, *I mustn't lose sight of it, damn it,* despite the fact that the conjunction of events had robbed him of any claim to the corpse that bore the name of his son. Mr Qorbani Hajjaj had formally and publicly claimed all title of next of kin, and arrogated to himself all matters of probate, both present and future, pertaining to the death of the martyr. He had stitched everything up beforehand, it appeared.

The colonel struggled to haul himself out of the mud and

up on to some high ground before he got trampled by the mob, and he watched the mob and the train of biers held aloft by the pallbearers. Curiosity made him try to count the coffins once more, to see if he had missed one out. He thought that, if there were more, a trouble shared would be a trouble halved, but he quickly abandoned this fantasy and looked away from the procession. Not least because he felt so dizzy, and he could not stand the sight of Qorbani's hairy arms sticking out of his shirt sleeves, looking like a pair of goat's legs. Everything went black in front of him. He shut his eyes and waited for the crowd to halt and put the coffins down. He guessed that these graves had been dug in advance. Perhaps the ghosts he had been seeing in the cemetery over the past few nights had been gravediggers at their work.

He rubbed his eyes, but it made no difference. The most sensible thing would be to get away from the crowd and head for home. The bigger the crowd became, the more noisy and chaotic it got. He was cracking up and beginning to feel that neither his son's corpse nor his death had anything more to do with him. He was a stranger in the crowd. Before he could make up his mind, he found that he was once more firmly wedged in the midst of the mob, shoulder to shoulder, with no way out, backwards or forwards. Where they were putting the coffins down, he could see a contraption like a stage being put up and made ready for speeches. He could just make out Qorbani going to the microphone and, with his very first words, expertly whipping up the crowd into an outpouring of emotion, *as if his family had been mullas and carrion-eating professional graveside mourners for generations.*

Qorbani launched himself into his funeral oration: "Masoud Forutan… this young man, so dear to us, yearned for martyrdom... he swore... that until... extinction... to avenge the blood of... never retreat... on the sacred path... till the last drop of his blood..." And then he held up Masoud as "the very model of righteousness and selflessness, whereas his sister and his brothers Taqi and Amir, well..."

"I'm feeling dizzy."

The colonel's world was spinning round and he was trying desperately to cling on to the idea that he had not lost his senses. He remembered that it had been sunny the day they buried Mohammad-Taqi. The sun was so bright that Mohammad-Taqi's blood turned the colour of mountain honey and the bare arms of the men carrying the flower-strewn coffin to the graveyard were dappled with bright colour, and the shoals of hands and arms reminded him of fish leaping out of the water and dancing for joy before dropping back down again. And in amongst all this, his son's coffin looked like a piece of driftwood being clung to by a thousand drowning men trying to save themselves from the deep. What a racket they made! They had whipped up the frenzied crowd with such a mixture of threats and exhortation that you felt that these lads flagellating themselves, with blood coagulating on their shirts and in their curly hair, wanted to dive into that flower-bedecked, tapestry-draped coffin and find eternal rest there themselves, in place of Mohammad-Taqi. *It would not be far-fetched to say that some of those young men, deep inside, felt short-changed by not being where my martyr hero Mohammad-Taqi was.* He had no idea where his other children had got to in that raging sea of people. He guessed that the young lads had sucked them in. Every so often, one of their faces would catch the sunlight and float briefly into his field of vision, only to disappear once more. But Parvaneh was nowhere to be seen, because she had been swallowed up entirely by waves of black-clad women. Once or twice he saw Farzaneh's face coming up for air and disappearing out of sight again. The last time he saw Farzaneh and Parvaneh together, he noticed that they had lacerated their faces with their fingernails and fresh warm blood was streaming down their faces, shining like golden honey in the dazzling sunlight. What an unexpectedly sunny day that was!

"I'm dizzy. And my eyes are going dark, misting over…"

His head was spinning as he heard the waves of shouted abuse hurled by the crowd at all his offspring, apart from Masoud of course, ringing in his ears. Hardly had he recovered from this blow than he heard his own name being called over the loudspeakers, gaping like open-mouthed skulls. And before he knew what was going on, he felt strong, practised hands lifting him up and carrying him onto the makeshift dais where the coffins were laid out. In that instant, two things convinced him that he had not yet lost his wits. The first was that he felt as light as a pigeon feather and that his bones really had become hollow, and the second was that he felt a burning sensation on the sole of his left foot. His shoe had fallen off and he had no idea where he had lost it. When he got to the microphone beside Qorbani, he raised his hand to his hat and jammed it firmly on his head. The crowd below him became a faceless blur. In his dizziness, everything went dark in front of him.

Things were now out of his control, and he was forced to listen to the sound of Qorbani Hajjaj's voice, and that of his own voice too, both booming out over the loudspeakers, stuck on their poles like the heads of traitors, and echoing meaninglessly over the serried ranks of the blank-faced mob that faced him. For several long minutes he was stuck there, having to endure the giddiness and the aching in his head, which was so painful that he felt his eyeballs were about to explode.

What a racket they were making!

And may God have mercy on the soul of Qorbani's father, for he can see what state I'm in after that son of his has forced me to deliver a string of insults against my Parvaneh, my Mohammad-Taqi and my Amir. At least he doesn't insist on my applauding Masoud and revelling in the reflected glory of having had such a selfless son. He has let me go and handed me back to the crowd, so that my place can be taken by a string of fathers, mothers, aunts or uncles of the other glorious fallen martyrs. I must go and look for my shoe.

The colonel jammed his hat more firmly on his head, to stop it being knocked off by the crowd of admirers that now surrounded him. As he worked his way through them, he kept having to nod to the left and right to thank them all for their sympathy and support.

In all this uproar, he had not even had a chance to spare a thought for Masoud, be it one of sorrow, grief, pride or even envy. He was shocked at his own apathy and callousness. Like an automaton, he worked his way out of the crowd, away from their steamy breath and the dust they kicked up in their own eyes. He was gripped by a panic that was new to him in the face of a crowd that was so patently infatuated with death. They were ravenous for either condemnation or adulation; it was terrifying. This new panic was quite different to that curiously fermenting feeling of common-or-garden fear that beset him these days.

He had been permanently fearful for years. It all started

when he buckled on his revolver for the first time and became aware of carrying a weapon. He had had to start thinking about life. The fear had been in him even before he had become aware of it. Perhaps he refused to recognise this fear as something much more ancient and primeval that had been passed down to him through generations, whose cryptic presence affected everything he did. *Mankind spends all its life in a state of permanent insecurity, knowing no peace, and it never knows why. And in the end you die, but you don't take that fear with you to the grave as you should. No, you pass it on to the next generation. When I became aware of fear, I had to accept it and gradually come to terms with it and split it up into different elements.*

But this new dread of the crowd did not fit into any of the old familiar categories. It had laid claim to a new place in his head and he had to get it out of there. He had to get away from them all and go home.

Home… but where is home, now?

* * *

It was night before they finally buried Mohammad-Taqi. The colonel could not remember what had happened in the cemetery, or how the funeral had ended. When he got home his mind was full of the maddened, roaring tumult of the strange and unfamiliar faces. His lungs felt weighed down by a tombstone and he searched for enough fire in his belly to start a fight.

My children!

They had brought Mohammad-Taqi in, still in his bloody clothes, dumped him in the middle of the room, then sat round and waited.* This gave the colonel a chance to take a breather and unloose the knot in his chest. The family were allowed to have him for the night and, after mourning him together, they each had a chance to sit in the corner and commune alone with him.

The next morning – the air was full of dust – I took an old photograph of Mohammad-Taqi out of my pocket and tucked it into the frame of The Colonel's portrait, right under his polished field boots. I looked up into The Colonel's all-seeing eyes and saw that he had closed them. Now all that was left for me to do was organise the funeral and the seventh-day memorial service for my son, you would have thought.

He did not know where he was, or even what time of day or night it was. He could hardly keep his eyes open and his hands were shaking. He felt he had shrunk to the size of a partridge and he craved a cigarette. But he was happy to have got away. Not caring about the mud, the potholes or his frozen shoeless foot, he kept on running, not looking where he was going, intent on putting distance between himself and the funeral crowd. He just wanted to be anywhere, it didn't matter where, so long as it was far away from those voices belching out of the massed skulls and pursuing him through the streets. As he ran from the madding throng, the noise of the speakers steadily faded behind him. The voices became more and more unrecognisable as he went, until, to his horror, he heard them now as his own voice, cursing his own children.

No, this cannot be… I want to hear my own voice again: my own voice, The Colonel's voice!

* * *

He was like a drowned rat again and his eyeballs were bursting with pain. The brim of his hat had curled up in the rain, he still had one shoe missing and his trouser legs were soaked and muddy right up to the knees. His coat tails had sagged even further with the weight of water they had taken up, and he stumbled as he sloshed his way through the mud. His mouth had dried up and his tongue tasted of snake venom. He had not eaten for the last day or two. He retched, but brought nothing up. What must he look like? The fear, confusion and exhaustion that filled the space between his hat and his coat made him think of a picture he had once seen somewhere of an old Jew who had just been let out of a concentration camp, with no idea of where he should go.

"This is the main square, Colonel, the courthouse square."

"But where's my home... and my son?"

"It was over there, Colonel."

Were his eyes deceiving him? In that wide and empty square, in between rows of shrines to young martyrs of the revolution, stood serried ranks of constables, sheriffs and executioners from the old days, all lined up as if for his inspection. *Yes, strange though it may seem, they really were there.* In any case, his way home took him past a row of these shrines. The last and newest of them, presumably provided by Qorbani, was for his own Kuchik. The colonel felt sure that Mr Qorbani Hajjaj-the-Tyrant had also erected an even more lavish shrine to Kuchik in front of his house. Now he understood why Qorbani had made such a fuss about getting an enlargement of Kuchik's photograph made, and why he had had a gilt frame made for it and had set it on the mantelpiece in his new living room. The colonel was beginning to suspect that maybe everything, down to the last detail, had been arranged beforehand. This worried him.

How can they even think like that?

As the old man entered the courtyard of his house, he stopped dead in his tracks. He could not believe his eyes. There, ghostlike, set up on boards over the pond,* stood the headless torso of Amir Kabir. So, thought the colonel, Amir has finally managed to finish something. The statue was over six feet tall. Amir must have brought it up from the poky little basement in sections, to assemble and finish off outside. But he had not yet mounted the head on the torso. The Colonel was on the verandah, holding it in his hands and inspecting it. Warm blood, that warm glistening blood of old, was seeping slowly from The Colonel's neck. Every now and then, with his customary dignity, he dabbed at it with a clean white handkerchief, never taking his eyes off the face of the great Amir Kabir.

Standing on the verandah steps, right in front of The Colonel, Amir did not notice that his father had returned. He squinted back and forth, at The Colonel and at his creation, as if seeking approval, even praise, for his work. It was a naïve expectation to have of The Colonel, thought his father, even though The Colonel had the most refined artistic taste. Amir clearly did not know him very well for, as far as The Colonel was concerned, if a man had done something well, he had done no more than was his duty.

Nobody should expect a reward for just doing his duty. No, Amir had not yet understood what The Colonel was all about.

Even so, as The Colonel gave Amir back his head, he smiled at him as if to show that he was pleased with him. Amir, pleased by this, carefully took his head back from him. The Colonel folded his arms across his chest and stood rigidly at ease in his black polished boots, clutching his white, but slightly pink handkerchief, as if watching to see how work on his statue progressed.

Standing on his stool, and without taking his eyes off his creation, Amir placed the head on Amir Kabir's sturdy shoulders, ran his hand over his beard and moustaches, arranged the tall black hat on top of his curly hair, and then stepped down.

On that sunny day, the colonel saw in Amir's eyes a glow such as he had never seen in a man's eyes before. Amir's eyes now sparkled with life. As if in a trance, Amir walked backwards to the bottom of the verandah steps, unable to take his eyes off his splendid statue. He halted in front of The Colonel's boots and, folding his arms across his chest like him, stood there for a time that seemed would never end and inspected his creation.

I don't mind about my poor feet. I just don't want to let a sudden movement of mine shake Amir out of his trance. I'll just wait here until Amir looks my way and see if he notices me.

He did not have to wait long for Amir to notice him standing there in the rain, with water dripping from the brim of his hat, soaking into his collar. Stirred to take pity on the old man, he came up, took him gently by the arm and led him from the pond up the steps onto the verandah. To show his father and The Colonel due respect, Amir stood by the doorway and waited for them to go through ahead of him. But The Colonel had vanished, right from where he had been standing. Amir led his father inside and sat him down by a table next to the stove. The stove was warm and the colonel could see from Amir's behaviour that a complete change had come over him, for his son was now treating him like a hospital patient. First he took from him his hat, heavy and wet from the rain, took it outside to wring it out, and put it by the stove to dry. Then he took from him his overcoat and hung it over a chair by the stove. Then it was the turn of the old man's jacket, waistcoat, trousers and long-johns. Finally he brought him a blanket to get warm, *something that had never occurred to me all the time I'd been wrapped up shivering in that old sheet*, and held it round him so that he could strip down to the buff and hang all his clothes out by the stove to dry.

There was no doubt as to how the stove had been kept going. It must have been Farzaneh who had brought over a drum of paraffin for us while Qorbani wasn't looking.

Amir poured a glass of tea and put it on the table in front of his father. He then brought the sugar bowl and put it within reach, so that his father could help himself without having to unwrap the blanket.

That's all very well, but Amir hasn't noticed that my mind is on something else. I want to find one of the old photographs of Masoud and put it next to the ones of Parvaneh and Mohammad-Taqi, beneath the Colonel's toecaps. I know where to look for it. Under the bed in the side pocket of a suitcase. I've even got the key on me…

Amir was sitting opposite his father with his elbows on the table, his chin resting on his fists and squinting intently at him as if to convey to him that the important part of his life's work was now done and that he now wanted to embark on something new. The colonel could hardly believe that he had chosen this juncture to undergo this sudden change, and was now looking life in the face again, but neither did he want to dismiss it out of hand. Nothing ever surprised him, and he was well aware that nobody could remain totally quiet and passive for ever, for no one could ever survive like that.

Experience, sir, experience.

He and his whole generation were scarred by the events that had followed 1953.* After that disaster, they were all paralysed by a pervading sense of pessimism, which had lasted for about twenty years. It only lifted when the generation responsible for the catastrophe had been worn out by defeat and had given way to a new one. In the second half of that period, the fight between the two generations had been quite something to behold.

Not that the new generation that emerged after that fight were any more sensible or realistic. The next generation had been founded on rejection as well, rejection of everything. Out of this decay had been born revolt. The fathers had rejected everything except their nostalgia, while the conduct of their sons made everyone repudiate them; they even repudiated themselves. The fathers were crippled, while their sons were apathetic and rootless. Neither generation wanted to know anything about the other, and the result was that they blinded one another to both the future and the past. One lot were passive rejectionists, while the other lot were catastrophic in their activity. The parents no longer had the energy or ability to explain things or pass on their experience, while the children did not have the faith or the patience to take such lessons on board. *It was like the game when children bet on an uncut watermelon being ripe or not. Some bet it would turn out to be "as green as soap," while others reckoned it would be "ripe and red as blood." Neither party had a reliable knife to cut it open and see, or sufficient courage or even permission to do so. So history remained unopened and unknown, until it rotted.*

And now Amir's face was a mirror, reflecting that

rottenness, and it reminded the colonel of many people in his distant past. Both the colonel and Amir could think of many fathers and sons, all at loggerheads with one another, not quiet and perplexed, like so many now. Every time they met, an argument ensued. They would attack and abuse one another and then go their separate ways. They knew each other's sore points and were expert in finding precisely the insult that would cause the maximum hurt. But now Amir and the colonel were faced with a quite different problem: for a long time now, there had been no quarrel between them. Present circumstances had levelled all their differences – like a modern plough that, when driven across any kind of land – be it fallow land, irrigated, dry land or barren ground, or just a vegetable plot – turns it all over the same. The two generations were going over the most important points of a debate about the period of "decay" without there being any differences between them. What was left out of the debate however, was the matter of how each one faced up to this rottenness, for there was no argument between them as to the existence or not of this rottenness, or of its massive scale. The only question now was how each of them would deal with it.

What I see with my own eyes, Amir sees just as clearly in his worst nightmares, even though he can't express it out loud.

"I'm afraid the old man might not find the strength to kill himself. It is the one act that requires careful planning. He's falling apart, you can see it in his face. I think I am only now beginning to realize how much I loved my father…"

* * *

When Amir got off the bus after being let out of prison,

he saw the colonel leaning against the brick wall of the bus station in his overcoat and fedora. It was dawn and drizzling. He was stooped over and studying Amir from under his salt-and-pepper eyebrows, and he was hiding a smile under his moustaches. Amir walked up to his father and held out his arms to embrace him, but the colonel's face showed no sign of pleasure. *No tears of joy; his eyes were dry.* Amir, too, was out of sorts and could not be bothered to put on a show of happiness. Just when everyone else was fired up with hope, he was plagued by doubt. And yet, alongside the self-doubting, despairing Amir, who wanted to do away with himself, there was another Amir, who wanted more than anything else to play at being happy and reveal his real self.

They were not far from home. Mohammad-Taqi, who had also come along to the bus station to welcome Amir back, took his bag and bundle and led the way, and the three of them set off in the silence of the dawn. There was nobody about and, in the emptiness of the morning, the town square seemed larger. Along the way the colonel began to talk to himself:

"Right, at least that's all over and done with, then."

"Yes… it's all over. Fifty years of it."*

"More like six thousand years…"

There was no sorrow or regret in the colonel's words, but no joy either. He sounded indifferent. Amir knew of his father's conviction that Iran had a six-thousand-year history of government.

I can understand what my father felt.

But no! I have become a fisherman, with long rubber waders, a beret, a big nose and a bushy moustache, lugging nets on my back, and with an Oshnu Special cigarette in my hand as I

*splash along beside the colonel in the heavy silence that he carries
with him. I am beginning to speak:* "There is no place for
doubt on the battlefield of history and revolution, papa! The
glorious history of the forty year struggle of the workers is a
shining example of…" *and I hate myself for such ridiculous,
meaningless jargon. I shudder to hear that oaf inside me uttering such rubbish, but I carry on:* "We must continue to hope,
papa, hope… A man without hope is nothing but an insect,
a mindless creature with no future. And a man without a
future can only go backwards. In prison we spat at the fence-
sitters for being men with no honour."

The colonel had turned round and was glaring at his
son from beneath his salt-and-pepper eyebrows. Amir felt
trapped. The nets on his back had gone, his Oshnu cigarette
had disappeared, there were no rubber boots to give him
the air of a mature man of experience, and his top lip was
no longer covered with a bushy moustache. He was a little
boy again, being smelted by the glare of his father's wise old
gaze. In vain, he tried to break the threatening silence of the
morning with a pretend cough, but then he had to meet his
father's withering stare. He tried to continue:

"Yes, in prison…"

*One look from my father was all it took and there I was
once more – back to feeling humiliated, beset by doubt and,
worse still, even by despair. All my soaring hopes had vanished
into thin air: Why do I prattle away like that without thinking? Why am I always preaching at others to try and win them
over, or provoking people, or haranguing them? Don't I just end
up hurting myself? And to speak like that to my father, of all
people! Am I the only person in the world who doesn't just lack
the courage to admit his own doubt but who is also so despicable*

as to impute it to other people – even my own father – and then attack him for it?

This behaviour really came to a head when he was sitting in the living room, surrounded by friends and relations. The one thought burning in his brain was "where is Nur Aqdas, my wife?" but he couldn't bring himself to say it. Instead, he was banging on in the same vein: "The incontrovertible truth is that we are living in a century of radical change, and there's no place for intellectual vacillation in a revolution, my friends!" His other self did not appear to him in the guise of a fisherman this time; this time he saw a man with a grey beard, a drooping moustache, and wearing a beret as he smoked his first pipe of the morning. Every now and then he gave a little cough.

Looking back on it, the person most attracted to that man smoking his pipe after breakfast was the lovely little Parvaneh. It was just bad luck that it was me, her brother!

That was when people started talking: it was the duty of any respectable family to repudiate a girl like that and send her packing. She was now *mahdour ud-dam*, fair Islamic game. It would be an honour killing.

* * *

In the warmth of the stove, the colonel's back and shoulders, wrapped in the steaming blanket, were now thawing out. Even his left foot was warming up. He was feeling lethargic and hardly able to keep awake for so much lack of sleep. The only thing that gave him any comfort, and moved him from time to time, was the memory of what he had said about Parvaneh over the unseen, echoing loudspeakers at Masoud's funeral. He could not believe that he would ever have been capable of uttering those words against a child who was not even fourteen, a girl to whom he was both a mother and a father. Had it really been his own voice that had yelled: "This girl is *mahdour ud-dam*… She must be killed. She is impure, possessed by the devil and now lost to us all…" It was as if he had been talking about Forouz.

How could I have said that? Perhaps there's been someone else lurking inside me for my entire life, just waiting for a chance to say it? Was it really my voice that I heard coming out of the loudspeakers? How could such a thing be possible?

* * *

"Well, Amir, what do you think?"

But Amir was not there. He was lost in thoughts of Parvaneh, who was not there either. A sick curiosity gripped him as to how Parvaneh had been killed. He wondered what level of torture she had been subjected to before dying, and what she had said about her heroic brother to her fellow prisoners. A brother who had a good name and reputation, who was loved by so many young men who had been to school with him, a noble brother who had been released from the chains of "the murderous régime."

But how silent this brother had now become, his mind filled only with isolated scraps of the past. And whenever a voice did begin to speak inside him, all it did was settle accounts, pronouncing a death sentence on a catamitic life that would shortly be at an end. In his tormented self-analysis, he became aware of a tendency to speculate on his own complicity in the crimes perpetrated against his brother and sister. And the only way out he could see was to see Khezr again, to hear from him what had happened to his little sister, just as he had finally found out about his wife Nur-Aqdas.

"If you executed her, then you should have given me some clue as to where she was buried. She was my wife, after all, Khezr Javid. My wife, and your prisoner."

This was possibly the first time that he had looked properly at Khezr. This time he stared intently into his eyes, begging him to answer

Khezr's answer was curt, dry, without remorse:

"We let her go. It was afterwards that she killed herself. She had done a deal with us, it seems, but couldn't come to terms with herself. The first night after she was let out, she did herself in. It was quite some time before we found her. The only recognisable bit of her was her hair. Everything else was swollen, black and putrid."

* * *

Amir had got home late, after midnight. He had a key. He opened the door and went silently up the stairs into his room. Nur-Aqdas recognised his footsteps, so she was not frightened, but she stared in amazement at the bloodstained knife. Amir stood by the door for a moment, and then looked at the table. His heart was pumping hard, but he saw that he had to come out with it. He sat down opposite his wife and looked at her, with her lecture notes spread all over the dining table. This was the image which reminded him most of her. She looked at him sternly, as if he were not her husband. She had decided to treat him like a complete stranger.

A minute later Mansour Salaami came in from the kitchen. He had been washing his hands and face and he went to get a towel from the hook on the wall. His eyebrows and moustache were wet and his sleeves were rolled up. He dried his face and hands, sat down on the nearest chair and pulled a packet of cigarettes out of his shirt pocket. He took a match from a box on the table and lit it. Amir noticed how the wet hairs on his arms were lying flat. Mansour puffed at his cigarette, and Amir registered the pleasure with which he blew a smoke ring, as if he was exhaling all the tiredness from his body. The oppressive, pregnant stillness in the room reduced Amir to silence. He began to wish he had never come to Tehran that night. But it was too late. He had got himself into a bad fix, and had been a witness to certain events that pointed to a crime. In any event, his mere presence would mark him down as an accessary after the fact.

"I had nothing to do with that business, Mr Javid. You were torturing me for nothing."

* * *

Amir was knocked out. Knocked out and hollowed out, with nothing more to live for. He was sitting on the floor leaning against the damp basement wall with his head down. He felt as if Khezr Javid had taken over his home, his bed, his life and his loneliness. At every snore from Khezr, he felt his own breath becoming shorter. Even more paralysing was the feeling that he had lost the strength to do anything, that all the vigour had been knocked out of him, even the ability to feel any hatred against the killer of his wife.

"You and your kind were dangerous, and you were getting

more dangerous. With the Shah behind you, you were untouchable, but then God saw fit to save the country."

Khezr got up to look for his cigarettes and lighter. He went on:

"For thirty years, pressure had been building up in the country, but the lid was firmly screwed down on top of it. It was like a swelling abscess that sooner or later would burst and shower blood and pus everywhere. When the muck is squeezed out of a boil, the pain goes away and the body is soothed. Which is why this boil had to be lanced to make our beloved people calm down. Then you get a deluge of blood and guts, and only idiots and sheep stand in its way. Forty-seven percent of the population of this country were young and wriggling about inside this abscess, my friend, so it needed the lancet of God to burst it."

Amir was staring, glassy-eyed, seeing nothing, silent. All he could think about was what he had gone through with Khezr Javid. As for the colonel, he was still thinking about the mystery of his own voice over the loudspeakers, and was worried about who might have heard him – Amir for instance.

No, he couldn't have heard. He hasn't set foot outside the house. But why is he staring at me, then?

Why are you looking at me like that? What have I done wrong? Why don't you say anything? Me... I've dealt with Kuchik's funeral and when my clothes are dry, they'll probably come and take me to the mosque to welcome the mourners. You probably don't feel like coming with me, do you? Well, never mind. I'll go by myself. As soon as my clothes are dry I'll put them on and go to the mosque.

Ah, those mosques! The people living in the slums on the

outskirts of the Ahmed Abad district had hoped that, if they had a mosque, the new government might provide them with running water and electricity and put tarmac on the road at long last.* The bazaar traders needed a decent place to celebrate the martyrdom of the Imam Hossein, so the faithful got together and bought old cinemas here and there and turned them into mosques and... It's always like that; things just happen and people only notice after the event. Of course, if people were to notice things earlier on, nothing would ever change.

It was after that when the first woman was executed in Qasr prison, under the Shah's regime, so I shouldn't be surprised that my daughter, who was not even fourteen, has been put to death now.

"You... Amir, do you remember any of that? I don't suppose you do... Can't you remember what I told you? What they said about your sister? You don't understand me? Well, I don't understand why you don't understand what your father is talking about. What's up with you? Am I speaking in some alien tongue, or what?"

"I don't understand, I don't understand."

"Say it again, go on!"

"I don't know what you're talking about, papa."

"That's extraordinary, truly extraordinary, why don't I get it? Talk to me in words I can understand." *How is it that I don't recognize my son's voice or even understand what he's saying?*

"Papa, you seem to have a fever. You're becoming delirious. Lie down and rest for a while. These voices are getting on your nerves. Why upset yourself? You're just making it worse."

"Amir... Amir... Just try not to torture your father so

much. Just talk to me like you used to, Amir. Why can't I understand what it is you're saying?"

"Papa, go and lie down for a couple of hours, and then I'll talk to you. I've decided to have a long chat with you before I die. But now… it's impossible to talk to you right now. Because, in your present state, I'm not sure you'd be able to grasp what I'm trying to say."

"Amir… Amir… I never expected that you'd go so disastrously dumb at this stage in your life. Your jaw opens and shuts, your lips move, but there's no sound. I can't hear anything. What's happened?"

"Don't get in a fuss, papa… But what am I to do? I need to talk to you before I die. There isn't anybody else. I've only got you, papa. If I want to die, I just want to tell you this; it's because I feel I have lost faith in everything I ever believed in. I can't bear my past any longer, I can't go on living just hating myself. After all, how long do you imagine a person can go on living just filled with nothing but hate? So why should I go on living? What I am trying to tell you is this, that Farzaneh brought a can of paraffin round today and I tried telling her how I felt, but however hard I tried, I couldn't get through to her, I just couldn't, and she ran out of the house, crying. What I was trying to say was perfectly simple; I just wanted to tell my sister that I had had just as much to do with the deaths of my brothers and sisters as Qorbani had. But I couldn't get through to her, papa."

The colonel said nothing. He thought Amir could not grasp that he did not understand what he was saying; he did not recognise his language. And he thought that his son was not ready to pay attention to why his father might want to explain things to him before his death, and therefore "will" him to understand why he wanted to die. He wanted to tell Amir not to think about the tragedy that had befallen his father, and to know that he himself had brought all their problems on the family, and was still doing so. He had decided to die and his conscience was now at ease, for he had never shirked his duty. *I was a soldier, and I always will be, and I'll prove it in the manner of my going.* If he had decided to die, it was because he could not bear to be seen in the street in this state. Nor could he stand idle children throwing stones and hurling abuse at him any more.

I feel my voice is changing, which means that my transformation has now started. Out of all fairness, I should not be obliged to spend what is left of my life in the disgrace and pointless humiliation of madness and ridicule.

He also wanted to say that, if he decided to cut out his tongue before he died, nobody should be surprised, or think that he had gone mad. *No, I shall be punishing myself for what I was made to say over the loudspeakers at the cemetery, things which I could hear with my own ears.*

Even so, he clung doggedly to the belief that it had not been his voice, but someone else's, speaking through his mouth. Still, there was a risk that that voice might speak from his mouth again and become second nature to him. Before his final metamorphosis took place, he was determined to ward it off, so long as his mind was still clear and he had control of his wits. Before he died, he wanted to have a talk with Amir and hear from his son that he had not been a bad father to his children. He wanted Amir, as the closest person to him, to bear witness that he had willingly sacrificed his children to this country, even though they had ultimately fallen victim to a vile conspiracy.

He wanted to impress upon Amir that this devastating tragedy should not lead people to question or mock his children's own genuine readiness for self-sacrifice. For the only reason they had entered the game and had honestly and laudably risked their necks was because they believed that their lives were inextricably bound up with their country and their people. This was what made them different from those evil bastards who were still alive and kicking today... *This is what I wanted to say to Amir, so that those people who won't let history be written down should not think that we come into the world as donkeys and leave it as asses. But it's all too late. Amir can't understand what I'm saying and I don't even recognize his voice, or even his language. And I should have explained to him that my killing his mother was not a crime, but just a natural reaction on my part. I had to kill her, so I did it. I killed my humiliation. Anyway, if regrets could change anything, I would regret killing my wife, even though Amir knows — and might even bear witness to it — that I should not regret what I did.*

Amir shook his head, affected by this. He could see from the colonel's face that he had formed a sad judgement of him, but this feeling was not so much from the fact that he felt sorry for his father as from the way his father was changing. He appeared to be fading away and vanishing before him.

The colonel thought this was rubbish. He expected his son to have the intelligence to see, written on his face, his determination to fade away. Because a decision, even if that decision will result in certain self-annihilation, in itself counts as a sign of the will to live. Just because the colonel had decided to fade away, that was no reason for Amir to treat him as if he had already gone.

But what can I say, when he doesn't even understand me?

What was the colonel supposed to do? *Pen and paper!* He got pen and paper and began to put down what he had been unable to say to Amir. A will, after all, had to be on paper. That was why it was called a written will and testament. He was astonished to see Amir also take up pen and paper and begin writing. They were both busy writing now, but they did not look at each other's papers. They were both sure that what they were writing was for the writer's eyes only. The content of both wills was clear: "Death."

The colonel wanted to tell Amir that he intended to die and that, before he did so, he wished to give his son the benefit of some of his long experience of life. But what was it that Amir wanted to commit to paper? Not another nightmare, he hoped.

When he had put the last full-stop to his piece, the colonel looked up at Amir and saw that Amir had also finished writing and was looking up at his father. The colonel puts his sheet of paper in front of his son. Amir does the same. They pick up each other's letters and carefully study the writing. When they finish reading they stare at one another for an unusually long time, as if trying to get to know each other and place each other again. They seem like strangers in each other's eyes. Finally, they accept that they are two figures of death sitting opposite each other...

The tea had grown cold in the glasses. Matters were drawing to a close.

Taking care not to let the blanket slip from his shoulders, the colonel stood up. It occurred to him that he had long since been meaning to tuck Masoud's photograph into the frame of The Colonel's portrait, next to Parvaneh and Mohammad-Taqi. He found the key to the suitcase, knelt down beside the bed, pulled out the suitcase, opened it, found Kuchik's photograph, got up and placed it where he had thought a thousand times about putting it. Then he sat down again.

Amir had also stood up and was making ready to go out. He was in no hurry, but he did not dawdle either. As he was doing up his raincoat, he fished a scrap of photograph out of a notebook in his side pocket. He hesitated, then gave the colonel, who was now staring into his cold glass of tea, a look to seek his permission, before lining up a picture of himself as a boy on the mantelpiece, beneath the shiny black boots of The Colonel, right next to the photographs of his brothers and sister. Then, as though he were bidding farewell to himself, he began muttering under his breath: "Finally… at last…" and slipped quietly out of the house.

The colonel sat and stared for a long time at the half-closed door, trying to imagine Amir in the form of a grey coffin being carried out of the room. He was struggling to control his emotions. But at the same time, he felt a great sense of relief at Amir's departure. In his guts, he felt that Amir had consciously lifted the burden of his own death off his back. But a hidden feeling of fatherly love, *which there is no reason to hide*, took hold of the colonel and forced him to the window where, to stop himself worrying about his son, he stood by the cracked pane and looked out into the courtyard and at the sky, as ever filled with rain. The first thing his eyes lit on was the pick and shovel propped against the wall by the gate. He had imagined that Amir would pick them up and take them with him. But what completely flummoxed him was the fact that the bust of Amir Kabir, which had been standing on the platform over the pond, had vanished. At first he could not believe that Amir Kabir had been removed, but then, as he peered through the finely falling rain, he saw that both leaves of the courtyard gate had been wrenched from their hinges and the lintel had been smashed. This convinced him that Amir had been taken away. He could not stand it, and went out on to the verandah, careless of the blanket flapping round his naked body. He caught sight of a distraught Amir emerging from the cellar and looking frantically round the yard for the bust. Lifting an arm out from under his blanket, he pointed silently at the gap in the wall where the gate had been. Amir, as if he had just noticed the wreck of the gateway, rushed out into the alley, ignoring the pick and shovel.

The colonel stood there, bemused, with his arm still pointing at the gate. All thoughts of death were behind him now. The rain kept on coming down, echoing silently in the colonel's head, stirring no memories in his mind, not even a faint image of a sunset after the rain on the rusty tin roof. And then he saw Khezr Javid coming in through the gate, dragging someone behind him in handcuffs. Khezr stepped into the yard and paused by the pond for a moment, as if making up his mind. Then he turned back, as if to measure up his companion.

The sight so unnerved the colonel that he woke from his daydream. Who had Khezr Javid arrested? The man was looking nervously around. Khezr Javid clicked the handcuffs round the single, withered branch of the orange tree to secure his prisoner and then went down to the basement, presumably to search it. The colonel blinked, and blinked again, as if he could not believe what he was seeing. But no, everything was as he had seen it: handcuffed to the tree in the rain by the pond was a hunchbacked creature, all huddled up and wrapped in an old army blanket. The only parts of him that were visible were his tethered arm and his extraordinary eyes, one like Masoud's and the other like Abdullah Kolahi's, whom he had last seen with a packet of sugar plums in the living room. On closer inspection now, he saw that Abdullah's strange eyes divided his half-burned and mutilated face into two distinct halves, like two mismatched panes of glass. These extraordinary glassy eyes were darting anxiously around the yard. The colonel could still remember Abdullah's words:

"Colonel, I'm going away and I shan't be coming back. I have come to ask for your blessing, Colonel. Bless me, Colonel."

He had not seen Abdullah again since then. As he looked at him in his present condition, everything went black and the image of the young Abdullah vanished in a puff of smoke. The colonel's head felt like a millstone and he felt as if his heart had been plucked out of his body and, like a demented canary, was beating against the sides of its cage. When he came to, he found himself gripping the back of the chair tightly with both hands. The blanket had fallen off his shoulders and was lying on the floor, leaving him stark naked and shivering like a dog.

"He's sick, Colonel, sick! What a sight you are, Colonel, Sir! I wish I had a camera!"

It was the nasal voice of Khezr Javid. His mouth open in a silent laugh, his sharp, professionally insolent look pinned the colonel's naked, fragile body, bent double over the chair. The colonel came round. He was not confused now. He bent down, carefully picked the blanket up from the floor and pulled it over his shoulders.

He remembered that he had just been standing on the verandah and that Khezr had gone down to the basement to… Now he had freed the crooked little hunchback from the tree and was dragging him, like an insult, towards the passage, presumably to lock him up in one of the rooms inside. Then he remembered that Khezr had brought him round with the words: "He's sick, Colonel, sick." Now he saw more clearly that the strange, mismatched eyes, like two different pieces of glass, had split Abdullah's transformed face into two halves. He saw that those two fearful, apprehensive glassy eyes were seeing things as if through a kaleidoscope. He felt himself being dragged towards the door as Khezr led the deformed young man into the passage, muttering back at the colonel, "He's dumb, he's gone dumb."

A moment later, Khezr came out of the corridor onto the verandah and stood looking at the wrecked gate. Taking a deep breath, and avoiding the colonel's gaze, he announced:

"It's been decided to turn this house into a lunatic asylum, Colonel. Let's hope they're all as dumb as this one, otherwise it's going to get really noisy round here soon."

My God… Am I seeing what I'm seeing? Am I hearing what I'm hearing?

Yes, there was no mistake. Khezr went down the verandah steps, scratching his new beard, went over to the wall, where the pick and shovel had been left, paused briefly to piss against the courtyard wall and went out of the gate. The last sight that the colonel had of him was his new mulla's cloak billowing out behind him as he swept out into the alleyway.

How many moons have passed? It seems only yesterday that Abdullah came with the packet of sugar plums to say that he was going away for good, and that he hadn't even told his wife… Oh dear, the seasons have all run together in my mind; everything seems to have happened to me in a single instant. And now, what have I got to offer him except a few lumps of sugar plum? It's an illusion, it must be an illusion. My mind is going... Can this poor wretch really be Abdullah?"

It was Abdullah.

A terrified Abdullah, from one of whose eyes the colonel's little son was gazing out at him. He was squatting forlornly by the wall, beneath the canary cage. When the colonel brought him a glass of tea and a couple of sugar plums, Abdullah reached out from under his blanket, grasped the colonel's hand and spoke in a hoarse, hollow voice, begging him to tell his mother where he was. "Before I wrap these..." – he pointed at the handcuffs hanging from his right wrist – "round my neck and..." He told the colonel he wanted to see his mother before he killed himself: "So that I can suck her milk one last time!" Then he closed his parched lips and gazed round the room with his glassy stare, taking in every detail. As the colonel left the room, he heard Abdullah's cracked voice behind him: "And you, Ali Seif. You were the one who shot people down like dogs. I'll tear you to pieces with my teeth..."

* * *

Oh, the dangerous bravado of youth! The colonel reflected that if the boffins could one day manage to expunge from a man's life the years of youth, say from eighteen to thirty, then those in power, those behind all the exploitation and plundering of the nation, would have nothing to worry about. Because nobody would ever again come up with such dangerous ideas as justice or freedom. *Why has nobody ever thought of this before? But then again, they need the young. Who else could they send off to fight their wars for them? But of course there are endless numbers of young men, endless. Which of them would be shot first?*

The rattling of the chain... *the chain round the gate of the Shams ul-Emareh.* * Was he really hearing the jangle of the heavy links of the chain on the great gate? *Do my ears deceive me?* No, he was right. Clear for all to see, they had wound the chains of the old Shams ul-Emareh palace gate round Amir Kabir's neck. His hands were tied behind his back and they were hauling him into the colonel's yard. The Amir is a pitiful sight, in his white shirt, black frock coat and cap askew, standing a good head and shoulders above the two youths who are dragging him into the yard and raining blows and curses down on him. It is no surprise that, even with his hands tied behind his back, he does not fall to his knees. When he is just a step away from the pond, he lifts his head, thrusts out his burly chest and gazes at the colonel standing there under the canary cage. The colonel is so deeply moved by the sight that he does not immediately notice that the two guards in charge of Amir are Qorbani Hajjaj and Ali Seif, bringing the young criminal back to the scene of the crime to see if they can clear it up.

So it was you, Ali Seif, who took such pleasure in killing people like dogs!

The colonel lost track of how long he had been standing there by the cage, staring silently into space, but he knew that he had closed his mind to the chain of the Shams ul-Emareh palace, to Amir and to the others. He had been taken to the verandah, so it seemed, and he had been made to stand just where The Colonel used to stand from time to time with his white handkerchief.

He looked at the rain, and at the smashed gate and at the wall by the gate. There was no sign of the pick and shovel. So, Amir had taken them after all, and what he had just witnessed had been nothing but a dream. All he could hear now was the sound of the rain beating on the old tin roof, and all he could feel was the shadowy hands of Qorbani Hajjaj, with his coarse fingers, helping him put on his still-damp clothes to take him off to the mosque. For the memorial service…

I am not even thinking about shutting the gates, even if they were still there. I can't think of anything to hide in this house any more. Everything has been tipped out like the guts of a slaughtered sheep, for all to see. There's no point in bolting the door now.

I've lost the habit of locking the door, and I am not the least bit concerned by it. I've got nothing to hide from anyone. Locking the door used to be second nature, but now that I think about it, what I was really doing was locking up my private life. Now that I am leaving the house shoulder to shoulder with Qorbani, the sanctity of my home is the least of my concerns. I am just worried about how to behave when I get to the mosque, where I should stand, and what I should say to people. I am just thinking about how long it will be before it's over.

In fact, Qorbani had made it quite easy for him, by taking over his role and allowing the colonel to stand back for the entire service. He thanked all those who had come to offer their prayers for the martyr, while the colonel stood by the mosque door shivering like a dog. By the time someone had thought to bring him a paraffin stove, the service was over.

Qorbani did not come back home with him. He had a lot to do, marching the crowd of mourners to the town square,

"Justice Square." He came as far as the end of the alleyway with him where, out of sight of the crowd, he turned and spat at him:

"If it hadn't been for those two or three other bastard children of yours, this one alone would have allowed you to hold your head up high for the rest of your life. But now…"

And with that Qorbani stalked off. In any event, the colonel had nothing to say to him. He might have found an answer, if he had had any further interest in life. He might just have spat in his face.

I might, possibly, have tried to get on side with him, by pretending to agree with him that those other children of mine were indeed bastards, and try to see my days out living off the name of the one who wasn't a bastard. But who can say?

Who knows what goes on in another person's mind? Had Qorbani said what he had said out of sympathy for him? Or out of fear that his father-in-law might become a burden to him?

Qorbani knows, better than his wife does, that I don't have a pension. And another thing! It could well be that he hates me and my children because he thinks the connection with us might get in the way of his bid for the contract to renovate the mortuary.

But in any case, the colonel knew that Qorbani had no idea which way his mind was going, and how far he had got in his plan. If he had known how close the colonel was to his end, he would not have bothered to offer him any sympathy, real or otherwise. Whatever the case, the colonel had no wish to get involved in trading petty insults.

I still have one or two things to attend to. I ought to take that packet of wedding sugar plums round the town and share the tomans among the poor. Then I must let the canary go free, or at least leave its cage door open so that it can fly away if it wants to. Once I've done that, the only question left to settle will be what I am going to do about myself. Anyhow, the first thing to do is go home.

* * *

The gate is still wide open and the colonel has no need to search his pockets for the key. Nothing worries him now. He knows that the house will soon be taken over by the state and – maybe – used for charity. *Of course, Qorbani should have no expectations; he will get more than his fair share of the inheritance by winning the tender to do up the mortuary…*

Almost nonchalantly, the colonel strolls into the yard. He does not even regret not taking a last look at the photograph of Masoud in the new shrine they had put up outside the gate. Nor does he worry whether it was himself, or someone else, who has left the light on in the sitting room. He just hopes that the stove is still going. His feet untrammelled by care for life or death, his intention now clear, he strides towards his end.

But what he sees on entering the living room pulls him up short: The Colonel, and someone whom he addresses as "Your Excellency" are sitting opposite one another at the table.*

The Colonel is sitting in my old place, and His Excellency is on this side of the table, in Amir's usual place. I am standing under the arch and The Colonel is facing the door, while His Excellency has his back to it. I seem to have interrupted a secret meeting and I am embarrassed by my mistake.

The Colonel ignores my presence. His piercing black eyes are trained on His Excellency, as if to stop him turning round to look at me. I look at The Colonel for an answer. Ignoring me, he dabs at the blood on his neck with his handkerchief and carries on with his conversation. I listen in:

"You were told to leave the country, Colonel."

"Yes, you did tell me that, Your Excellency."

"I sent you that order via HQ. According to the order, you and Farrokh and Bahador* were to take two years' salary and go to Europe to complete your training."

"I had to deal with some outstanding matters that fell within my remit. That didn't require any further training."

"Outstanding matters, indeed! You take yourself far too seriously, Colonel… They could have been dealt with in your absence."

"I have never shirked my duty. I have many enemies always laying traps for me. I couldn't go away."

"If you'd agreed to leave Persia, your enemies would not have been a problem. After all, there's not one of them that isn't in our pocket."

"I came back from Europe to finish what I had to do, and had no wish to go back again. I saw no need to do so."

"I'm not interested in whether you want to go back to Europe or not. I am telling you to leave Persia."

"I am aware of that, Sir, but I won't leave my country. Iran is my country. Can't you see that?"

"When you talk about your country like that, you sound more arrogant and aggressive than you should be, Colonel. They don't stand for that sort of thing. And I won't put up with it, either. You disrupt our lines of communication, seize our weapons and you insult a friendly nation. And you then

ignore a friendly suggestion that you should leave Persia…
No, Colonel, you can't expect to get away with such inso-
lence. Not you, not anyone."

"I don't expect to, Sir. I blocked your communications
because it was my duty to do so. I impounded your arsenal
of weapons because they were illegal. And I commandeered
your cavalry and other equipment because I believed that you
were not entitled to set up an independent militia outside
state control. I was just doing my duty as an Iranian soldier."

"Your conduct was not that of a Persian officer, Colonel."

"What do you mean?"

"The orders you received from me came direct from Army
HQ."

"Whose HQ?"

"Persia's, of course."

"So, who the hell are you to give me orders, Sir? May I
enquire as to what your position is, exactly?"

"Colonel, kindly stop being so difficult and aggressive, not
to say insubordinate!"

"Insubordinate to you, maybe."

"It was a question of an understanding between two gov-
ernments, which you insisted on interfering with. Otherwise, why did you disobey an order?"

"What order? If an order had come from the government
of Iran…"

"Iran had no effective government at the time, my man.
Surely you can see that?"

"I'm well aware of that. And that is precisely why you and
I should have been trying to set one up!"

"What, some kind of 'government of national unity,'
no doubt? You lot philosophise like bloody pie-in-the-sky

German idealists, Colonel. You're nothing but romantic minstrels."

"I don't like your tone, Your Excellency. I know just what kind of a man you are and what sort of grand family you come from. Nevertheless, I am happy to try and show you that our country, mine and yours, has never lacked philosophers and musicians of its own."

"Always harking back to the past, aren't you? I can't stand your arrogance when you start going on about 'your country.' I should have got those Kurds to sort you out earlier."

"Well, in the end you did, and as usual you acted too soon. My mistake was in not throwing you out of the region I was responsible for and exiling you to Zahedan."

"Not so much a mistake as not having the capability of doing so, I suspect. You see, your giving orders to lay siege to the consulate of a friendly nation has not been forgotten, and the insult will not be forgiven, I can assure you."

"This attitude of yours is, of course, in your own interest. I'm sure you could teach us plenty on that score."

"You could have learned a lot from remembering how your namesake Taqi Khan Amir Kabir ended up."*

"We did indeed, Sir."

The Colonel gets up and leans on the mantelpiece, dabbing the blood off his neck with his handkerchief. His Excellency stands up too, picks his hat up off the table and lays it over the hand holding his walking stick. He straightens his grey bow tie under his Adam's apple, gives a little cough and, fixes his gaze sternly on The Colonel through his pebble glasses:

"If I were you, Colonel, I'd take better care of your head."

The Colonel turns round to look at him: "Will that be all?"

His Excellency simply smiles and looks at The Colonel

once more. To see him properly he has to look up a little. As he does so, the greasy hair on the back of his head and round his ears catches the light and shimmers like a cock's tail feathers. For a while he says nothing, and just stands there, wondering what to do next, as though finding the presence of The Colonel distasteful. Then he sits down, puts his hat and stick down and, with his elbows on the table, rests his chin on his hands and studies The Colonel through his spectacles. The Colonel's final impertinent question was a calculated affront, and he cannot let it stand and leave the room humiliated. But The Colonel stands, solid as a rock, by the mantelpiece, beneath his photograph, wiping the blood off his neck with his handkerchief every now and then and saying nothing. Knowing His Excellency's character, he is deliberately making him sweat.

This time His Excellency is more threatening:

"I stayed on, to make sure we did not lose the oil in the north.* But you and your like… your pride is too much. A special court has been set up to pronounce on all the crimes of the last century, from Amir Kabir right down to you, Colonel Mohammad-Taqi Khan, and my own cousin, Mossadeq. I hope that you will be able to maintain your usual sang-froid."

He stood up and went on: "I hope you've got the stamina for it, Colonel. The charges are serious indeed. A judicial review of the whole story is long overdue. Sealed files will not be opened, of course, but with a little patience… It will be local people running the court, Colonel, your own offspring, patriotic young men, all."

His Excellency is clearly trying to provoke The Colonel, who forces himself to control his temper. His eyes glowing two chalices of blood, he glares back, his voice shaking like a battle ensign in the wind:

"Enough play acting, Your Excellency! Come out and be frank."

His opponent has by now regained his composure. He even manages a smile, as he takes a sugar plum out of a soggy paper bag and pops it in his mouth. His tone is now winningly sarcastic:

"All in good time, Colonel, all in good time. No more of this old soldier business, now. Come on now, every old soldier knows never to leave your foxhole until you've dug another one first! You have dug yourself well in to your last hole this time, haven't you, Sir? Isn't that so?

Ah, I am indeed sorry for you, for your successes as much as for your defeats. You are too good for this vale of tears. To think, a man of your talents and your nice European education, with all that German romanticism, all that Wagner and Nietzsche... It pains me to see you brought so low. You were just too good for this country, too rarefied a flower for this stony ground. What a shame that you never took my advice. If you had, you wouldn't be an embittered old man faced with the wickedness and wrath of the mob, Colonel. Or with the anger and vengeance of your own offspring. You really should have left, you know..."

"I couldn't abandon my country, Sir. Logically, it should have been you who left..."

"I told you why I had to stay... But you... You'll be totally forgotten, Colonel. Your misbegotten children, villains all of them, will devour you like wolves. And all because of your patriotism, Colonel. Would you believe it? Your own children!"

"My children will pay you back for this one day, as will yours, I swear, Your Excellency."

"Your children are blowing another tune now, soldier. Can't you hear the mob out on the street? Your children are busy tearing each other to pieces like wolves. Not a pretty sight! It's frightening, isn't it? Look where I'm pointing, I'm showing you what tomorrow will bring!"

"We were trying to find our own way in life, Sir. But I'm telling the story backwards."

"Look out of the door. Your children are right outside at this very moment, waiting for you. It's a big show! If you want my advice, you'll be a bit more compliant. They will be more lenient if you are. After all, how many times can they cut off a man's head?"

His Excellency sits in silence under The Colonel's unblinking stare for a while, then, without meeting The Colonel's gaze, gets up and gathers up his hat and stick: "So, you've decided to tough it out, have you? I admire the stand you are taking, I really do – I'm honour bound to say that to you. But on the other hand, your stubbornness is exasperating. For the same reason, I would like to break those' fine upstanding legs of yours."

"Have you anything further to say?"

No, everything had already been said. The old man was shaking now and his eyes were clouding over and he had a splitting headache. Was madness descending on him once more? It all seemed so unreal, and yet it was all too real. Alone with the monotonous, unrelenting din of the rain, he felt the evening filling the room with a suffocating darkness. He saw shadowy hands strapping a horse's girth round The Colonel's shoulders and leading him out through the rain into the street and on to the square. The Colonel held himself up straight and strode purposefully along. He no longer made any attempt to staunch the blood running from his throat over his shoulders and on to his chest.

* * *

The room needed light. The old man stretched out a shaky hand to switch it on, and there was light. In the glow cast by the lamp, he saw that The Colonel's picture was missing from its frame and that the photographs of his children had fallen on the floor, where they had been crumpled and kicked about. Rain was hammering on the old tin roof. The flame in the paraffin stove was guttering. It seemed that it was all over. On the wall his sword and his *setar* were still hanging there, covered in a thick film of dust. He was seized by a wish to take down his *setar*, dust it off and strike up a tune, but… No, he had to get on with it now. There were things on the table waiting to be dealt with: the box of sugar plums, the 35 tomans. He picked them up and went out.

Outside, on the verandah, he was brought up sharp by a ghostly sound of disintegrating horror. Facing him was the eerie, misshapen, hunched-up creature with bulging mis-matched eyes, wrapped up like a clenched fist in an old army blanket. His face was seared, his teeth were smashed, and his claw-like hand was clutching at his jugular as he yelled: "It was you Ali Seif, who slaughtered people like dogs…" He rambled on: "And my mother… my mother… I just want to suck her tits… Colonel, tell my mother, before I chew my own throat…" Then he shouted: "Mother, Mother!" the colonel was no longer surprised by anything, not even by his next outburst:

"I killed him, I killed him a thousand times over. He had fallen behind a sandbag and was groaning. I realised that his magazine must have been empty, but I didn't bother to check whether the barrel of his machine gun was hot or cold. I didn't want there to be an excuse for not killing him. No doubts or second thoughts. I flung myself at him. It was just as well that I couldn't see his face, but it must have been screwed up with pain. All I could see was the gaping wound in his chest. I could have left him to die, or had him carried away by the medics. But no, I got stuck into him with a bayonet. The first blow got him right in the middle of his wound, I remember that. But after that, I don't remember a thing. When I'd finished him off, I had just enough strength left to take his watch and put it on my own wrist. Then I fainted. Nausea. I thought my father would be pleased with the present of a watch I was going to bring him. Ali Seif! Ali Seif!"

* * *

The colonel had opened the packet of sugar plums and held them out in front of Abdullah's scorched face and crazed eyes. But presently he felt himself to be quite alone on the verandah. He could no longer hear Abdullah's snuffling breath. He had gone… But no – he was still there after all. A misplaced curiosity drew the colonel towards the dark corridor, towards the misshapen, deformed creature standing, rock-like, under the canary's cage. Its mismatched eyes, one blue, the other yellow, glowed in the dark like a jungle cat's. It seemed to be speaking:

"I'm dumb, colonel, I can't speak."

"So am I, my son – but now I have things to do."

* * *

When the colonel reached the main square, he saw a large crowd moving along. In the darkness and the rain, he could not make out a single clear face. All he could see were their gaping mouths, baying fearsomely, and their terrifying hypnotised eyes. They seemed to be high on some lethal drug, but the colonel saw no need to be afraid, for there was nothing left in him for that drunken mob to destroy. What was there to fear now? *Anyway, I want to hand out those sugar plums to them.*

He opened the packet and held the coloured sugar plums out to the eager hands stretched towards him. They grabbed the sweets and stuffed them into their mouths. They would bring blessings on the show that was about to start. Shouting "Good Luck!" at him, they parted and cleared a way for the colonel to get through to the centre of the square, where the show was about to take place.

I'm not surprised, not in the least surprised!

The accused had been made to sit down on the wet cobblestones, like prisoners of war. Some of them, it appeared, had already been sentenced and had punishment meted out to them. Amir Kabir, who stood out from the others, had been made to kneel in the mud. In the centre stands The Colonel, erect as ever.

It was all like some nightmarish old historical panorama, rendered in shades of grey and black, with a landscape in the background shrouded in mist and rain. Even the blood – on

The Colonel's throat, flowing from the vein in Amir's arm, pouring from Heidar's heart and Sattar Khan's leg – was grey.*

Grey also was the blanket they had wrapped round Mossadeq's shoulders. The only colour came from some bright red vertical lines in the left-hand edge of the painting, where a man with a red scarf round his neck was hanging from a red gibbet.† His glasses had been shattered, but were still on his nose, and he was completely naked. The clear intention was to humiliate him. Unseen hands kept pushing his dangling body this way and that, so that it was lit from all sides by the glare of the spotlights. His naked body was just a bag of skin and bones, indicating that he had spent his youth locked up in damp and stinking jail cells. It was hard to see why the authorities were so insistent on publicly disgracing and torturing this man, as the performance did nothing to stop his mother from weeping and crying incessantly in Azeri: "*I don't recognize my son. That is not my son; show him to me!*"

This appeal has no effect whatsoever on the tyrant Hajjaj bin-Yousef Qorbani. He is bent on wiping these people out, and he has no intention of letting her Azeri gibberish penetrate his Arab brain.‡

His particular speciality lies in that, before violating the honour of a nation through its women, first he shits on them and then makes them eat each other alive, just like Morshed Kabir in Safavid times, and then he throws the last of them to the hyenas of the Dead Sea deserts to the north, who have been driven over here, like an unwanted gift.§ It was absurd to expect Hajjaj Yousef Qorbani to be moved by the lamentations of an Azeri mother on her knees before the naked body of her son, wailing that she could not recognize him and begging the hangman to show him to her: "*Muslims, Muslims! This is not my son. Taqi, Taqi… Mother!*"

Another speciality of Qorbani Hajjaj Yousef's is to allow his victims – after they have denounced themselves – to choose how they want to be put to death. *But on one condition – the victim's decision must be announced over the loudspeakers by the colonel, who is to be the spokesman of his son-in-law.* The colonel heard his own voice echoing over the square: "Praise be to Allah, there are many different forms of punishment, some two thousand four-hundred odd, each one designed for a specific crime." Qorbani, after the usual obsequious preambles praising the authorities, then listed the various crimes the prisoners were accused of.

At that moment, the colonel's gaze lighted on old Mossadeq, who was still sitting on the floor, wrapped in his old army blanket, with his right knee raised. The point of his walking stick was stuck in the ground, with the crook of it resting between his shoulder blades to support his back. He held his head down, looking at the ground. He looked like a dejected shepherd whose flock has been attacked by a pack of wolves. A knowing, distant smile played around his lips. Khezr's ghostly face can just be made out in the mist.

Now it was Heidar Amoghli's* turn: as a snowstorm began swirling over the square, he held the cold barrel of Mirza Kuchik's rifle against his heart and, standing there next to the kneeling Sattar Khan and Sheikh Khiabani,† gave Mirza the order to fire.

Then The Colonel appeared, holding his head and bloodied astrakhan cap above his head like a lantern. And finally it was the turn of the great Amir Kabir. Calm and grimly silent, he knelt down where he stood, as if on a prayer mat, or facing an execution block, bracing himself with his hands on the cold cobbles and looking at the ground. He seemed not to notice the brownish blood seeping out of his forearm. He is holding a eulogy in one hand, perhaps for the great Qaim Maqam…* He is looking down as Qorbani Hajjaj appears, clutching a dagger still greyish-red from the blood of Dadvi-yeh.† His sleeves are rolled up, and the folds of his cloak are girt up. The bands that hang down three sides of his pointed steel helmet are adorned with glittering rubies and emeralds. His bare, ugly feet are covered in mud and blood up to the ankles. Standing beside Amir, he speaks from the back of his throat, spraying out spittle with every word. With a string of foul imprecations, he lambasts him as a criminal of the first order and then asks him how he wishes to be executed. Without deigning to look up at him, Amir gives the order himself: "Off with my head!"

How could anyone take pleasure in the curve of a sabre in this savage method of separating a body from its head, still less when it is kneeling down with its palms nailed to the ground? It's a ghastly form of revenge.

The colonel recalled that when criminals were hanged in the old days in Execution Square or Artillery Square, people would scatter coins at their feet by way of expiation. There was something disgusting and self-abasing about the whole performance, for what they were really doing was trying to purge themselves of complicity in the act.

Without thinking, the colonel takes the last few sugar plums out of the packet and, like a farmer scattering seed, strews them over the bloody pile of severed heads. The world goes dark in front of him and, in the depths of the darkness, all he can see is the tall, upright figure of The Colonel holding his head high above him, blazing like a torch.

His head was still spinning as he lifted up his forehead from the cold cobblestones in the square. He hesitated and then, with some trepidation, opened his eyes. The rain had stopped and the square was empty. There was just the echo of marching boots on the bare flagstones. The whole square was spattered with blood. Looking up, he saw a procession, led by The Colonel, of the great men marching out of sight, each one holding his head under his arm. Their old field boots gleamed in the light of the street shrines erected in memory of their sons, and in the light of the flame that was The Colonel's head, held high above them all.

Oh, my forefathers… these are the men who went before us!

* * *

The colonel could not understand what Amir was saying. He was standing in front of his father, holding the pick and shovel on his shoulder like an old gravedigger. The colonel looked at him and Amir glanced back at his father. *We have nothing to say to each other. Although we belong to different generations, we have both witnessed the same things, so we are now as one. Except for one thing, which I hold dear, but do not have the courage to admit to…*

The colonel got up, not caring that his clothes were all stained with blood. He set off at an easy pace, shoulder to shoulder with his son. The sound of their footsteps was the only sound in the square. They stopped at the side of the square. It was as if they had both agreed to go their own separate ways.

In the Traditions of the Prophet it is decreed that corpses should not be buried at night.

Amir headed off in the direction of the cemetery, none-theless. The colonel watched his son as he disappeared. He did not give a moment's thought to feeling any sympathy for Amir, for he had plenty of other things to do now.

"I must get on."

* * *

The alleyway was completely lit up by the shrine to Masoud. As he passed it, the colonel realised that he was still clench-ing his left hand into a tight fist. He relaxed it. The 35 toman notes in his hand were damp with sweat. He laid them, all screwed up, at the foot of the shrine to his Little Masoud. "I can't stop, my boy. I've got to go home and see to your sister's canary." He knew that if he let the bird out of its cage, where it had lived all its life, it would not be able to fly away, let alone survive. But he would rather do that than leave it to a living death in its cage.*

He went straight up the steps into the corridor to open the cage. But as he did so he heard the mewing of the old black cat by the pond. He stopped to look at it. The cat looked back at him. He stamped and shouted, trying to shoo it away, but the cat refused to budge. It seemed to him the cat was quite shamelessly letting him know that it was just waiting for Parvaneh's canary to come out so that it could gobble it up.

The colonel would have cheerfully killed it, but he thought he ought to have a look at the canary first. He crossed the verandah and went into the passage, switched on the light and walked up to the canary's cage, which hung on the wall. No bird. He could not believe his eyes. He took the cage down and held it to the light, but the bird was gone.

"I'm so ashamed of myself, Colonel. You should treat me as you would your son. I… I've eaten it, but it was already dead."

It was the cat speaking, or so it seemed, with its mismatched eyes… or was it Abdullah? The colonel wasted no time dwelling on what might have happened to Parvaneh's dead bird. With a venomous "You're welcome to it!" he went out on to the verandah. He felt like stopping there for a while to breathe in the fresh air after the rain and recall that one day he had seen the sun setting over the ochre-coloured tin roof after the rain. He stood there with his arms crossed and thought that – hoped that – tomorrow would be a sunny day, like the day when they had brought home Mohammad-Taqi's body. He thought how lucky were the people who would still be alive tomorrow. He did not begrudge it to them for a moment, or wish that he was going to be alive the next day. No, he thought, why should he spoil the end of his life by letting envy of other people get the better of him? No, life's tribulations may open one's eyes and ears and torment one's soul, but they can also purge it of narrow-mindedness. And enjoying life makes death seem young and beautiful…

In these final moments, this thought took the stoop out of his back and he stood up straight and took a deep, delicious, breath of the air after the rain. *No, I never wanted to go out with a whimper. I refuse to go quietly, not after all this.*

He would have to take a shower and have a shave, brush his hair, and put on his old uniform, *I'm a soldier, damn it!* He was not going to forget his old standards now. He attached his aiguillettes, took his field boots out of the suitcase, polished them up and put them on. His insignia of rank had been stripped off when he was cashiered. He felt now that he had somehow preempted death by cleansing his body of all its slimy, grubby traces. He was purged. He just needed to dust off his beloved old *setar* and leave it hanging on the wall as a memorial.

I'm sure someone'll play it again one day. He took his sabre down off the wall, wiped the dust off it with the back of his hand and tested its bright, shining blade with his finger.

Before I die, I must turn on all the lights in the house. He wanted the house to be ablaze with light. It was time to go. He was turning on all the lights in his house, *in all my children's rooms, as well…*

He set off, picking up Amir's will from under the sugar bowl on the table as he went. He tried to read it, and also to remember what he himself had written: "If those who are to come were to take the time to pass judgement on the past, in all likelihood they would say: 'Our forefathers were powerful and impressive men, who sacrificed themselves to the great lie in which they fervently believed and which they spread. And the moment they began to doubt their beliefs, it was off with their heads! No doubt the bazaar merchants, businessmen and wheeler dealers among them will end up with the view that we would all be happy if we could just elect to be ruled by the least arbitrary of the thugs amongst us.'"

He put the sheet of paper back under the sugar bowl and, once more, held his sabre up to the light and studied its flashing blade. Running his freshly cleansed fingers along his jugular vein, he stepped out onto the verandah.

Now, have I turned on all the lights in the house? Yes, I have…

* * *

Ever after that rainless night, the street people and the bazaar folk heard the strumming of an old *setar* reverberating in the darkness of the alleyways. They said that in the dead of night one saw a man roaming the narrow little streets, holding a lantern in his hand as he chanted these ancient lines:

> If you see on your way a severed head
> Tumbling along to that square of ours,
> Ask it, just ask it, how we all fare;
> It will tell you that buried secret of ours!

چو در ره بینی بریده سرے   کغلتان رودسوی میدان ما

ازاوپرس ازاوپرس احوال ما   کز او بشنوی سرّ پنهان ما

Afterword

Mahmoud Dowlatabadi

Mahmoud Dowlatabadi is a colossus of contemporary Iranian literature. He cut his literary teeth on the great Persian poets like Hafiz and Rumi, imbibing their rich language and blending it uniquely successfully with modern everyday speech to create his own thoroughly contemporary voice. His language is poetic, rhythmical, metaphorical and allusive, and flows like a broad, mighty river, full of eddies, side currents, quiet backwaters and whirlpools. As he puts it: "Words are like the strings of a guitar. You have to let their clear tones ring out and not stifle their resonance with verbs."

Dowlatabadi began working on this novel 25 years ago, but kept filing the manuscript away in a drawer, taking it out periodically and revising it. In 2008, he finally declared the text ready for publication. He dismissed any notion that earlier publication might have changed the course of history as an unreasonable and fanciful expectation to place upon a literary work. He also feared that the novel might itself have fallen victim to the unchecked violence of the revolution.

The descriptions of torture are taken from the experiences of the author himself, or from those of his friends. It comes as no surprise to learn that *The Colonel* has never appeared in its original language in the author's native country. The manuscript remains in the hands of the censor, who has demanded a number of deletions and revisions, which the author has refused to make.

Dowlatabadi was born in 1940 into a peasant family in the small village of Dowlatabad, near the town of Sabzevar on the northern edge of the *Dasht-e Kavir*, the great Persian desert. His early childhood memories are of carrying sacks of melons by donkey for sale in the nearest market town. "It was a bitter struggle between the unyielding stone and the fragile glass within me, countless shards on the dry earth, people wracked by poverty and hunger…"

Aged 13, he left his native village and fended for himself, first in Mashhad and Sabzevar and later in Tehran, as a jack-of-all-trades. While keeping himself enrolled in school, he moonlighted variously as a hairdresser, checking tickets in cinemas and selling advertising space in local newspapers. He was homeless and often spent the night on the streets. In his spare time, he devoured every book he could lay his hands on, as much from the canon of Persian classical literature as from translations of the works of European political philosophers and novelists. He describes himself as self-educated. Though he never gained his high school diploma, he was accepted for a place at drama school and wrote his first short story, "The Night's Abyss." This launched him on his literary career.

Dowlatabadi's first collection of stories appeared in 1969, followed by a novel *Safar* (The Trip) translated into German as *Der Reise*. Eight more novels appeared before the revolution in 1979. Dowlatabadi's 1979 novel *Ja-ye Khali-ye Soluch*, translated into English as *Missing Soluch*, treated the decline of Iranian village life in the 1960s. This starkly beautiful novel looks at the trials of an impoverished woman and her children living in a remote village in Iran, after the unexplained disappearance of her husband, Soluch. Lyrical yet unsparing, the novel examines her life as she contends with the local political corruption, authoritarianism and the poverty of the village. This landmark novel, which pioneered the use of the everyday language of the Iranian people, revolutionised Persian literature in its beautiful and daring portrayal of the life of a marginal woman and her struggle to survive.

Dowlatabadi's most ambitious work, completed in 1984, is a 10-volume, 3,000-page epic entitled *Kelidar*, an account of life in the village of that name in north-eastern Iran in the 1940s. The village people are impoverished Kurds, who were moved there in the 17th century by Shah Abbas to guard the frontier against incursions by the Turkmen raiding from the north. Neither two years in prison under the Shah's regime, nor the upheavals of the revolution nor the death of his much-loved father could interrupt his tireless work on this *magnum opus*. Its publication was a sensation and catapulted Dowlatabadi to instant fame. He noted at the time: "I was totally exhausted and wanted nothing so much as to take a long rest, but I was compelled to go on writing." *Kelidar* has been translated into German.

While he was writing *Kelidar* Dowlatabadi tried to shut himself off from events in the post-revolutionary outside world. His own politics, which evolved over time, could be loosely defined as leftward-leaning liberal nationalism. He became totally disillusioned by the outcome of the revolution that toppled the Shah: "I felt a great sense of unease within me, an inner compulsion that drove me to the brink of insanity." Then came the fateful night when everything came to a head and *The Colonel* was born:

It was a dream, or rather a nightmare. I saw all the various characters, the colonel and his children and sensed the atmosphere before and after the revolution, as the whole recent history of Iran ran like a time-lapse film before my eyes. But when I awoke, the nightmare didn't go away. I immediately began writing down what I'd seen, if only to relieve the terrible ferment I felt churning inside me.

Dowlatabadi now lives in Tehran. His children live in Europe and the USA. He travelled to Europe in 1990 and visited the United States in 1991, lecturing on literature and politics. In 2009 he visited Germany for the launch of the German translation of *The Colonel.*

The place

Readers who think of Iran as a dry country may be surprised by the constant rain in the narrative. The story unfolds in Rasht, the capital of Gilan province on the Caspian, where rice grows on the coastal plain and tea is cultivated on the foothills of the Alborz mountains, which separate the coast from the high, dry central Iranian plateau. The seaward side of the range is covered by heavy rain forest, which for centuries has given cover to bandits, rebels and dissidents. In 1920 Rasht was the base of the short-lived Socialist Republic of Gilan, under Kuchik Khan. Shortly after the revolution of 1979, the mountain forests gave cover to refugee Marxists. The time of the novel is placed towards the end of the Iran-Iraq war (1980–88).

The historical background

The Iranian Revolution of 1979 saw the end of the 2,500-year-old Persian monarchy. The hundreds of thousands who poured into the streets expected that the revolution would bring them better times, social justice, freedom and independence from foreign interference. The revolution was more than just a change of regime; it was also an act of revenge, the settling of a number of accounts that had been outstanding since the early years of the 20th century.

The history of modern Iran begins with the constitutional revolution of 1906, where the fault lines between the royal court, conservative clerics, liberal clerics, western-oriented liberals, nationalists and Leftists first became apparent. In this struggle between progressive and reactionary forces, the royal court emerged as the winner. The Iranian Left was born in the oilfields of Russian Baku, where most of the labourers had come north from the Iranian province of Azerbaijan to find work. These labourers were very much part of the first Russian revolution of 1905.

After World War I the British, seeing that the Bolsheviks were moving into Iran from Baku, tried to turn Iran into a protectorate, under a triumvirate of two princes and Vosuq ad-Dowleh, the brother of Ahmad Qavam, who were paid enormous sums of money to push a treaty agreeing to this through the Majlis, which never approved it. In 1921 an army colonel, Reza Khan, mounted a coup with Seyyid Zia, who became prime minister. Reza Khan became minister of war and in 1925 he became Shah. Reza Shah was an admirer first of Ataturk and later of Nazi Germany. He dragged the country into the modern age and promoted technological progress. His dictatorial reign stifled all opposition, particularly from the Muslim clergy, whom he saw as the biggest barrier to progress. He made women remove their traditional veils, while mullahs who displeased him had their turbans knocked off in the street and their beards forcibly shaved – acts of public humiliation that left deep scars and a wish for revenge.

The Second World War brought a change. Allied forces from Great Britain and the Soviet Union occupied Iran, forced Reza Shah to abdicate and banished him to Mauritius. There were two reasons for this: the Allies felt that, although Iran was officially neutral, Reza Shah was too close to the Axis and secondly, Iran was needed as a transit route to send war material to Russia, to prevent the Nazi occupation of the oilfields in the Caucasus, and their possible advance into Iran and her oilfields. The old dictator, who had made great play of national independence, was succeeded by his young, inexperienced, largely apolitical and malleable son. For a short spell, there ensued a power vacuum, which gave various nationalist and leftist movements the chance to make their reappearance on the political stage.

During this brief phase of Iranian history at the height of the cold war, liberals and democrats were able to operate freely. Under the prime ministership of Mohammad Mossadeq, the British-owned oilfields were nationalised, the British were forced to leave the country and the British dominance over Iran came to an end. The new Shah also decided to leave. Believing that Mossadeq was now under communist influence, the CIA orchestrated a coup in 1953, which toppled his government and brought back the young Shah. This gave the United States the opportunity to fill the vacuum left by the British departure. The Americans, with the help of the Israelis, built up SAVAK, the highly efficient secret service, which devoted itself to the suppression of all opposition, particularly of the communist Tudeh party, which was supported by Moscow.

The popular uprising that broke out in 1978 was initially inspired by the various leftist movements, but it was not long before the Islamic clergy under the leadership of Ayatollah Khomeini managed to position themselves at the forefront of the opposition movement and seize power after the overthrow of the Shah. Having been in the game much longer, and being far closer to the people than the European-educated student leftists, the clergy were far more experienced in the art of crowd manipulation. Bridging the divide between Islam and secular socialism had been the preaching of Ali Shariati, who concocted a synthesis of the two in order to make socialism palatable to the traditionally-minded masses. He was killed in England in 1975. Some say that SAVAK killed him, while others say that it was the work of the Islamic hard-liners.

Their aim was the complete Islamization of Iranian society and the dismantling of all the democratic-liberal reforms that had been enacted in the country in the last few months of the Shah's reign. For the Islamists, this was the time to settle old scores: not only did they ruthlessly stamp out all other political movements and liquidate their representatives, they also instigated a thorough-going "cultural genocide," designed to expunge from Iran every last trace of the modern world and its institutions. The revolution was to be Islamic, not Iranian. The old, secular nationalists compared this to the Arab invasion of Persia in the 7th century, which was so lamented in the *Shahnameh*, the great Persian epic written in the 11th century.

Iran had never been a formal colony, but it had been caught between the Russian empire and the British empire in India until 1917. After the collapse of the Tsarist regime Iran had been run *de facto* by the Anglo-Iranian Oil Company (later BP). Even after the oil industry had been nationalised in the 1950s, foreign control continued in the form of US influence. American "advisers" occupied positions of power in the administration and dictated the country's political direction. The most telling taunt of Khomeini was that a junior American corporal who committed a crime in the street was, by virtue of being American, immune from prosecution. The wounds caused by the daily humiliations that the Iranian people had had to endure for almost a century at the hands of their foreign overlords ran deep. The one thing that united all the different factions during the revolution, aside from their opposition to the Shah's régime, was their utter rejection of hated foreign rule. Soviet propaganda, which whitewashed out the history of the pre-1917 Russian domination of Iran, was able to play heavily on these emotions. It is one of the great tragedies of Iran's history that the agenda of liberation, clearly expressed in the revolutionaries' demands for freedom and independence, was later co-opted and twisted by the Islamists to legitimize their ideology. So it was that the revolution, far from sweeping away ossified and outmoded ideas, actually succeeded in breathing new life into them. The biggest tragedy of the Iranian left was that their final achievement after fifty years – the removal of the Shah – served only to clear the way for the Islamists, who in 1988 duly slaughtered them, something that the Shah had never managed to do. *The Colonel* is Dowlatabadi's lament for this disaster, this living example of the law of unintended consequences. "Be careful what you wish for."

The Colonel

The protagonist, the unnamed colonel, was an officer in the last Shah's army. He was a soldier with principles, a patriot who had remained true to his oath to serve only the interests of his country, modelling himself on a historical figure, Colonel Mohammad-Taqi Khan Pesyan, a legendary patriot, who resisted the corrupt central government in the period immediately after the First World War. His story is in the Notes.

The Persian title of the book is *Kolonel*. Pesyan, who received his military training in Europe, was always referred to as *Kolonel*, rather than the Persian *Sarhang*. The colonel of the title has been given the affectionate nickname of *Kolonel*, since everyone knows how much he admires, and has almost become, Pesyan.

The principal characters

The colonel's five children represent the divergent political tendencies of the revolution. During the 1979 revolution and in the years that followed, almost every family in Iran was riven by such ideological disagreements.

Amir, the eldest, represents the orthodox communist Tudeh party, which toed the Moscow politburo line and, for a few years after the revolution, collaborated closely with the new regime. Until, that is, its support was no longer needed and it had outlived its usefulness, whereupon they were executed in droves. Amir's shortcomings not only reflect the demise of the Tudeh, but also the terminal decline of Iran's intellectuals, who for the most part supported this movement. Their opportunistic collaboration to the new régime in the early days was a wholesale betrayal of their own ideals. Ever after, most of them were sunk in semi-catatonic nihilism.

The colonel's second son, Mohammad-Taqi, is a member of the communist-leaning People's Fedayan. Killed during the uprising, he is at first fêted as a fighter but later condemned as a "dissident," as were many thousands of non-Islamist anti-Shah resistance fighters who were liquidated by the new régime.

The youngest son, Masoud, is a Khomeini supporter. He volunteers for the Iran–Iraq war (1980–88) and upon his death is celebrated as a "martyr."

Parvaneh, still just a child, is a member or at least a fellow-traveller of the People's Mujahedin, an organisation whose roots were in the Islamist camp, but which was markedly more left-wing than the conservative clergy. During the Iran-Iraq war they took the Iraqi side and established themselves in a military base at Camp Ashraf across the border. Condemned as traitors to their country by many, and in deep trouble with the new Iraqi government, they are today busy reinventing themselves as friends of the west.

The People's Mujahedin and the People's Fedayan, the two underground groups that took up arms against the Shah's regime and also played a leading part in the revolution, were among the first organisations to be targeted and eradicated by the new theocracy. They kept up resistance for a while, but the régime had the masses on its side. In 1988 huge numbers of leftists were rounded up and executed, something that the Shah, even when SAVAK was at its most savage, never did.

The revolution ate its own children as, in Persian legend, Rostam killed his son Sohrab.

Farzaneh, the colonel's elder daughter, is married to Qorbani Hajjaj, who encapsulates the world of deceit and specious dogma. The colonel's son-in-law is one of those people who always manage to come out on top, whichever way the wind is blowing. Such hirelings will shamelessly cheerlead for whoever happens to be in power, and will do whatever is required to keep themselves in favour. Farzaneh has submitted to this line, even though it is now beginning to frighten her.

Equally adaptable and lacking in principles is the secret policeman, Khezr Javid, whose personal inadequacies drove him into the arms of SAVAK. He was happy to interrogate and torture any number of dissidents under the Shah, and yet had no scruples about throwing in his lot with the new régime to keep his job. Nobody knows for certain how many Savakis, and informers, there were under the Shah, but there were thousands of them, with agents in every government organisation and in private companies. They created an atmosphere of fear and distrust, even within families. The senior ones were educated and urbane, while the torturers were recruited from the unwanted children born in the official brothels.

What makes this novel unique in modern Persian literature is its directness. The author spares nothing and no-one, and flies in the face of all kinds of literary, moral and social taboos, even those that are deemed sacrosanct in Islamic culture. By doing so, he highlights the deep-seated contradictions that have condemned a whole society to failure.

The colonel is a liberal who has taught his children to think for themselves and go their own way, with the result that they end up killed. At the same time, hidebound by conventional morality, he murders his wife because she has impugned his honour by having affairs. This contradiction between the old and new values is the essential Iranian tension today. Iran is a society based on family loyalties yet, after the Islamists seized power, they tried to turn the whole country into a nation of spies: the Supreme Leader demanded that everyone should keep a close eye out among their family and neighbours for anyone who stepped out of line or transgressed against the precepts of *shari'a* law. On television, he publicly proclaimed a woman who had betrayed her own child as "Mother of the Year." The methods of Stalin had been visited upon the leftists who had brought about the revolution.

Acknowledgements

I am indebted for help with the translation and with the historical references to a number of Iranian and British friends and colleagues. I am also indebted to Peter Lewis for his tireless collaboration and editing. By the nature of the language, much has inevitably been lost in translation, but I hope that sufficient poetry remains to do justice to the power and feeling of the original.

Tom Patterdale

Notes

Pg. vii [Translator's Note]
*Colonel Mohammad-Taqi Khan Pesyan. His aristocratic family came to Iran from the Iranian Caucasus after the Russians conquered it in 1828. His grandfather had worked closely with Amir Taqi Khan (Amir Kabir). After military training in Germany he was given a command in the Swedish-officered Iranian gendarmerie on the western Kermanshah front in World War I. Although Iran was neutral, this sector of Iran was occupied by Russian forces. Pesyan fought them but lost and then took his men over to the German-Turkish side. From there he went to Berlin and joined the German air force. After the war he was appointed head of the Khorasan gendarmerie in NE Iran, with the rank of Colonel. As a nod to his European training, he was given the nickname Kolonel (derived from the French, "*Colonel*"), which stuck. Even official documents referred to him as Kolonel. Pesyan was on bad terms with Ahmad Qavam, the governor of Khorasan, who later became prime minister. The colonel had thrown in his lot with Seyyid Zia, the fiercely nationalist post-war prime minister and in 1921 he arrested Qavam for failing to acknowledge Seyyid Zia as prime minister, and dismissed all his appointees. Seyyid Zia then appointed Pesyan as military governor of the province.

Pesyan sent Qavam under arrest to Tehran. After the fall of Seyyid Zia, Qavam became prime minister. Pesyan rejected his appointees to the governorship of Khorasan and declared the province independent of the central government, going so far as to print his own currency. He attempted to finance the improvements he wanted to make to the province by taxing merchants, landlords and tribal leaders. He cleaned up the finances of the Shrine at Mashhad, which were being embezzled by the officials running it, and returned them to their proper charitable use. Totally honest himself, he led an austere life and encouraged education, including for women.

When the central government was fully stretched dealing with the Jangali rebellion in the north, Pesyan threatened to attack the undefended Tehran with 4,000 men, accusing Qavam of being a servant of foreign interests. Tehran would have welcomed him. He made overtures to Kuchik Khan and to the Bolsheviks of Central Asia for assistance, but the Soviet government of Moscow offered to assist Tehran against him. Qavam offered Pesyan amnesty, safe passage out of the country and even monetary compensation, but the colonel refused to compromise. He accused Qavam of double dealing with the tribes against him and broke off all relations with the British, who were trying to act as intermediaries between him and Qavam, through their consul at Mashhad. Pesyan arrested all those who had worked with or for the British.

Qavam, with Reza Khan (later Reza Shah) as minister of war, induced the local tribes to raise a force against him, which defeated him and his gendarmes at Quchan. The colonel escaped, but was caught and killed in a subsequent skirmish. His head was sent to Tehran. Pesyan was buried in a shrine erected in memory of the great Nader Shah, the conqueror of India. Ever since, he has been a hero to Iranian nationalists, who have always resented the continuing interference of the Great Powers in the affairs of Iran. Although nationalistic, the Islamic regime has never taken this secular man to its heart.

†The monumental 60,000-stanza Iranian national epic, *Shah-nameh* (Book of Kings), is the work of the Persian poet Ferdowsi (940–1020). He was one of the first exponents of a new literary form in the Persian language, which had fallen out of use following the Arab invasion of Iran in the 7th century. The *Shahnameh*, completed in 1011, glorifies pre-Islamic Iran. It ends with the Arab invasion of Iran in AD 640, regarded by Iranian nationalists as the nation's greatest tragedy, in that it practically destroyed Persian culture and language. Ferdowsi's verse is notable for employing almost no Arabic words.

Pg. 4
*Jangal means "forest." Kuchik means "little." There is an allusion here to Kuchik Khan, founder of the revolutionary Nehzat-e Jangal (Forest Movement), a guerrilla army that operated in the heavily wooded regions of northern Iran, attacking the Shah's regime, and the foreign (Russian and British) forces supporting it, from 1914 onwards. Khan established the Socialist Republic of Gilan in 1920, which was crushed the following year by government forces. After the Islamic revolution the secular guerrillas retreated to the same forests.

†These "hejlehs" – bridal chambers – are garishly illuminated shrines, erected for 40 days at street corners to honour young men who have died unmarried and unfulfilled. They are usually brightly lit, small red-tented pavilions. A photograph of the martyr, surrounded by lights, is the centrepiece. The shrines were put up to honour both the soldiers who fell in the Iran-Iraq war and those Khomeini supporters killed in armed street clashes after the founding of the Islamic Republic. During the war, almost every street in the poorer parts of town had a hejleh.

Pg. 11

*There is a play on words with the name of Farzaneh's husband. Quorbani means "sacrificial sheep." And Al-Hajjaj ibn Yusef was a draconian 8th century Arab governor under the Umayyad caliphate, responsible for many deaths, particularly of thousands of pilgrims to Mecca. He was later made governor of the Persian provinces, where he savagely put down a number of rebellions. Written in Persian, Hajjaj can also be read as Hojjaj, meaning pilgrims to Mecca. "Qorbani Hajjaj" can be read as a sheep tied up for sacrifice by a returning pilgrim. Such a sheep would naturally be worried about what is about to happen to it.

†Like the poisoned shirt given to Hercules unwittingly by his wife, which killed him.

Pg.12 Heroes of the *Shanameh*: Iradj, Salm and Tur are sons of King Fereydoun, who divides up the known world between them. Incited by Salm, Tur kills Iradj. Manuchehr, the son of Iradj, then kills Salm and Tur in revenge.

Pg. 14 Amir Kabir was a major reformer and prime minister of Iran under Naser al-Din Shah from 1848 to 1851. He established new ministerial departments, reorganised the financial system, founded the country's first newspaper and first modern university and introduced compulsory vaccination against smallpox. In 1851, he was accused of conspiracy, dismissed from office and sent into exile in Kashan where, at the Shah's instigation, he was murdered in a bath house. Amir Kabir is widely regarded and revered as the founder of modern Iran.

Pg. 17 In the Qoran, Khezr, who has drunk the water of life and is therefore immortal, is the teacher of Moses. Khezr sees things that Moses cannot see or understand. Taking him on a journey,

Khezr nearly sinks a boat, then murders a young man and, in a town where no one will give them hospitality, he repairs a broken wall. Moses does not understand why, and protests. Khezr tells him that many seemingly malicious acts are beneficial: he has damaged the boat to prevent the crew from falling into the hands of a pirate king; he has killed the boy to stop him from bringing disgrace and danger to his parents, for God would give them a better son; the wall was to cover buried treasure left for the orphan of righteous parents, which was about to be exposed to thieves. In subsequent legends Khezr appears in various guises, at the last moment, often dressed in green, to guide or save the faithful when they are in trouble. In this novel, with hideous irony, Khezr Javid is the eternal and indestructible secret police-man, necessary for the survival of every régime, of whatever political hue.

Pg. 18 The setar is a traditional three-stringed instrument, similar to a small lute.

Pg. 20 Lalezar Avenue in the old days was the most European of the streets of Tehran.

Pg. 22 The Dhofar province is in the south-west of the Sultanate of Oman, next to the border with South Yemen. In December 1973, a force of 3,000 Iranian elite troops went to help Sultan Qaboos bin Said put down a rebellion by PFLOAG (People's Front for the Liberation of Oman and the Arabian Gulf), insti-gated by South Yemen, which housed a substantial Soviet base at the time. The Omani Army was trained and led by British officers.

Pg. 26
*The author is alluding to the "west-toxification" of modern Iranian youth, the title of a book of the same name by Jalal Al-e Ahmad.

†In Muslim burials, the body is taken out of the coffin and buried only in a shroud.

Pg. 27 Nationalized in 1951. Until then, the oil of Iran was in the hands of the Anglo-Iranian Oil Company, which later became BP.

Pg. 30 Parvaneh means "moth."

Pg. 34 Rostam, the great Persian hero of the *Shanameh* epic, defeated the Turanian champion Ashkabus in single combat. Paridokht was a heroine who fought with Rostam's son, Sohrab. His tragedy was that he unwittingly killed his son Sohrab in single combat, recognising him only as he lay dying. In the period of Iranian nationalism from the 1920s to the 1970s, progressive nationalist families eschewed the old Islamic names in favour of names of heroes of the *Shanameh*.

Pg. 46 Birjand is the capital of South Khorasan province in eastern Iran, close to the Afghan border.

Pg. 48 That is, the Caliph Omar, enemy of the early Shi'ites. As an insult to him, the old outdoor privies were known as "The Caliph's house."

Pg. 53 The prophet Khezr, by contrast, is believed to follow people who are in danger, to intervene and save them.

Pg. 65 This recalls the ordeal of Siyayah in the *Shahnameh* epic.

Pg. 75 These are districts of Tehran. Salsabil is a fountain of nectar in paradise and Jey means "pure."

Pg. 76 The Mossadeq period. Mossadeq was Prime Minister of Iran from 1951 to 1953. A staunch defender of Iranian independence, he nationalised the country's oil industry and ended British dominance in Iran. After the forced British withdrawal, the United States, with British help, organised a coup against Mossadeq. Shah Mohammed Reza Pahlavi, who had been forced into exile, returned and, with American help established a modernising régime, regarded by leftists as a dictatorship, which lasted until his overthrow in 1979. After Mossadeq was deposed in 1953, he was sentenced to three years of solitary confinement in prison, followed by permanent house arrest on his estate until his death in 1967. He is revered as the only truly democratic statesman in the early history of independent Iran. A number of political commentators in the US now say that it was a mistake to have overthrown him.

Pg. 78 Rezaiyeh (modern name: Urumiah) is the capital of the Iranian province of West Azerbaijan. Under the founder of the Pahlavi dynasty, Reza Shah, Urumiah was renamed Rezaiyeh. The original name was restored with the advent of the Islamic Republic.

Pg. 80 These minarets are a few miles outside Isfahan and can be made to shake.

Pg. 81 Westernised Iranians drink tea from a cup.

Pg. 83 Flagellants in mourning, commemorating the death of the Imam Hossein at the battle of Karbala, AD 680. It was often said that a number of Palestinians and Lebanese came to join the revolution.

Pg. 88

* Shapour Bakhtiar was prime minister for 30 days in the transition period between the departure of the Shah and the return of Khomeini. He ordered the release of all political prisoners and the dissolution of SAVAK.

†After the Islamic revolution, the communist Tudeh party decided to publish the names of government informers. SAVAK, created by the CIA and Israeli security experts after the 1953 coup against Mossadeq, was the equivalent of the KGB. Its charter committed it to "defending the state and preventing all conspiracies against the public interest." SAVAK was used by the Shah's regime to stifle all forms of opposition. It was a huge organisation, with informers everywhere, creating an atmosphere of suspicion and distrust between families and friends. Dissidents were rounded up, tortured and, in some cases, executed. In the last few years of the Shah's reign, when Jimmy Carter was president of the US, they became noticeably more tolerant of opposition.

Pg. 89

*In some remote small towns, mourners for the Imam Hossein at Kerbela cover themselves in mud to show their annihilation of self.

†A cheap brand of Iranian cigarette, mostly smoked by working people. Also Homa cigarettes.

Pg. 100 This refers to the death of Colonel Mohammad-Taqi Khan Pesyan. See first note, "Translator's Note," above.

Pg. 104 The half-brother of Rostam, the great hero of the Shahnameh epic. Shaghad and the king of Kabulisatan dig a pit full of swords and entice Rostam to ride into it, with his famous horse

Rakhsh. Both are impaled on the swords. The dying Rostam persuades Shaghad to give him a bow and arrow. With his last breath, he shoots an arrow at Shaghad, who is hiding behind a tree. So strong was Rostam that the arrow pierced the tree and killed Shaghad from behind, pinning him to the tree.

Pg. 110 The universities were closed in 1981 to prevent student disturbances.

Pg. 111 One who has made the pilgrimage to Kerbela, the site of the martyrdom of the Shi'i Imam Hossein in AD 680.

Pg. 113 "Lead" harks to the period of stagnation of the Italian communist party 1969–79, known as the *anni di piombi*, the years of lead.

Pg. 119 President Truman's development aid programme intro-duced in 1949 as the fourth mainspring of American foreign policy. It was designed to provide aid – initially mainly economic and technical, but later military – to countries in Latin America, Africa and Asia as a way of countering the influence of Soviet Russia and China.

Pg. 132 Big noses are ugly to Iranians. The Shah was famous for his big nose, but because he was Shah, he could not be despised for it. It became quite acceptable, even admirable, for men to have big noses in his day.

Pg. 133 In 1953, Sha'ban the Brainless was a Tehran gang leader paid by the CIA to bring the crowds out against Mossadeq. Khosrow Rouzbeh was an army officer in the communist Tudeh party, which was waiting for orders to come from Moscow to start an insurrection, which never came. Mossadeq was overthrown and the Shah returned. He earned his popular nickname Bimokh (the Brainless) for his witless thuggery. After the successful coup and the restoration of the Shah, Sha'ban was handsomely rewarded for his services.

Pg. 136 The first of the legendary kings to rule Iran after the breakup of the empire of his great-grandfather, Fereydoun.

Pg. 140 "The Paradise of Zahra" the largest cemetery in Iran, located in the southern suburbs of Tehran. During the Shah's reign, resistance fighters who were executed or killed in guerrilla fighting were buried there. It was the site of Ayatollah Khomeini's first major rally after his return from exile in France in 1979. Behesht-e Zahra is also the final resting place of the "martyrs" who fell in the Iran-Iraq War of 1980–88 and of political opponents executed after the establishment of the Islamic Republic.

Pg. 147 After the revolution, Islamic revolutionary committees were created in most neighborhoods. Initially they seemed answerable to nobody, and ran their patches with a heavy hand, invading houses to check for alcohol, "immoral" parties etc.

Pg. 149
*Russian-made rocket propelled grenade.

†This refers to the abortive plan of some air force officers to shoot down Khomeini's plane on his return from Paris.

‡The Turkmen live along the NE border of Iran. Being Sunni, they made a short-lived resistance to the Shi'i Islamic revolution. On the other side of the border was Soviet Turkmenistan, which tried to provoke the Iranian Turkmen into an uprising against the Islamic government.

Pg. 151 The Mojahedin-e Khalq went over to Iraq during the Iran-Iraq war, and are still considered by many to be traitors.

Pg. 153 Friday is the day of rest in Iran, making Thursday night a night to celebrate.

Pg. 154
*Nima Yushij, the father of modern Persian poetry (1869–1960).

†Hungarian Marxist philosopher.

Pg. 155 The teachers Khezr Javid describes in his early days, before he joined SAVAK, were part of the *Sepah-e Danesh*, the Army of Learning, which was established by the Shah in the 1960s. As an alternative to military service, educated young men and women were sent to remote villages to teach basic literacy and hygiene. Some of these teachers were very energetic and idealistic and fit in well with village life, becoming useful links between the village and outside officialdom, while others were unable to adapt to the primitive conditions in the villages of those days, and became desperately homesick and lonely.

Pg. 158 Shortly after the revolution, a number of Marxists took refuge from the Islamic regime in the forests along the Caspian, following an ancient Iranian tradition. The regime labeled them as the "hypocrites of the jungle."

Pg. 165 They indicate that he had not raped the colonel's daughter. Sugar plums are offered when a young man's family comes to ask for the hand of a girl in marriage.

Pg. 169
*Mohammad-Reza Shah, the last Shah of Iran. He outlawed the Communist Party of Iran in 1931.

†In the Shah's time, power was exercised top down, but in the post-revolutionary period orders came in a mish-mash of top-down and bottom-up: from above, through the mullas and their associates, and from below, through the newly empowered "Komités of the oppressed."

Pg. 176 Martyrs are buried in the clothes they died in, not in a shroud.

Pg. 178 It was the custom to make a stage for entertainment by placing boards over the pool in the yard.

Pg. 181 The year of the coup against Mossadeq.

Pg. 183 i.e. the reigns of the last two Shahs.

Pg. 190 Municipalities are obliged to provide services wherever there is a mosque.

Pg. 200 Shams ul-Emareh. A palace added to the Golestan Palace compound and finished in 1867. It was ordered by Nasir al-Din Shah, who had been impressed by the tall buildings he had seen in Europe. The first five-storey building of old Tehran, it was lavishly decorated with tiles and mirror work. It served both as royal harem and, later, as a place for official receptions.

Pg. 203 This is Ahmad Qavam, the prime minister who ordered the assassination of Colonel Mohammad-Taqi Khan. See also: first note, "Translator's Note," above.

Pg. 204 Mutasim al-Saltanah Farrokh was the Mashhad karguzar, the government official responsible for relations with the foreign consulates, and a supporter of The Colonel. Major Ismail

Khan Bahador was the colonel's closest and staunchest supporter among the gendarmes.

Pg. 206 He was assassinated by order of Nasir ud-Din Shah. See note for page 14, above.

Pg. 207 In 1946, to persuade the Soviets to withdraw from Iranian Azerbaijan, which they had occupied during the war, the brilliant and wily prime minister Qavam granted the Soviets an oil concession in the north of Iran. After the troops moved out, the Majlis (parliament) refused to ratify the arrangement and the Russians got nothing. Qavam, outwardly subservient to foreign interests—and criticised for it—was in fact a patriot, who earned the nickname of The Wily Fox.

Pg. 213
*Heidar Amu-Oghlu, a founder of the communist Tudeh ["Masses"] party, killed in 1921. Sattar Khan was a nationalist hero of the Constitutionalist movement of 1906. Under his guidance, a "High Military Council" was proclaimed in 1908. However, after revolutionary forces took Tehran, he and his followers refused to lay down their arms. In an ensuing armed clash with former comrades, Sattar was fatally wounded and died a few days later.

†This is Taqi Arani, considered by many to have founded the Tudeh party. Like many communists, he studied in Germany, then came back to found *Donya* [*The World*] magazine. In 1937, he and 53 others were arrested for communist activities, and he later died in jail.

‡The Azeri language, a form of Turkish, is now spoken mainly by the indigenous inhabitants of the north-western Iranian

provinces of Azerbaijan and Zanjan, though Persian remains the official language there. Many Azeris migrated to Tehran and their language can be heard in much of the south of the city and in the bazaar. Tabriz, the capital of Iranian Azerbaijan, was Iran's gateway to the west, through which many European ideas were imported. The Constitutional Revolution of 1906 was started by Azeris, and many of the founders of the Iranian communist party were also Azeris. Colonel Mohammad-Taqi Khan was an Azeri. Until the Russians conquered it in 1828 most of what is now modern Azerbaijan was Iranian territory.

§The Hezbullah in Lebanon.

Pg. 214
*Heidar Khan Amoghli was a leading member of the Communist Party of Iran, which was founded in the northern port of Bandar-e Anzali in 1920, and founder of the short-lived Gilan Soviet Republic of 1921. The party was outlawed by the government of Reza Shah in 1931.

†A renowned patriot from the early days of independent Iran. Active during the 1906 Constitutional Revolution, at the age of 30 he was elected as a member of the Democrat party to represent his native Tabriz in north-western Iran in the Iranian parliament. Revolting against the 1919 treaty that handed effective control of the country to Britain, he set up the breakaway republic of Azadistan ("the land of liberty") in Tabriz. The revolt was soon crushed, and Khiabani was put to death.

Pg. 215
*Qaim-Maqam (1779–1835), renowned statesman, essayist, and poet of the early Qajar period. Mirza Taqi Khan Amir Kabir essentially adopted his outlook on politics and diplomacy. He

was the architect of a "no war no peace" policy with Russia, which drew on religious and nationalist sentiments to rally support behind the crown prince and his military modernisation programme, to create a credible defence against Russia. His policies facilitated funding for military reforms and guaranteed British support against Russia.

†One of the first Iranians to convert to Islam during the lifetime of the Prophet Muhammad. After the death of the Prophet, he was betrayed and assassinated.

Pg. 217 A Living Death [*Zendeh be-gur*] is a famous novel by Sadeq Hedayat.

MAHMOUD DOWLATABADI is one of Iran's most important writers of the last century. The author of numerous novels, plays and screenplays, he is a leading proponent of social and artistic freedom in contemporary Iran.

Born in 1940 in a remote farming region of Iran, the son of a shoemaker, his early life and teens were spent as an agricultural day laborer until he made his way to Tehran where he started working in the theater and began writing plays, stories and novels.

Dowlatabadi pioneered the use of the everyday language of the Iranian people as suitable for high literary art, and he often examines the lives of the marginal and oppressed in his work, as in his previous Melville House title, *Missing Soluch*, his first work translated into English. That book was written via memorization while he was in prison. (Dowlatabadi had been arrested in 1975 while on stage performing in a play seen as critical of the Shah.)

Ten years in the writing, his newest novel *The Colonel* has been shortlisted for the Haus der Kulturen Berlin International Literary Award, and longlisted for the Man Asian Literary Prize.

He lives in Tehran.